Written by:
ALEX SIMMONS

Pencils by:
DAN PARENT

Inking by:
RICH KOSLOWSKI

Lettering by:
JACK MORELLI

Coloring by:
DIGIKORE
STUDIOS

Co-CEO: Jon Goldwater
Co-CEO: Nancy Silberkleit
President: Mike Pellerito
Co-President / Editor-In-Chief: Victor Gorelick
Director of Circulation: Bill Horan
Executive Director of Publishing/Operations: Harold Buchholz
Executive Director of Publicity & Marketing: Alex Segura
Project Coordinator & Book Design: Joe Morciglio
Production Manager: Stephen Oswald
Production: Rosario 'Tito' Peña, Jon Gray, Kari Silbergleit, Pat Woodruff
Proofreader: Jamie Rotante

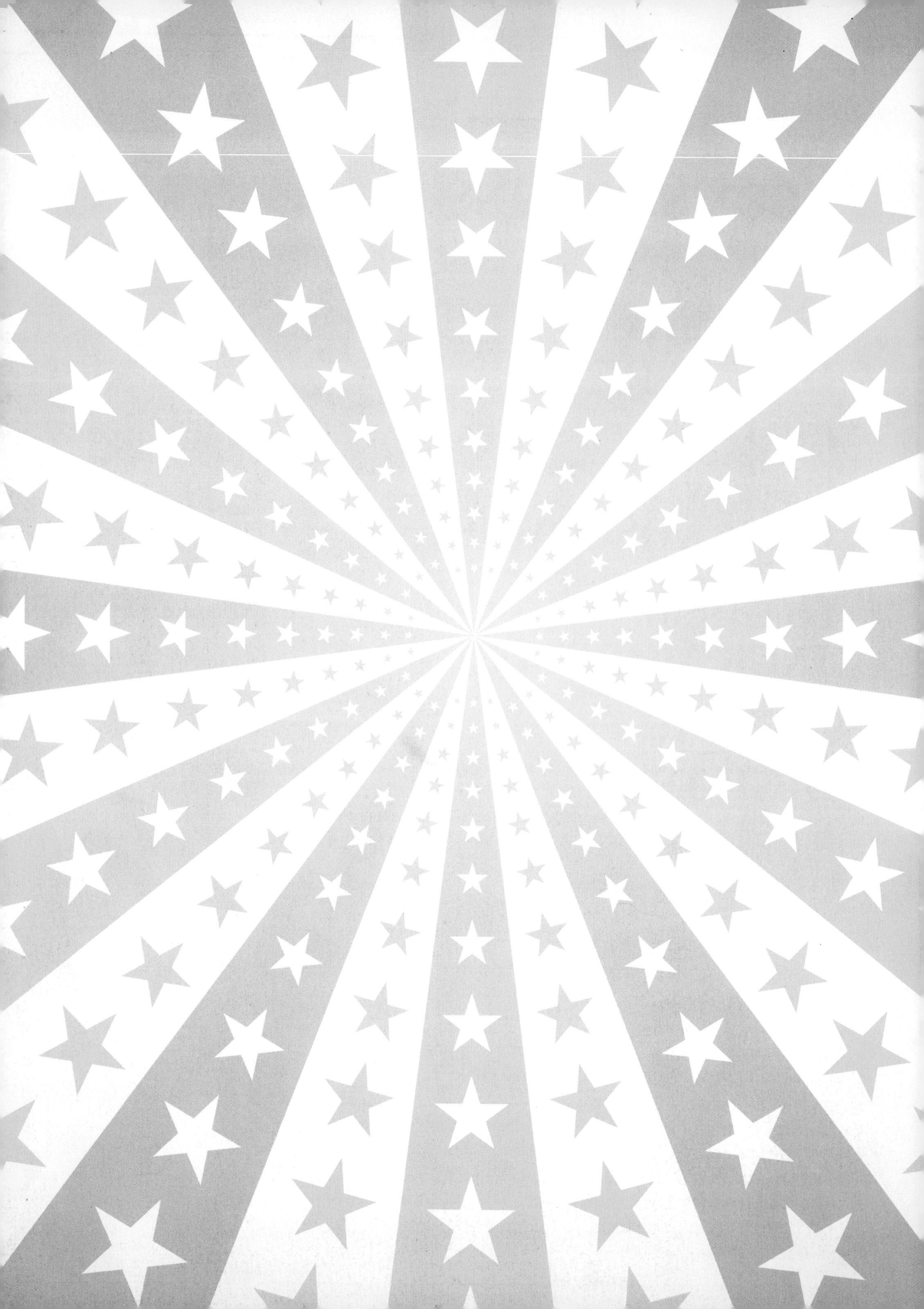

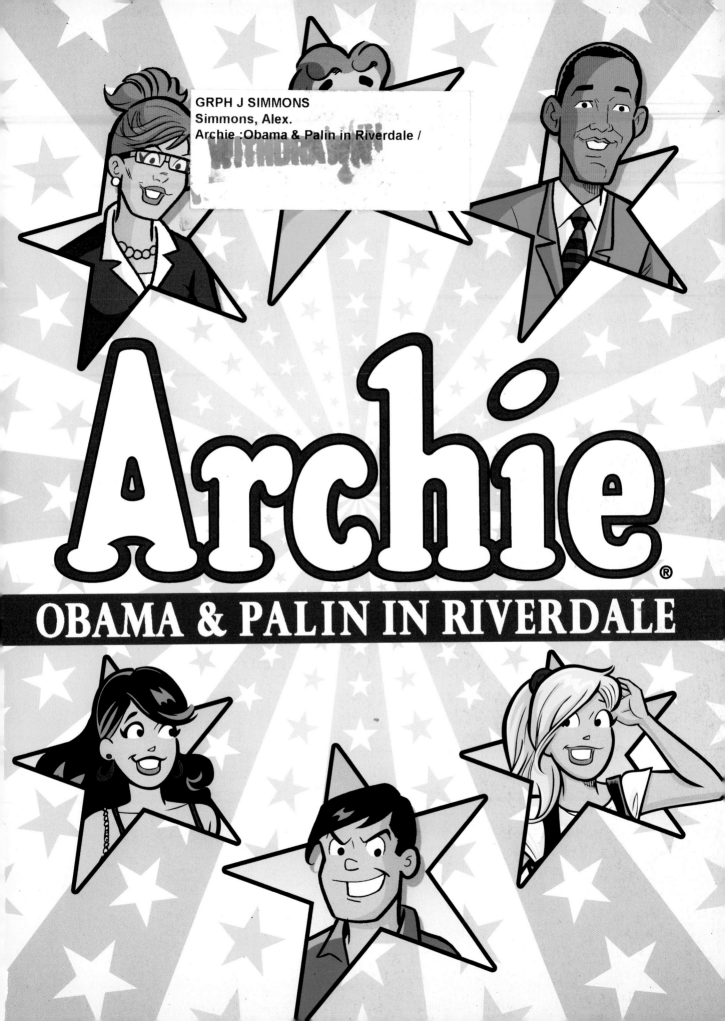

Archie®

OBAMA & PALIN IN RIVERDALE

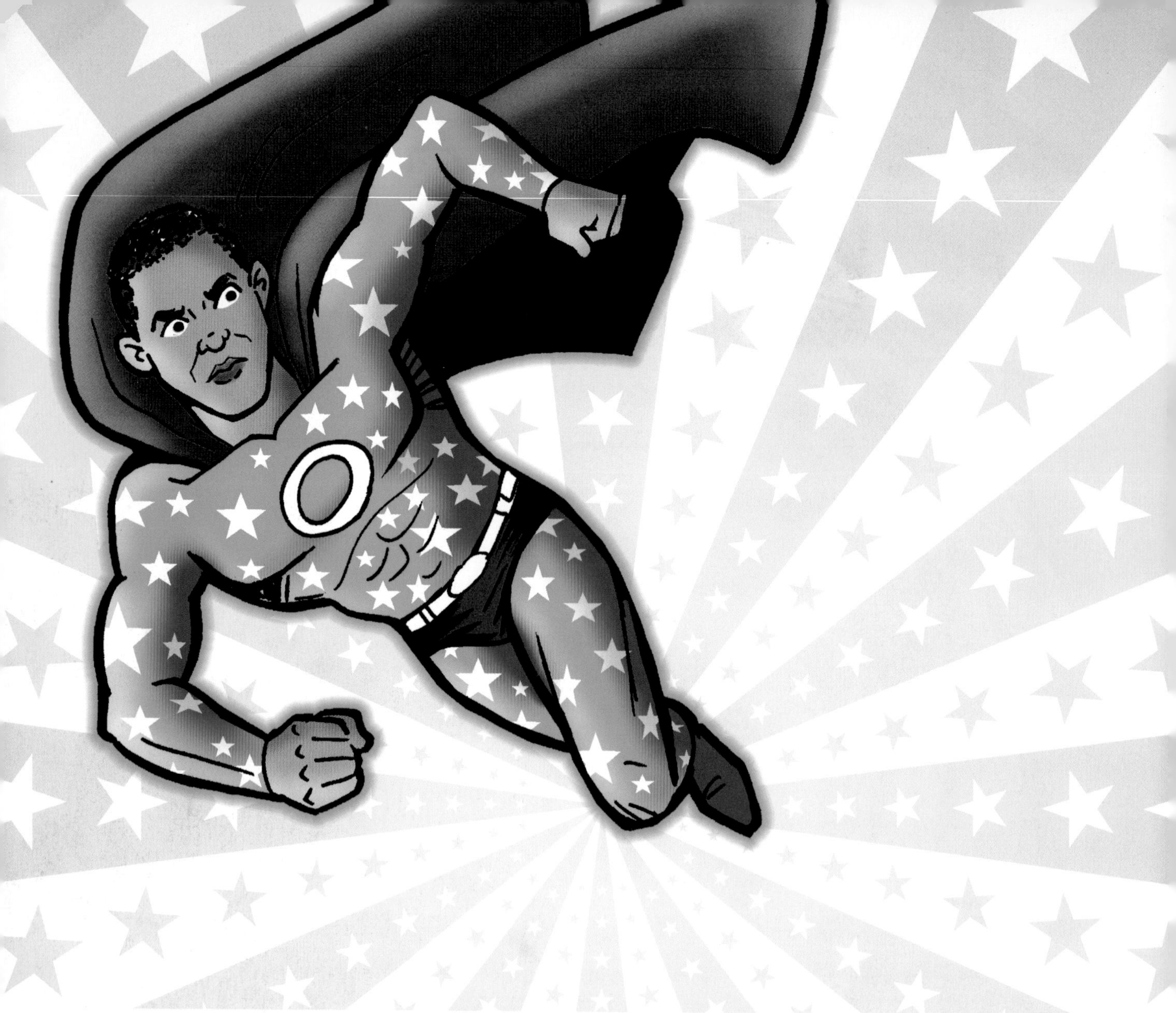

Archie & Friends All-Stars Vol. 14,
ARCHIE: OBAMA & PALIN IN RIVERDALE
Published by Archie Comic Publications, Inc.
325 Fayette Avenue, Mamaroneck, New York 10543-2318.

ISBN: 978-1-879794-87-0

10 9 8 7 6 5 4 3 2 1

Printed in U.S.A.

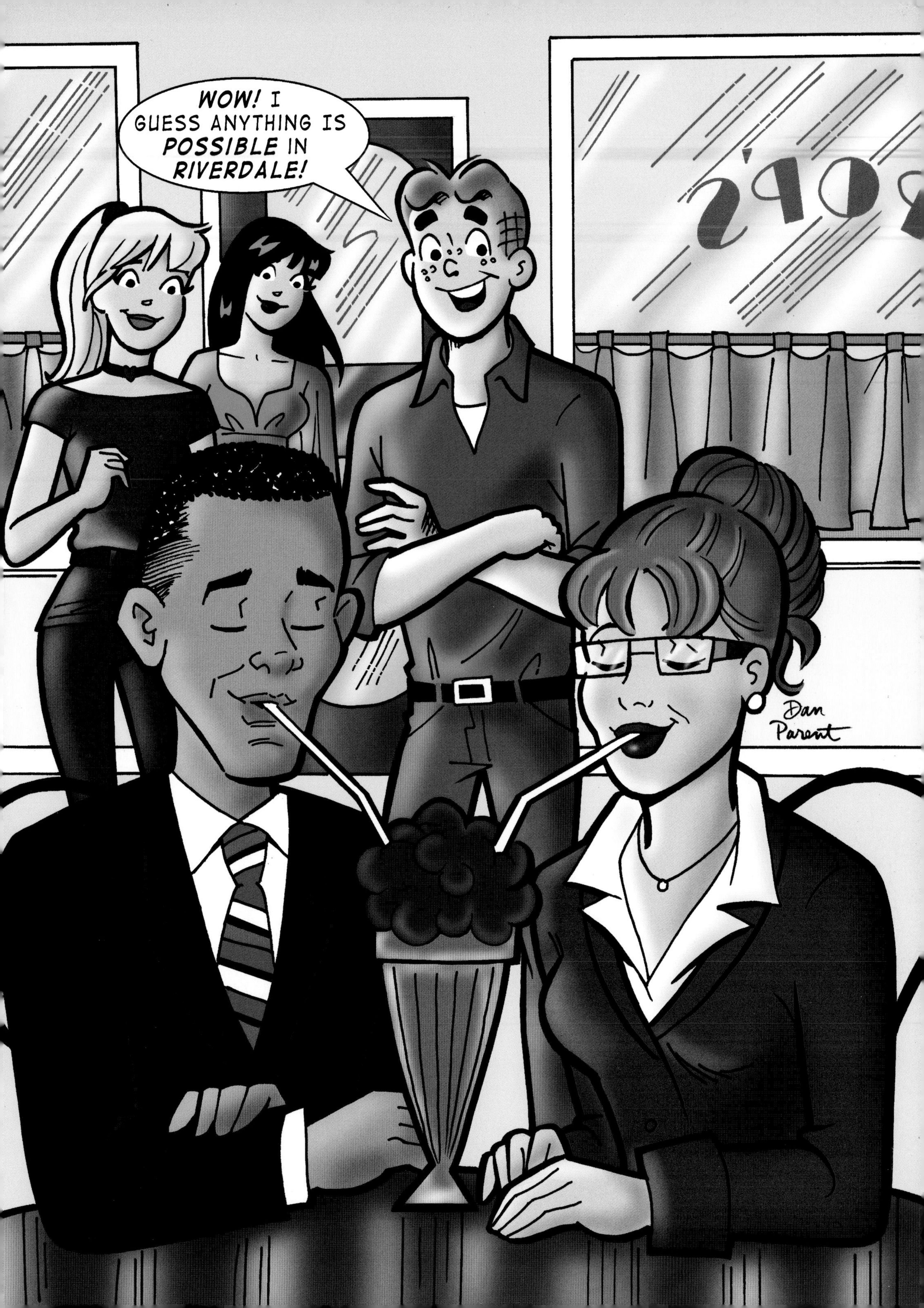
WOW! I GUESS ANYTHING IS POSSIBLE IN RIVERDALE!
Dan Parent

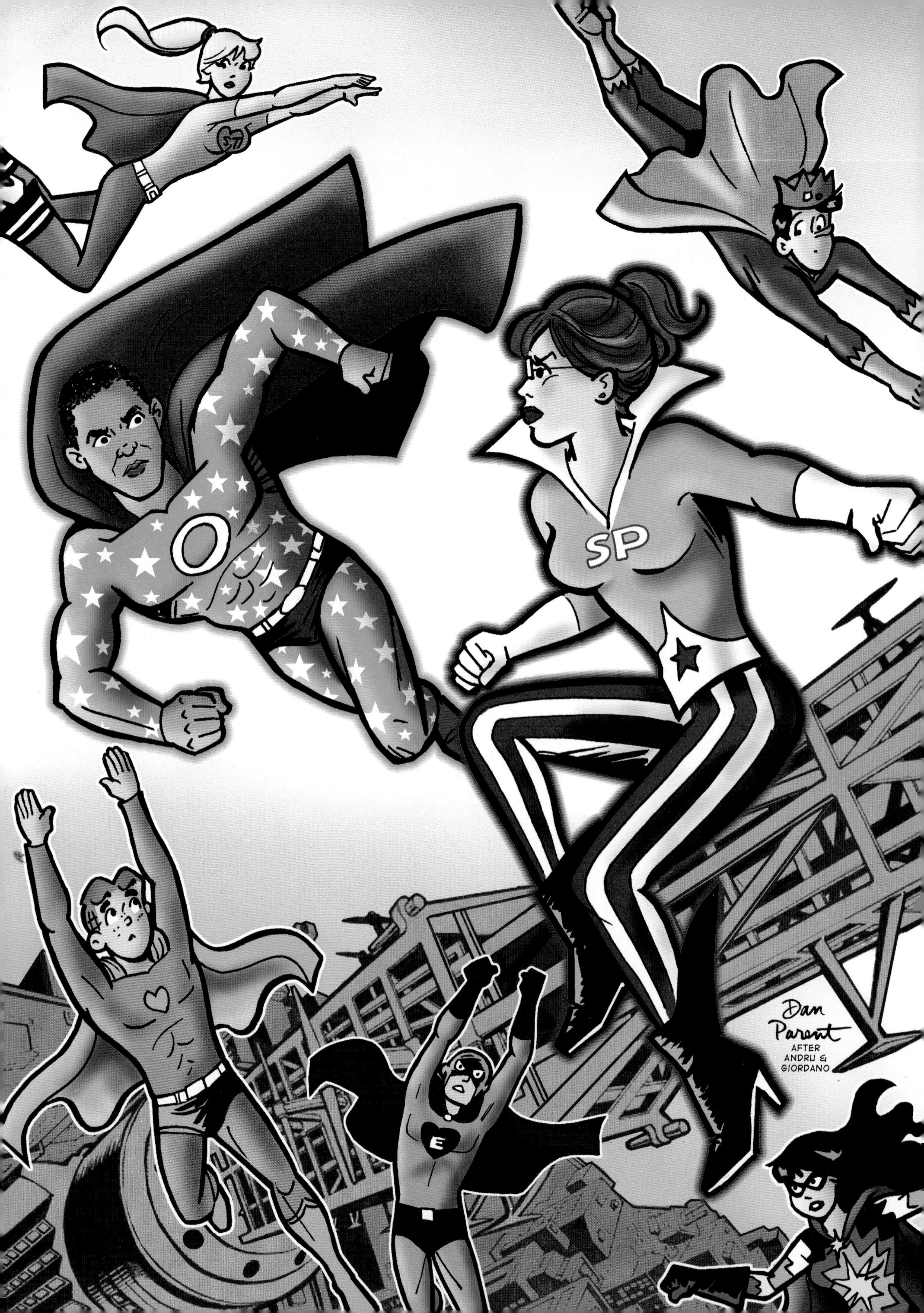

S7
O
SP
E
Dan Parent
AFTER ANDRU & GIORDANO

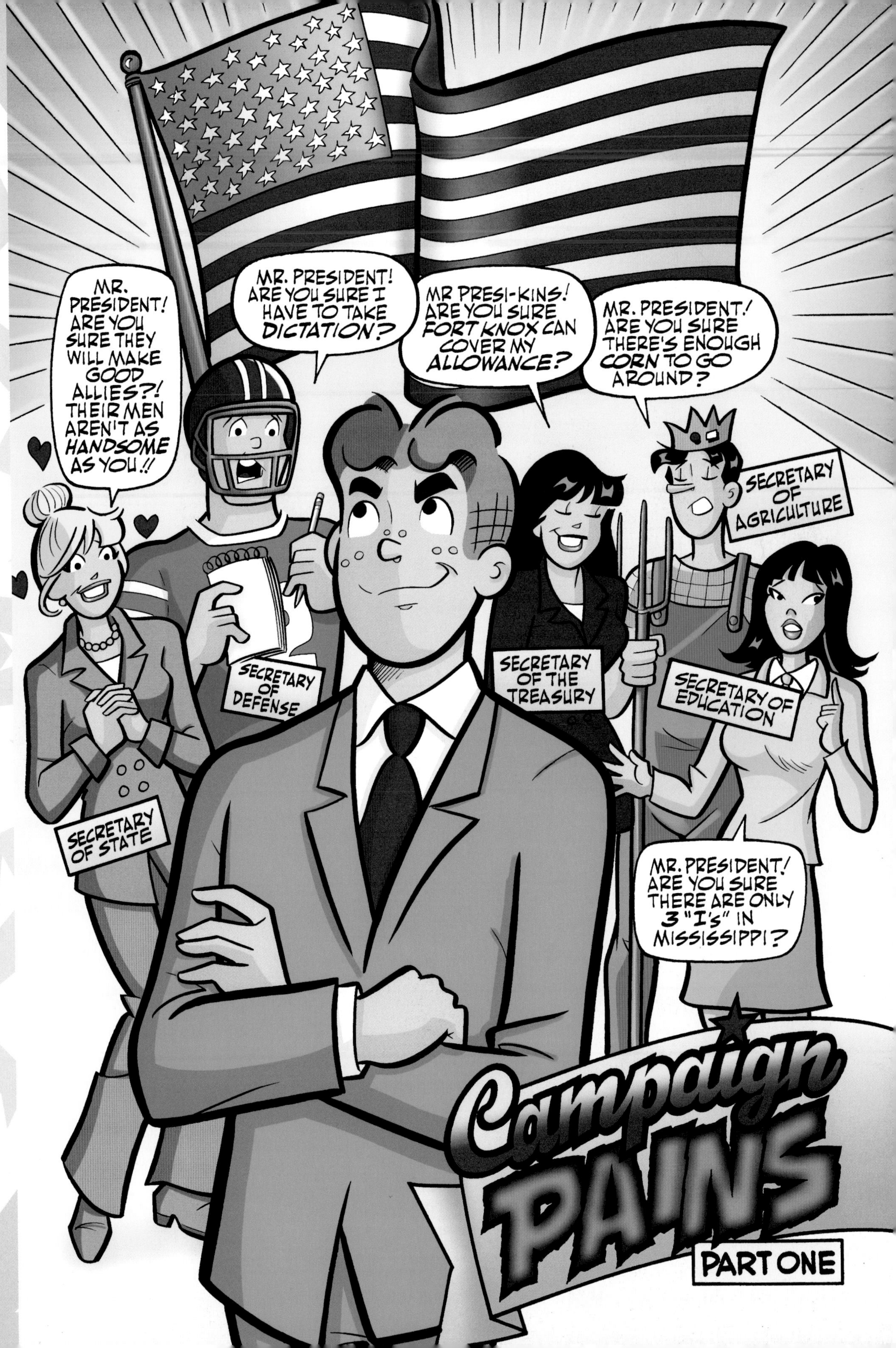
MR. PRESIDENT! ARE YOU SURE THEY WILL MAKE GOOD ALLIES?! THEIR MEN AREN'T AS HANDSOME AS YOU!!
MR. PRESIDENT! ARE YOU SURE I HAVE TO TAKE DICTATION?
MR PRESI-KINS! ARE YOU SURE FORT KNOX CAN COVER MY ALLOWANCE?
MR. PRESIDENT! ARE YOU SURE THERE'S ENOUGH CORN TO GO AROUND?
SECRETARY OF AGRICULTURE
SECRETARY OF DEFENSE
SECRETARY OF THE TREASURY
SECRETARY OF EDUCATION
SECRETARY OF STATE
MR. PRESIDENT! ARE YOU SURE THERE ARE ONLY 3 "I's" IN MISSISSIPPI?
Campaign PAINS
PART ONE

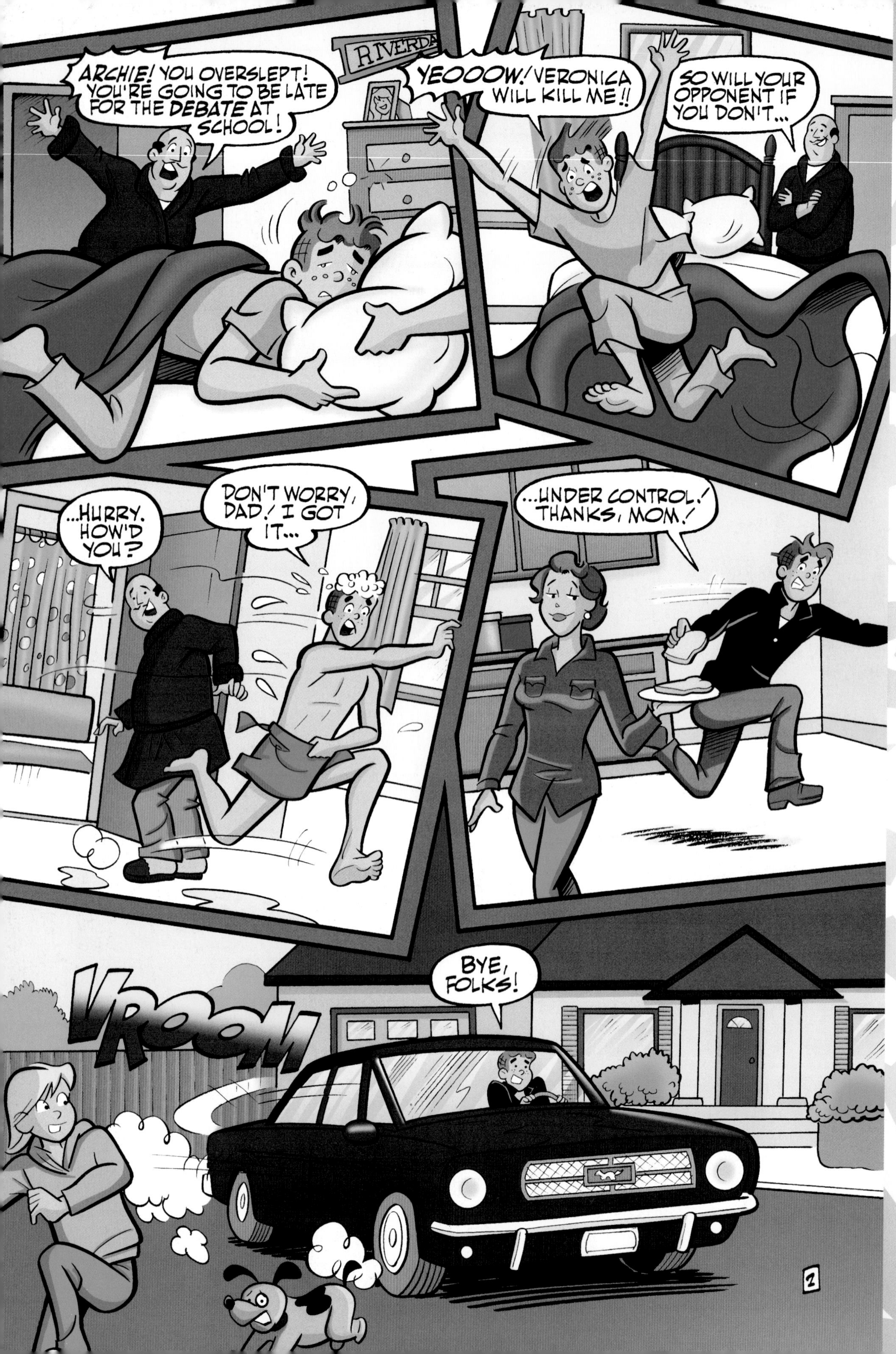

RIVERDA
ARCHIE! YOU OVERSLEPT! YOU'RE GOING TO BE LATE FOR THE DEBATE AT SCHOOL!
YEOOOW! VERONICA WILL KILL ME!!
SO WILL YOUR OPPONENT IF YOU DON'T...
...HURRY. HOW'D YOU?
DON'T WORRY, DAD! I GOT IT...
...UNDER CONTROL! THANKS, MOM!
VROOM
BYE, FOLKS!

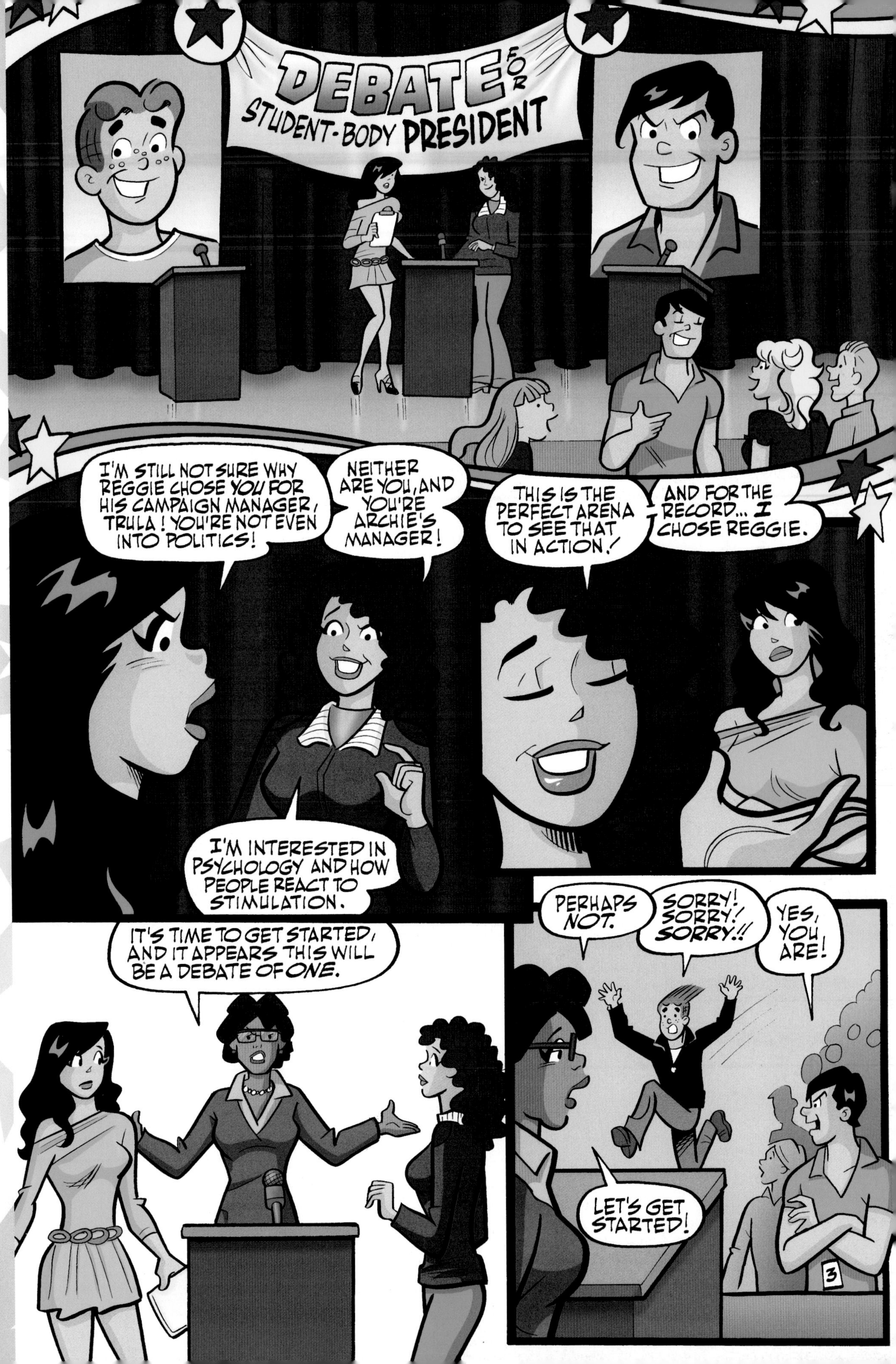
DEBATE FOR STUDENT-BODY PRESIDENT
I'M STILL NOT SURE WHY REGGIE CHOSE YOU FOR HIS CAMPAIGN MANAGER, TRULA! YOU'RE NOT EVEN INTO POLITICS!
NEITHER ARE YOU, AND YOU'RE ARCHIE'S MANAGER!
I'M INTERESTED IN PSYCHOLOGY AND HOW PEOPLE REACT TO STIMULATION.
THIS IS THE PERFECT ARENA TO SEE THAT IN ACTION!
AND FOR THE RECORD... I CHOSE REGGIE.
IT'S TIME TO GET STARTED, AND IT APPEARS THIS WILL BE A DEBATE OF ONE.
PERHAPS NOT.
SORRY! SORRY! SORRY!!
YES, YOU ARE!
LET'S GET STARTED!
3

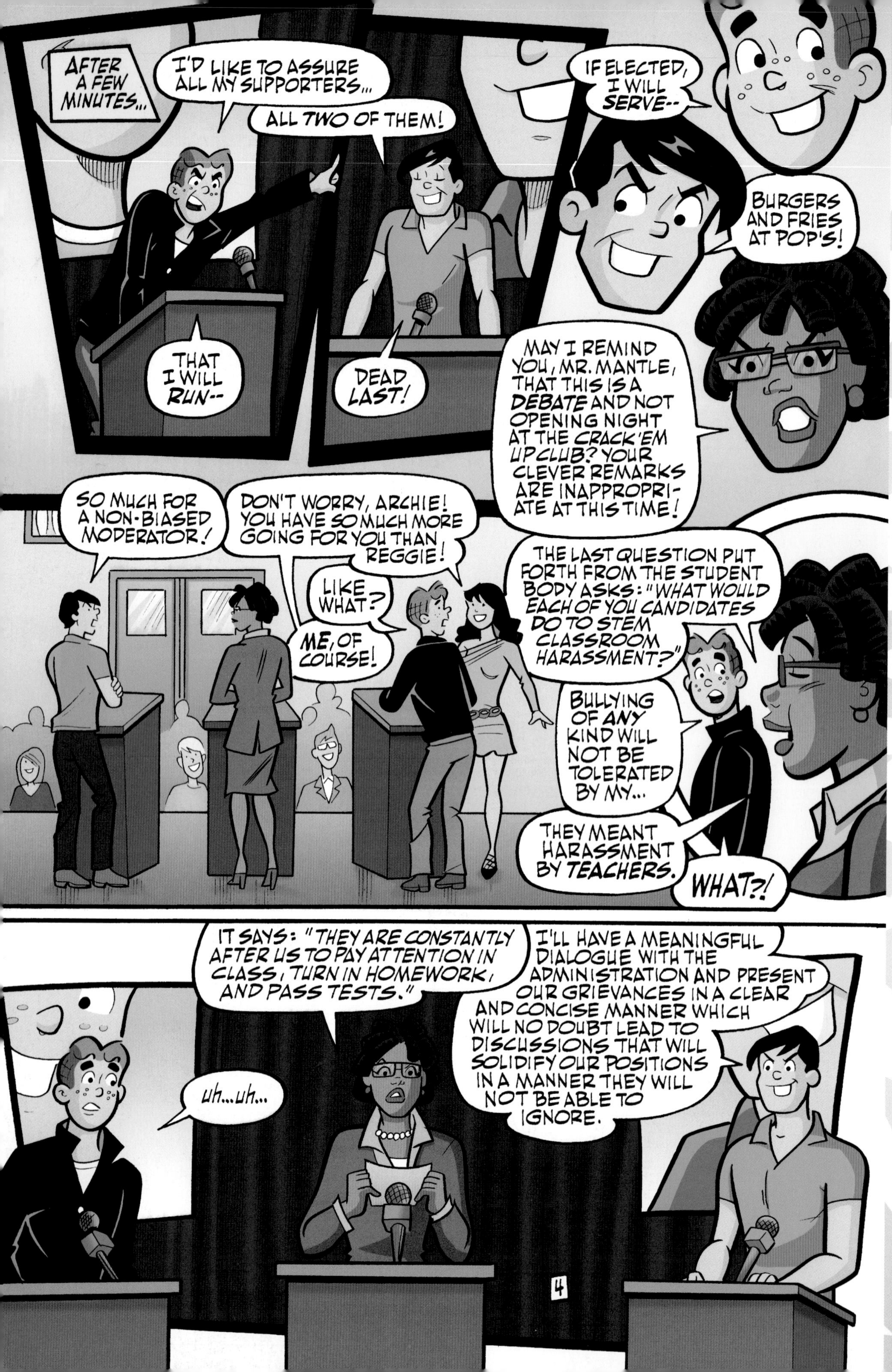
AFTER A FEW MINUTES...
I'D LIKE TO ASSURE ALL MY SUPPORTERS...
ALL TWO OF THEM!
THAT I WILL RUN--
DEAD LAST!
IF ELECTED, I WILL SERVE--
BURGERS AND FRIES AT POP'S!
MAY I REMIND YOU, MR. MANTLE, THAT THIS IS A DEBATE AND NOT OPENING NIGHT AT THE CRACK'EM UP CLUB? YOUR CLEVER REMARKS ARE INAPPROPRI-ATE AT THIS TIME!
SO MUCH FOR A NON-BIASED MODERATOR!
DON'T WORRY, ARCHIE! YOU HAVE SO MUCH MORE GOING FOR YOU THAN REGGIE!
LIKE WHAT?
ME, OF COURSE!
THE LAST QUESTION PUT FORTH FROM THE STUDENT BODY ASKS: "WHAT WOULD EACH OF YOU CANDIDATES DO TO STEM CLASSROOM HARASSMENT?"
BULLYING OF ANY KIND WILL NOT BE TOLERATED BY MY...
THEY MEANT HARASSMENT BY TEACHERS.
WHAT?!
IT SAYS: "THEY ARE CONSTANTLY AFTER US TO PAY ATTENTION IN CLASS, TURN IN HOMEWORK, AND PASS TESTS."
uh...uh...
I'LL HAVE A MEANINGFUL DIALOGUE WITH THE ADMINISTRATION AND PRESENT OUR GRIEVANCES IN A CLEAR AND CONCISE MANNER WHICH WILL NO DOUBT LEAD TO DISCUSSIONS THAT WILL SOLIDIFY OUR POSITIONS IN A MANNER THEY WILL NOT BE ABLE TO IGNORE.
4

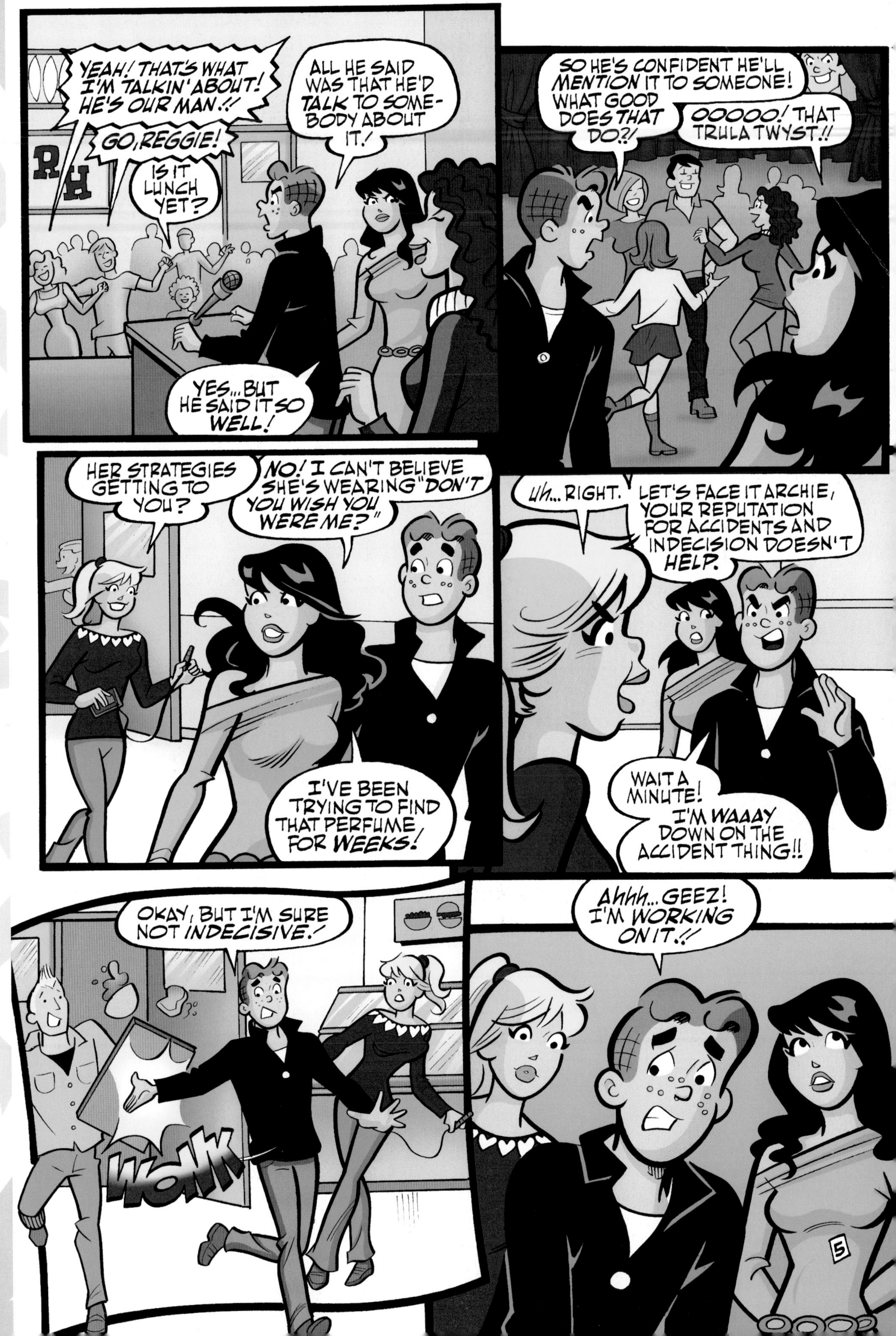
YEAH! THAT'S WHAT I'M TALKIN' ABOUT! HE'S OUR MAN!!
GO, REGGIE!
IS IT LUNCH YET?
ALL HE SAID WAS THAT HE'D TALK TO SOME-BODY ABOUT IT!
YES... BUT HE SAID IT SO WELL!
SO HE'S CONFIDENT HE'LL MENTION IT TO SOMEONE! WHAT GOOD DOES THAT DO?!
OOOOO! THAT TRULA TWYST!!
HER STRATEGIES GETTING TO YOU?
NO! I CAN'T BELIEVE SHE'S WEARING "DON'T YOU WISH YOU WERE ME?"
I'VE BEEN TRYING TO FIND THAT PERFUME FOR WEEKS!
UH... RIGHT.
LET'S FACE IT ARCHIE, YOUR REPUTATION FOR ACCIDENTS AND INDECISION DOESN'T HELP.
WAIT A MINUTE!
I'M WAAAY DOWN ON THE ACCIDENT THING!!
OKAY, BUT I'M SURE NOT INDECISIVE!
WONK
AHHH... GEEZ! I'M WORKING ON IT!!
5

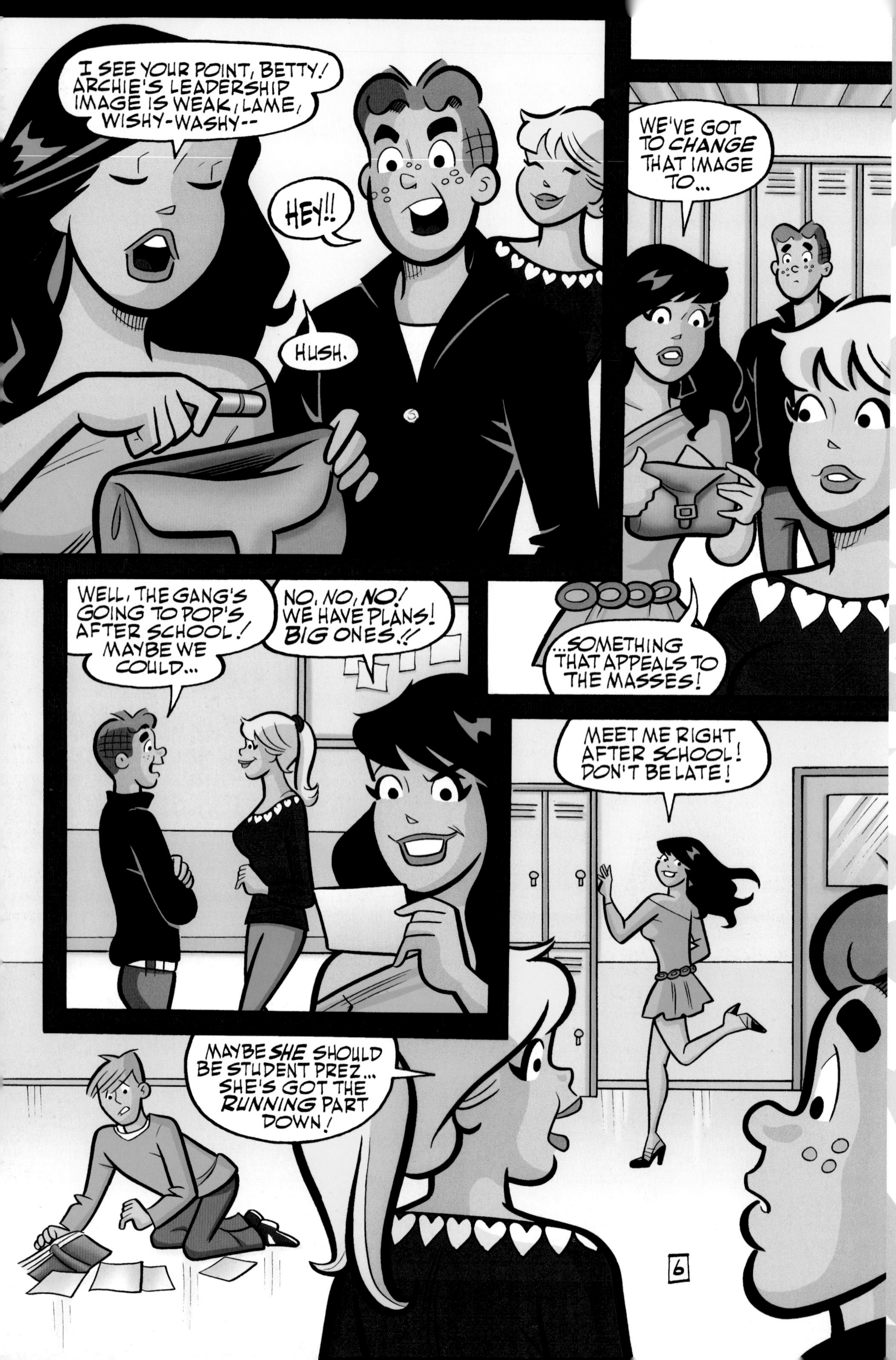
I SEE YOUR POINT, BETTY! ARCHIE'S LEADERSHIP IMAGE IS WEAK, LAME, WISHY-WASHY--
HEY!!
HUSH.
WE'VE GOT TO CHANGE THAT IMAGE TO...
...SOMETHING THAT APPEALS TO THE MASSES!
WELL, THE GANG'S GOING TO POP'S AFTER SCHOOL! MAYBE WE COULD...
NO, NO, NO! WE HAVE PLANS! BIG ONES!!
MEET ME RIGHT AFTER SCHOOL! DON'T BE LATE!
MAYBE SHE SHOULD BE STUDENT PREZ... SHE'S GOT THE RUNNING PART DOWN!
6

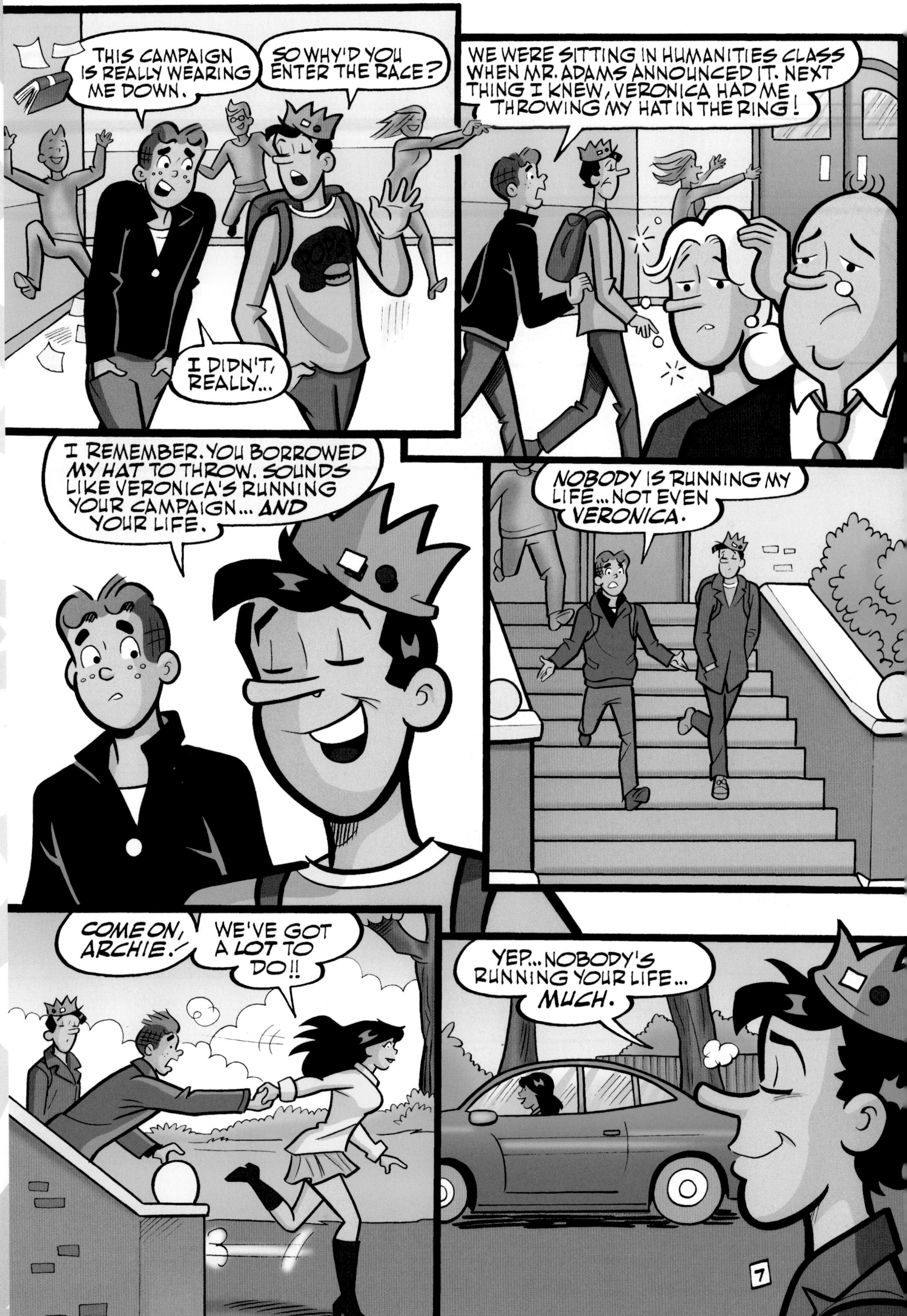

THIS CAMPAIGN IS REALLY WEARING ME DOWN.
SO WHY'D YOU ENTER THE RACE?
I DIDN'T, REALLY...
WE WERE SITTING IN HUMANITIES CLASS WHEN MR. ADAMS ANNOUNCED IT. NEXT THING I KNEW, VERONICA HAD ME THROWING MY HAT IN THE RING!
I REMEMBER. YOU BORROWED MY HAT TO THROW. SOUNDS LIKE VERONICA'S RUNNING YOUR CAMPAIGN... AND YOUR LIFE.
NOBODY IS RUNNING MY LIFE... NOT EVEN VERONICA.
COME ON, ARCHIE!
WE'VE GOT A LOT TO DO!!
YEP... NOBODY'S RUNNING YOUR LIFE... MUCH.

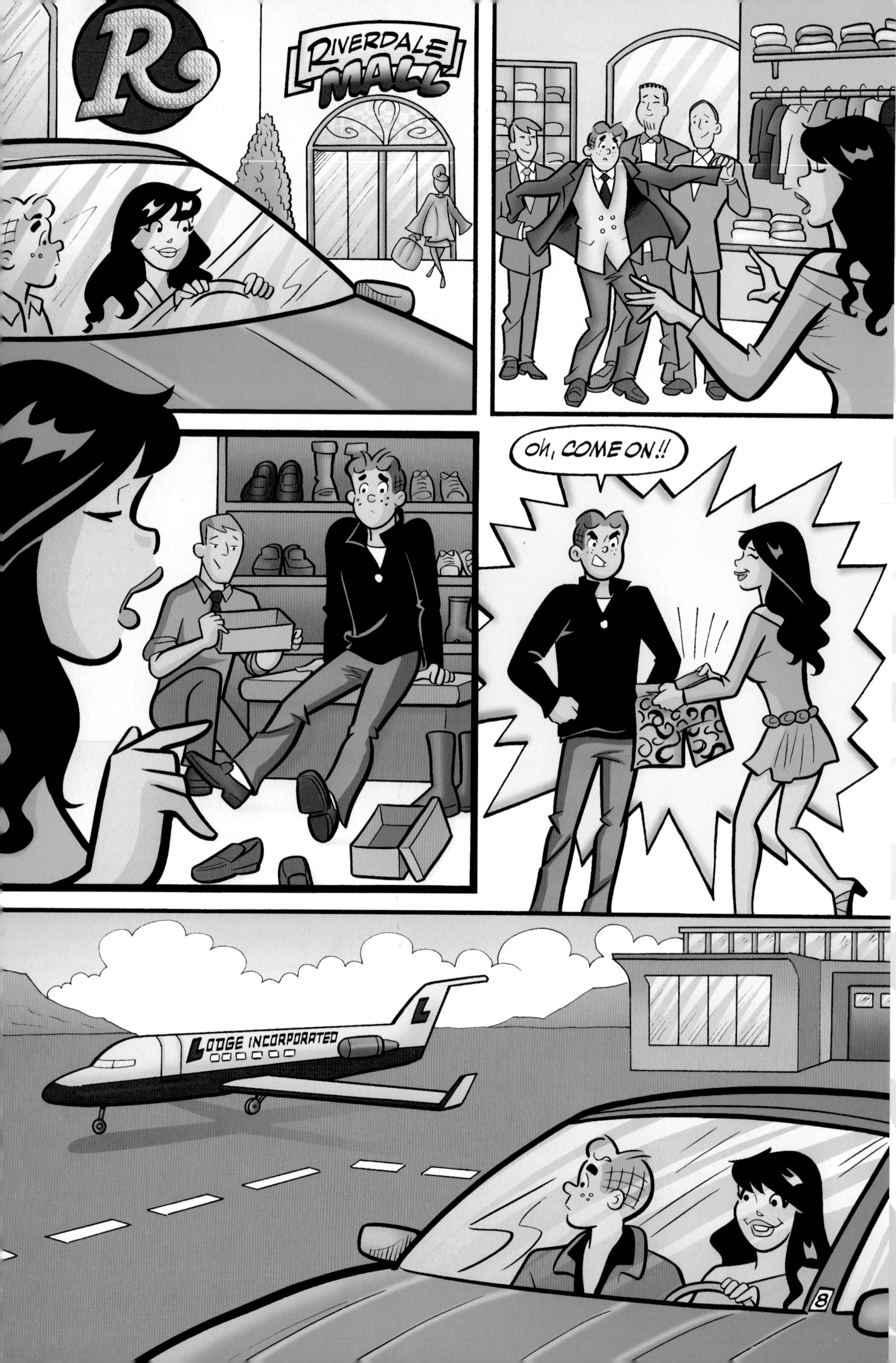
RIVERDALE MALL
Oh, COME ON!!
LODGE INCORPORATED
8

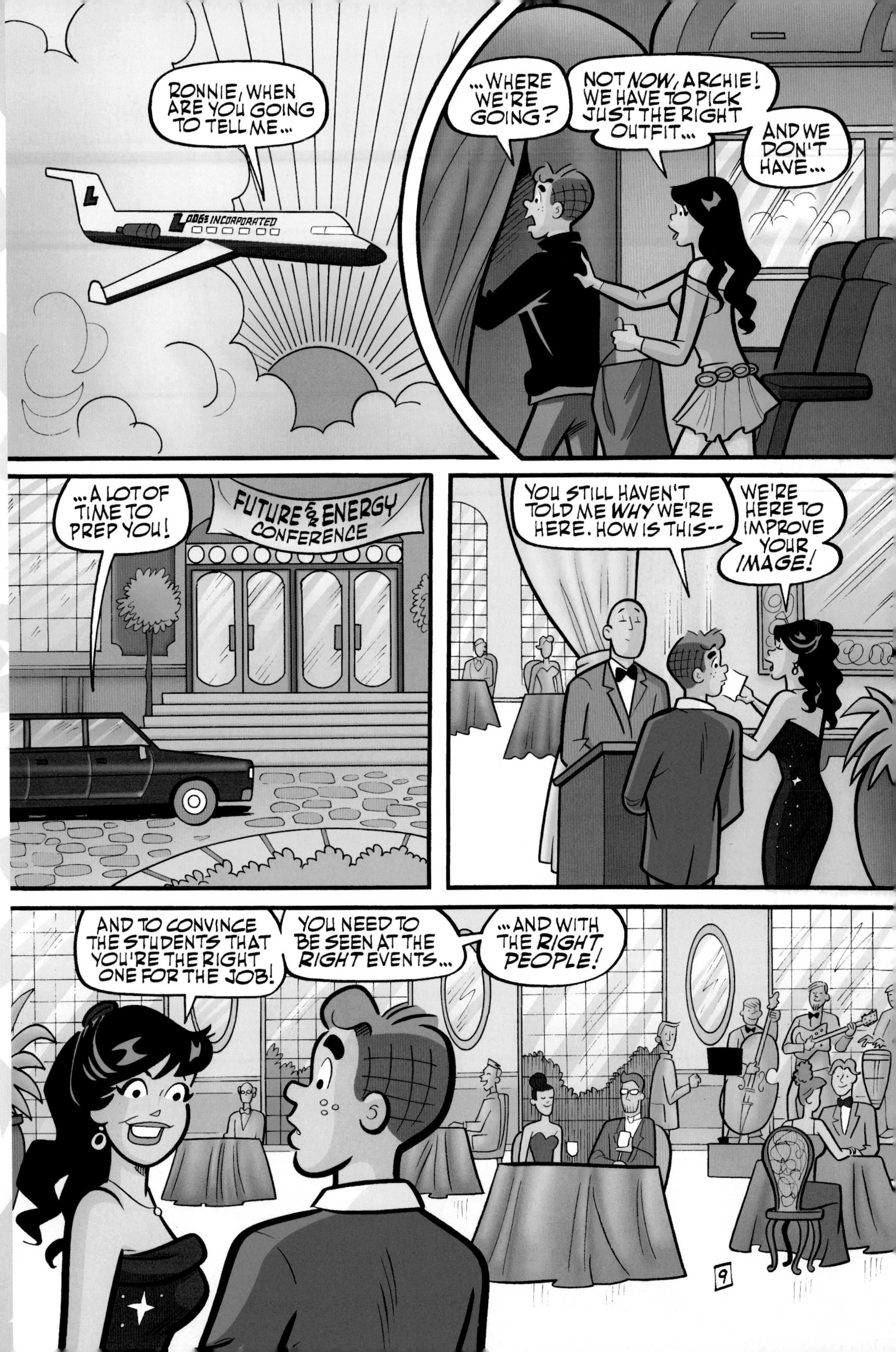
RONNIE, WHEN ARE YOU GOING TO TELL ME...
LODGE INCORPORATED
...WHERE WE'RE GOING?
NOT NOW, ARCHIE! WE HAVE TO PICK JUST THE RIGHT OUTFIT...
AND WE DON'T HAVE...
...A LOT OF TIME TO PREP YOU!
FUTURE OF ENERGY CONFERENCE
YOU STILL HAVEN'T TOLD ME WHY WE'RE HERE. HOW IS THIS--
WE'RE HERE TO IMPROVE YOUR IMAGE!
AND TO CONVINCE THE STUDENTS THAT YOU'RE THE RIGHT ONE FOR THE JOB!
YOU NEED TO BE SEEN AT THE RIGHT EVENTS...
...AND WITH THE RIGHT PEOPLE!

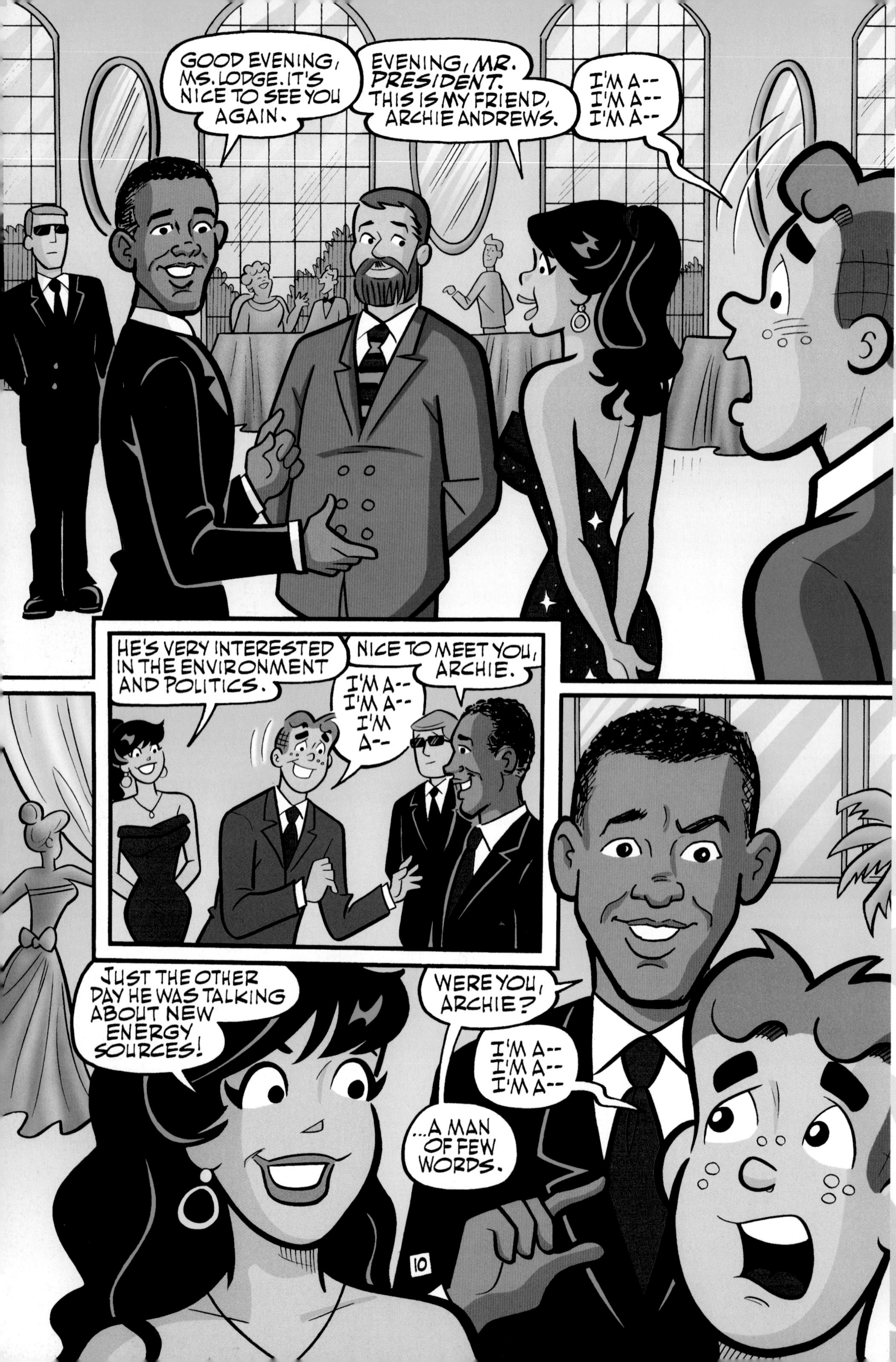
GOOD EVENING, MS. LODGE. IT'S NICE TO SEE YOU AGAIN.
EVENING, MR. PRESIDENT. THIS IS MY FRIEND, ARCHIE ANDREWS.
I'M A-- I'M A-- I'M A--
HE'S VERY INTERESTED IN THE ENVIRONMENT AND POLITICS.
NICE TO MEET YOU, ARCHIE.
I'M A-- I'M A-- I'M A--
JUST THE OTHER DAY HE WAS TALKING ABOUT NEW ENERGY SOURCES!
WERE YOU, ARCHIE?
I'M A-- I'M A-- I'M A--
...A MAN OF FEW WORDS.

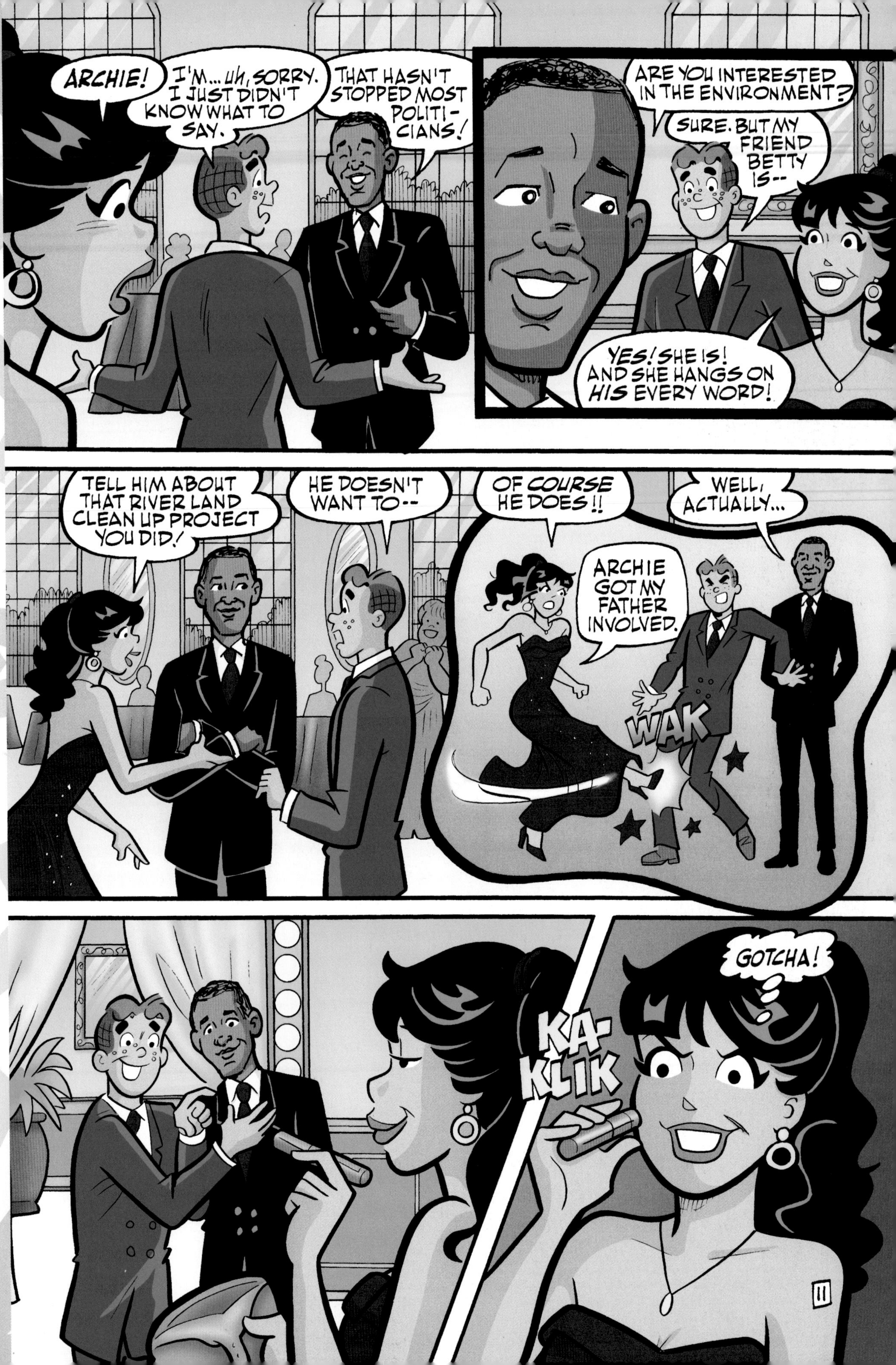
ARCHIE!
I'M... uh, SORRY. I JUST DIDN'T KNOW WHAT TO SAY.
THAT HASN'T STOPPED MOST POLITI-CIANS!
ARE YOU INTERESTED IN THE ENVIRONMENT?
SURE. BUT MY FRIEND BETTY IS--
YES! SHE IS! AND SHE HANGS ON HIS EVERY WORD!
TELL HIM ABOUT THAT RIVER LAND CLEAN UP PROJECT YOU DID!
HE DOESN'T WANT TO--
OF COURSE HE DOES!!
WELL, ACTUALLY...
ARCHIE GOT MY FATHER INVOLVED.
WAK
KA-KLIK
GOTCHA!

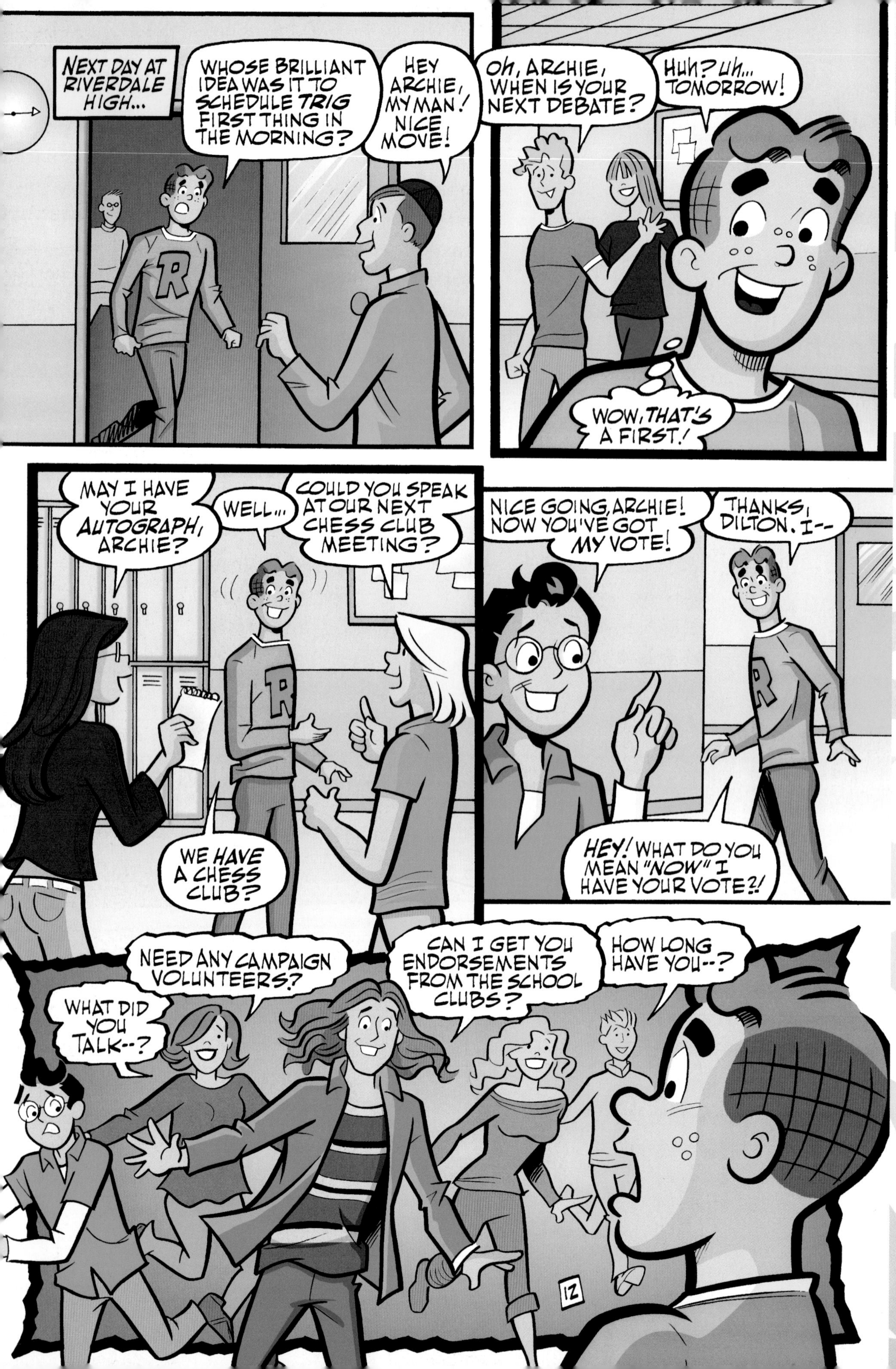
NEXT DAY AT RIVERDALE HIGH...
WHOSE BRILLIANT IDEA WAS IT TO SCHEDULE TRIG FIRST THING IN THE MORNING?
HEY ARCHIE, MY MAN! NICE MOVE!
Oh, ARCHIE, WHEN IS YOUR NEXT DEBATE?
Huh? uh... TOMORROW!
WOW, THAT'S A FIRST!
MAY I HAVE YOUR AUTOGRAPH, ARCHIE?
WELL...
COULD YOU SPEAK AT OUR NEXT CHESS CLUB MEETING?
WE HAVE A CHESS CLUB?
NICE GOING, ARCHIE! NOW YOU'VE GOT MY VOTE!
THANKS, DILTON. I--
HEY! WHAT DO YOU MEAN "NOW" I HAVE YOUR VOTE?!
WHAT DID YOU TALK--?
NEED ANY CAMPAIGN VOLUNTEERS?
CAN I GET YOU ENDORSEMENTS FROM THE SCHOOL CLUBS?
HOW LONG HAVE YOU--?
12

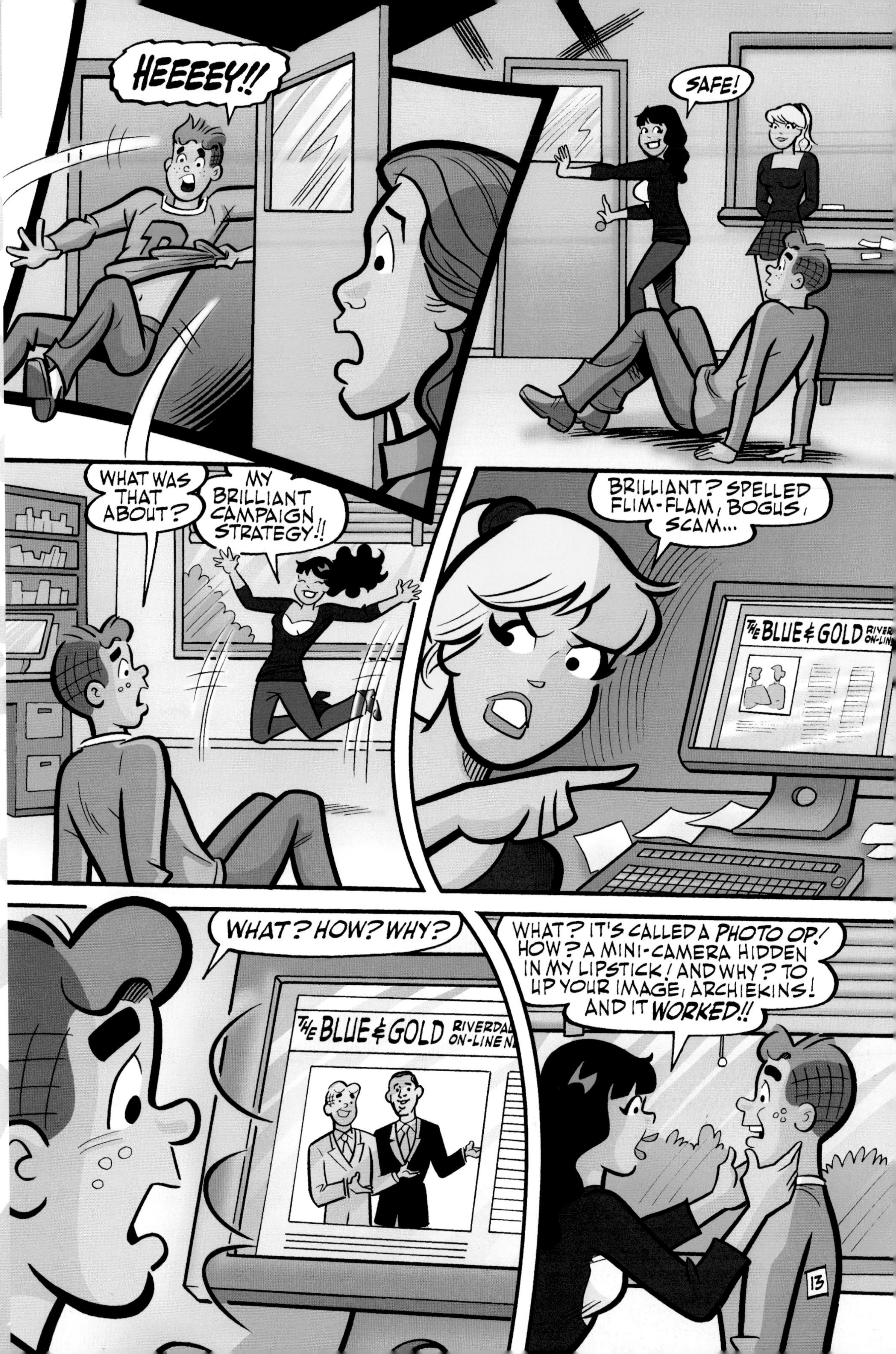
HEEEEEY!!
SAFE!
WHAT WAS THAT ABOUT?
MY BRILLIANT CAMPAIGN STRATEGY!!
BRILLIANT? SPELLED FLIM-FLAM, BOGUS, SCAM...
THE BLUE & GOLD
WHAT? HOW? WHY?
WHAT? IT'S CALLED A PHOTO OP! HOW? A MINI-CAMERA HIDDEN IN MY LIPSTICK! AND WHY? TO UP YOUR IMAGE, ARCHIEKINS! AND IT WORKED!!
THE BLUE & GOLD RIVERDAL ON-LINE N
13

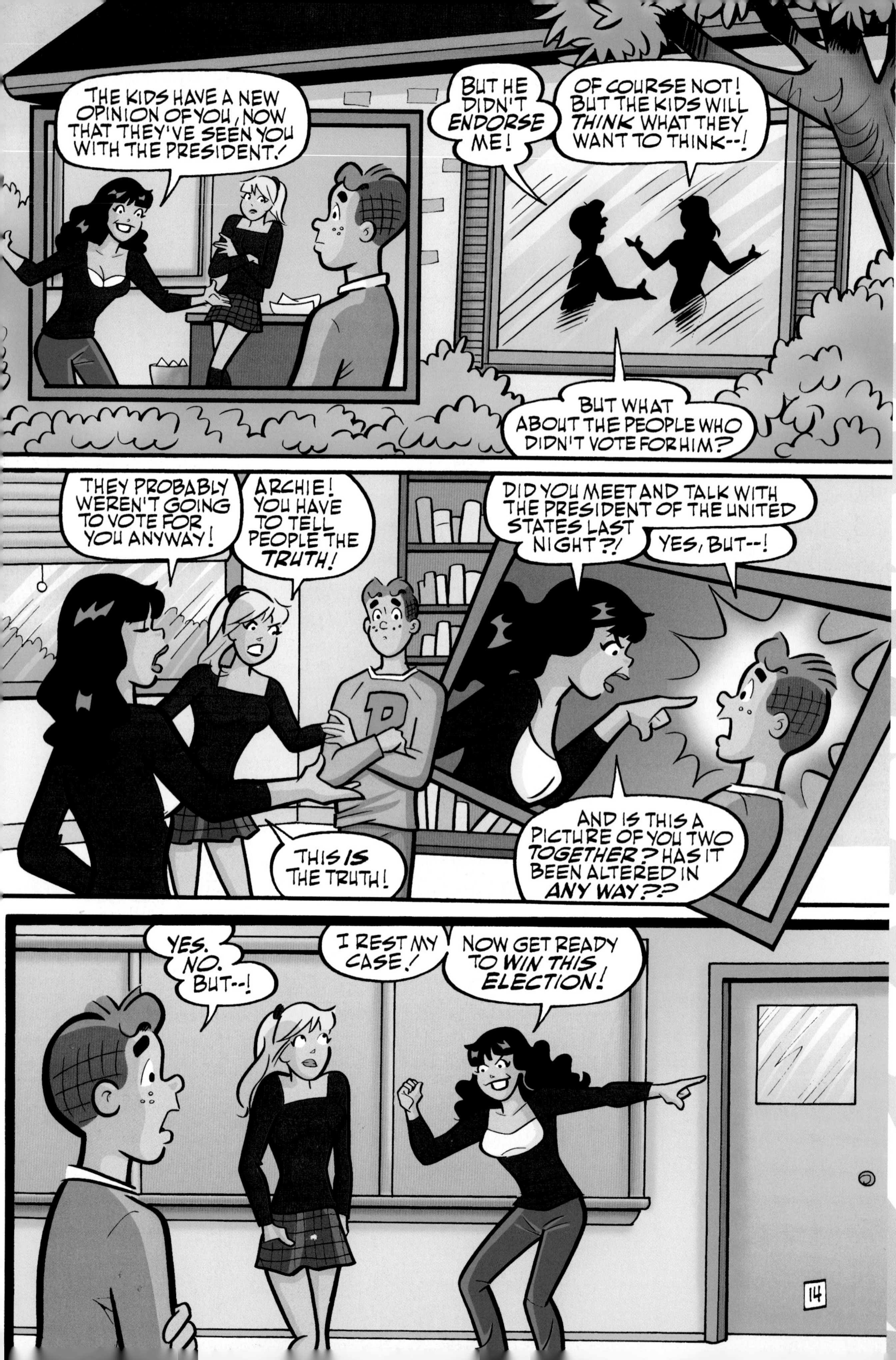
THE KIDS HAVE A NEW OPINION OF YOU, NOW THAT THEY'VE SEEN YOU WITH THE PRESIDENT!
BUT HE DIDN'T ENDORSE ME!
OF COURSE NOT! BUT THE KIDS WILL THINK WHAT THEY WANT TO THINK--!
BUT WHAT ABOUT THE PEOPLE WHO DIDN'T VOTE FOR HIM?
THEY PROBABLY WEREN'T GOING TO VOTE FOR YOU ANYWAY!
ARCHIE! YOU HAVE TO TELL PEOPLE THE TRUTH!
DID YOU MEET AND TALK WITH THE PRESIDENT OF THE UNITED STATES LAST NIGHT?!
YES, BUT--!
AND IS THIS A PICTURE OF YOU TWO TOGETHER? HAS IT BEEN ALTERED IN ANY WAY??
THIS IS THE TRUTH!
YES. NO. BUT--!
I REST MY CASE!
NOW GET READY TO WIN THIS ELECTION!
14

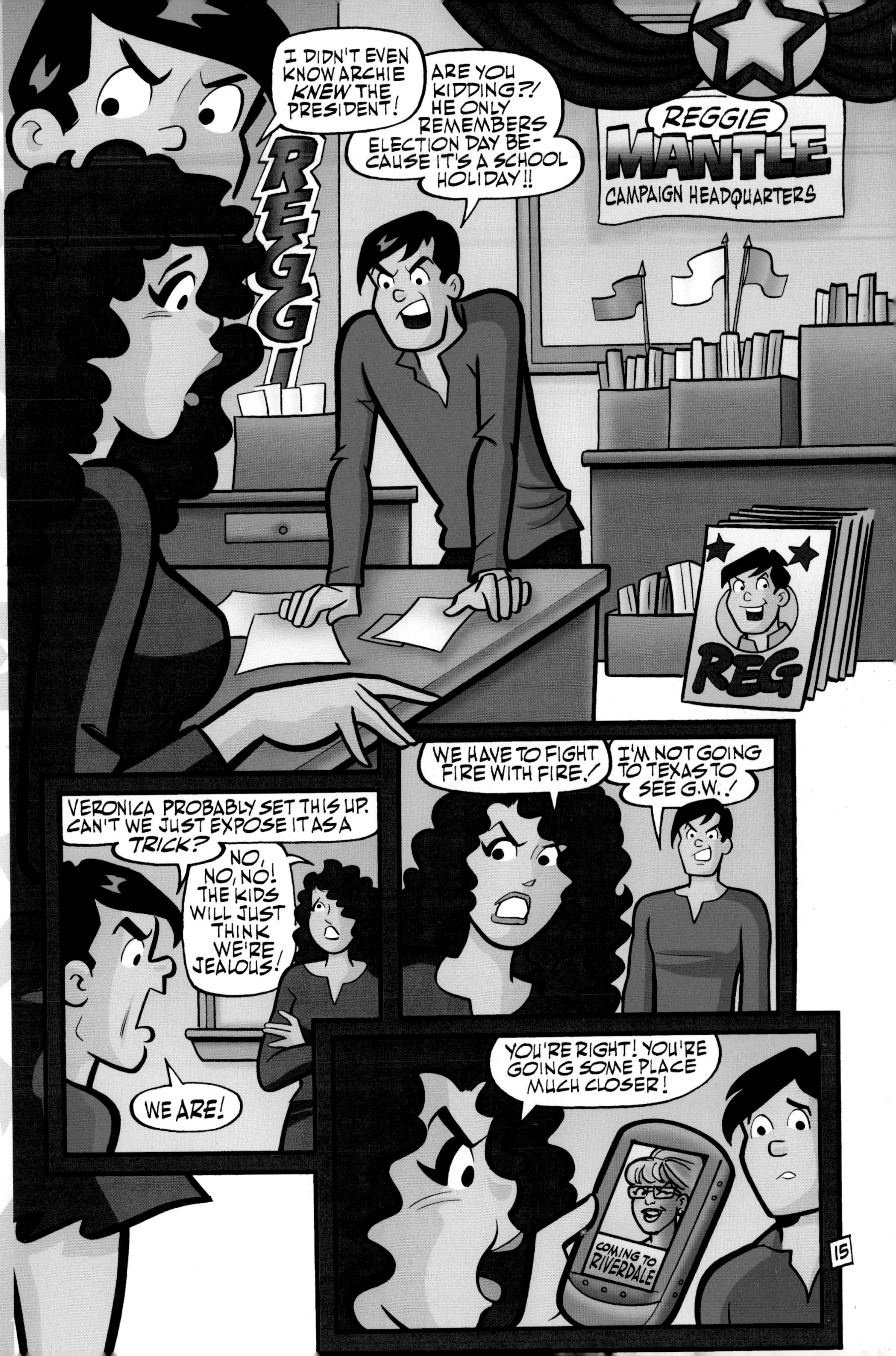

REGGIE MANTLE CAMPAIGN HEADQUARTERS
I DIDN'T EVEN KNOW ARCHIE KNEW THE PRESIDENT!
ARE YOU KIDDING?! HE ONLY REMEMBERS ELECTION DAY BECAUSE IT'S A SCHOOL HOLIDAY!!
REGGIE!
REG
VERONICA PROBABLY SET THIS UP. CAN'T WE JUST EXPOSE IT AS A TRICK?
NO, NO, NO! THE KIDS WILL JUST THINK WE'RE JEALOUS!
WE ARE!
WE HAVE TO FIGHT FIRE WITH FIRE!
I'M NOT GOING TO TEXAS TO SEE G.W.!
YOU'RE RIGHT! YOU'RE GOING SOME PLACE MUCH CLOSER!
COMING TO RIVERDALE

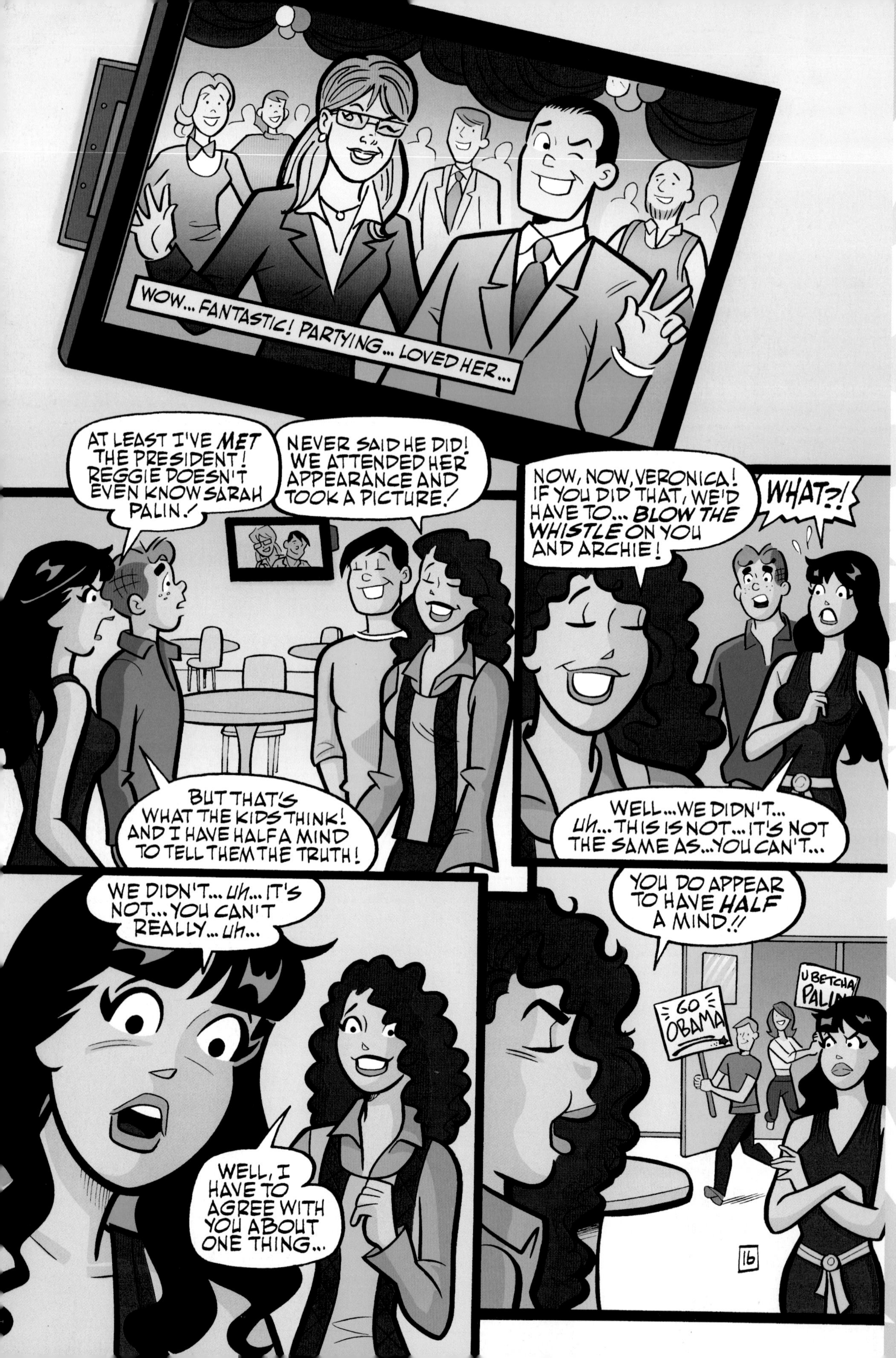
WOW... FANTASTIC! PARTYING... LOVED HER...
AT LEAST I'VE MET THE PRESIDENT! REGGIE DOESN'T EVEN KNOW SARAH PALIN!
NEVER SAID HE DID! WE ATTENDED HER APPEARANCE AND TOOK A PICTURE!
BUT THAT'S WHAT THE KIDS THINK! AND I HAVE HALF A MIND TO TELL THEM THE TRUTH!
NOW, NOW, VERONICA! IF YOU DID THAT, WE'D HAVE TO... BLOW THE WHISTLE ON YOU AND ARCHIE!
WHAT?!
WELL... WE DIDN'T... UH... THIS IS NOT... IT'S NOT THE SAME AS... YOU CAN'T...
WE DIDN'T... UH... IT'S NOT... YOU CAN'T REALLY... UH...
WELL, I HAVE TO AGREE WITH YOU ABOUT ONE THING...
YOU DO APPEAR TO HAVE HALF A MIND!!
GO OBAMA
U BETCHA PALIN
16

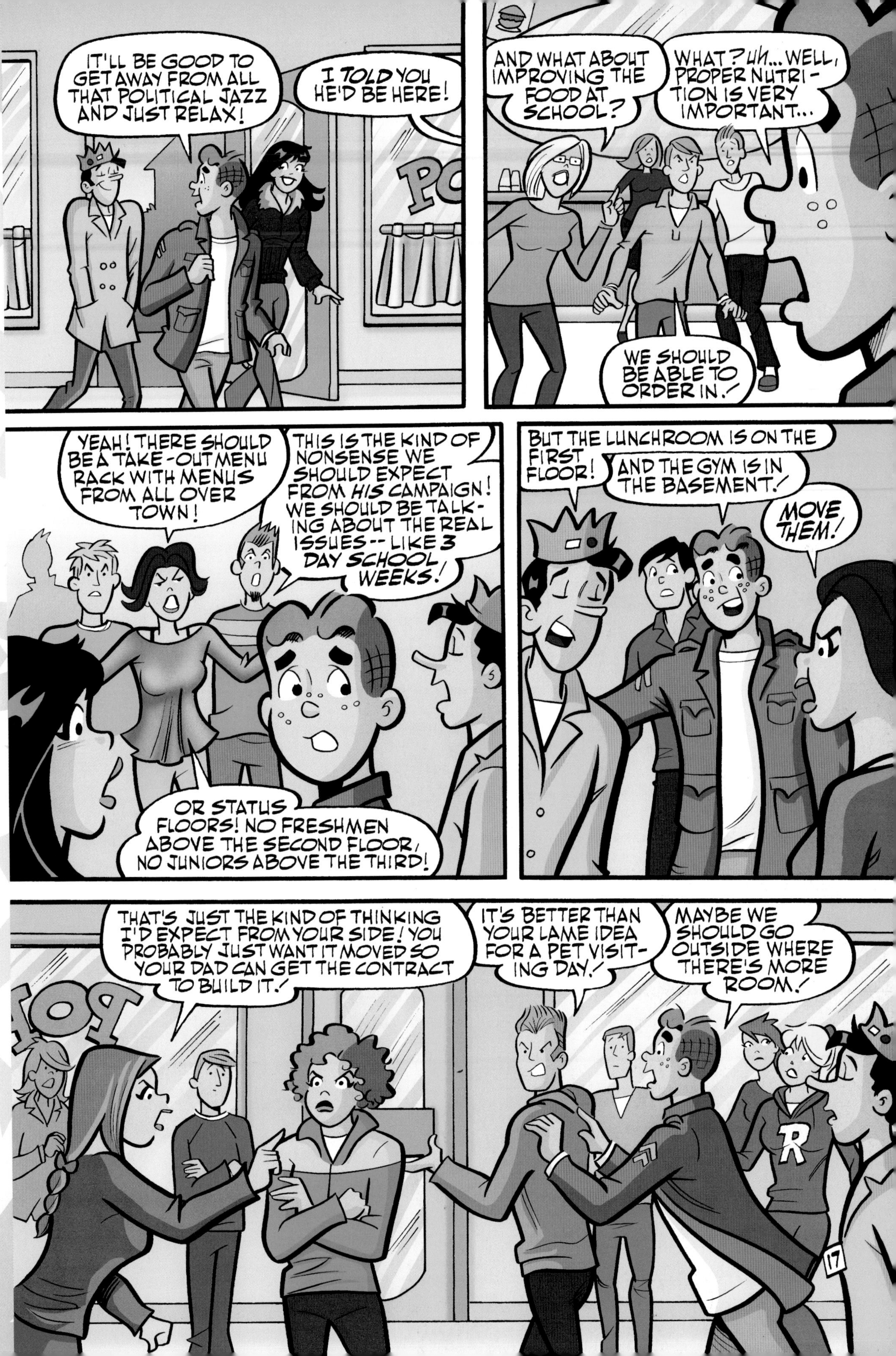
IT'LL BE GOOD TO GET AWAY FROM ALL THAT POLITICAL JAZZ AND JUST RELAX!
I *TOLD* YOU HE'D BE HERE!
AND WHAT ABOUT IMPROVING THE FOOD AT SCHOOL?
WHAT? *UH*... WELL, PROPER NUTRITION IS VERY IMPORTANT...
WE SHOULD BE ABLE TO ORDER IN!
YEAH! THERE SHOULD BE A TAKE-OUT MENU RACK WITH MENUS FROM ALL OVER TOWN!
THIS IS THE KIND OF NONSENSE WE SHOULD EXPECT FROM *HIS* CAMPAIGN! WE SHOULD BE TALKING ABOUT THE REAL ISSUES -- LIKE 3 DAY *SCHOOL* WEEKS!
OR STATUS FLOORS! NO FRESHMEN ABOVE THE SECOND FLOOR, NO JUNIORS ABOVE THE THIRD!
BUT THE LUNCHROOM IS ON THE FIRST FLOOR!
AND THE GYM IS IN THE BASEMENT!
MOVE THEM!
THAT'S JUST THE KIND OF THINKING I'D EXPECT FROM YOUR SIDE! YOU PROBABLY JUST WANT IT MOVED SO YOUR DAD CAN GET THE CONTRACT TO BUILD IT!
IT'S BETTER THAN YOUR LAME IDEA FOR A PET VISITING DAY!
MAYBE WE SHOULD GO OUTSIDE WHERE THERE'S MORE ROOM!
17

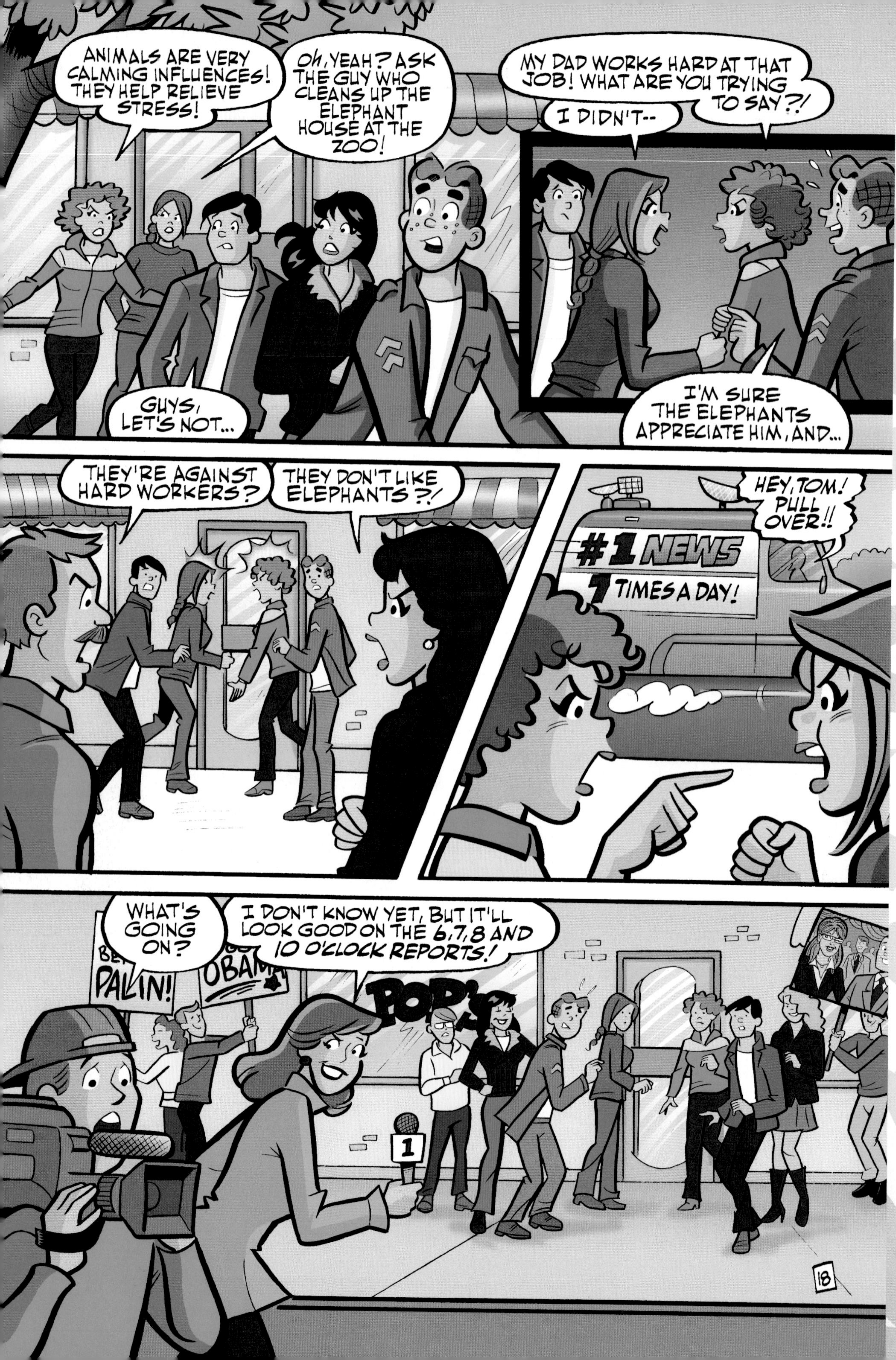
ANIMALS ARE VERY CALMING INFLUENCES! THEY HELP RELIEVE STRESS!
Oh, YEAH? ASK THE GUY WHO CLEANS UP THE ELEPHANT HOUSE AT THE ZOO!
GUYS, LET'S NOT...
MY DAD WORKS HARD AT THAT JOB! WHAT ARE YOU TRYING TO SAY?!
I DIDN'T--
I'M SURE THE ELEPHANTS APPRECIATE HIM, AND...
THEY'RE AGAINST HARD WORKERS?
THEY DON'T LIKE ELEPHANTS?!
HEY, TOM! PULL OVER!!
#1 NEWS
7 TIMES A DAY!
WHAT'S GOING ON?
I DON'T KNOW YET, BUT IT'LL LOOK GOOD ON THE 6, 7, 8 AND 10 O'CLOCK REPORTS!
PALIN!
OBAMA
POP'S
1
18

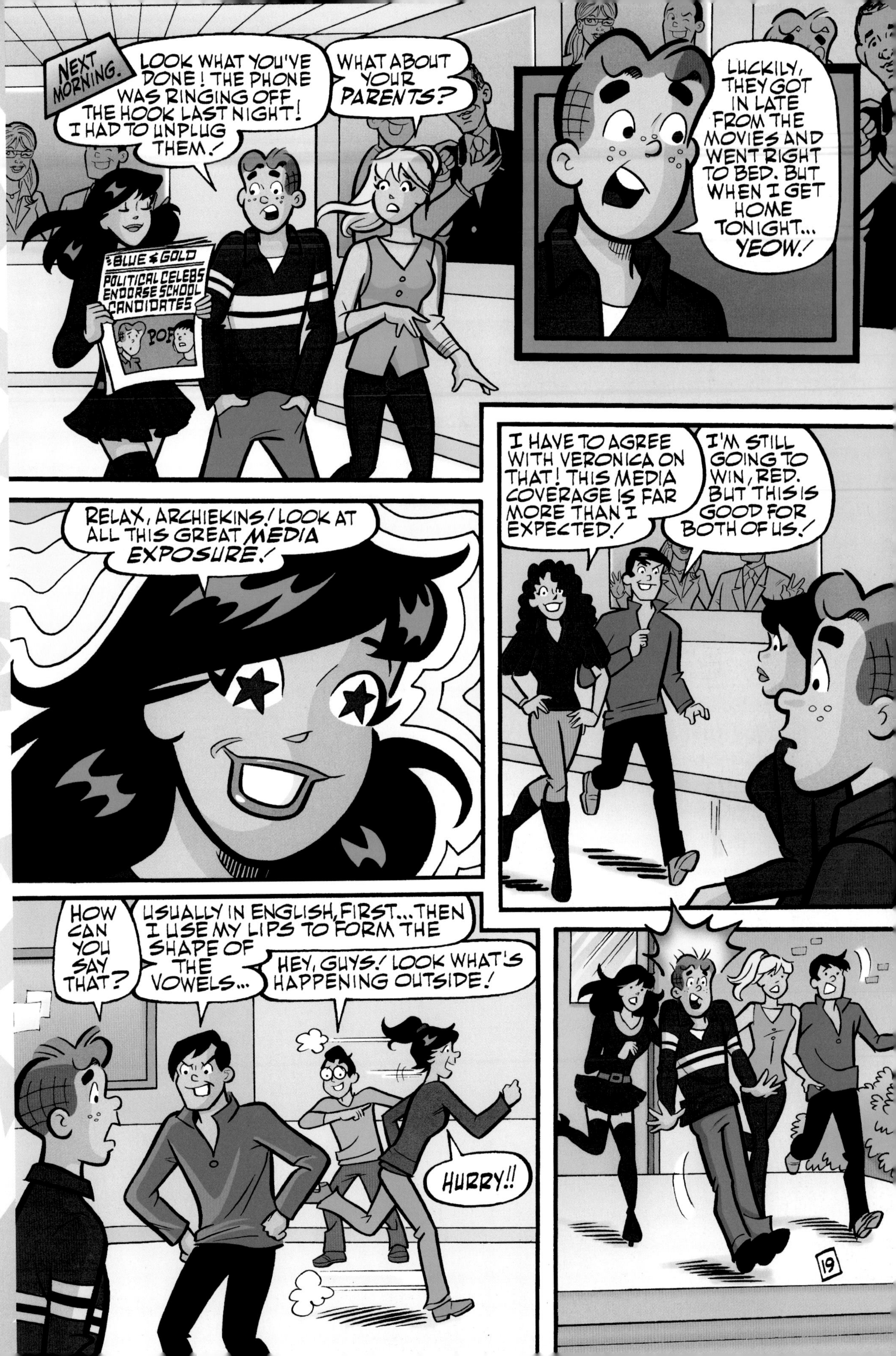
NEXT MORNING.
LOOK WHAT YOU'VE DONE! THE PHONE WAS RINGING OFF THE HOOK LAST NIGHT! I HAD TO UNPLUG THEM!
WHAT ABOUT YOUR PARENTS?
BLUE & GOLD
POLITICAL CELEBS ENDORSE SCHOOL CANDIDATES
POP
LUCKILY, THEY GOT IN LATE FROM THE MOVIES AND WENT RIGHT TO BED. BUT WHEN I GET HOME TONIGHT... YEOW!
RELAX, ARCHIEKINS! LOOK AT ALL THIS GREAT MEDIA EXPOSURE!
I HAVE TO AGREE WITH VERONICA ON THAT! THIS MEDIA COVERAGE IS FAR MORE THAN I EXPECTED!
I'M STILL GOING TO WIN, RED. BUT THIS IS GOOD FOR BOTH OF US!
HOW CAN YOU SAY THAT?
USUALLY IN ENGLISH, FIRST... THEN I USE MY LIPS TO FORM THE SHAPE OF THE VOWELS...
HEY, GUYS! LOOK WHAT'S HAPPENING OUTSIDE!
HURRY!!

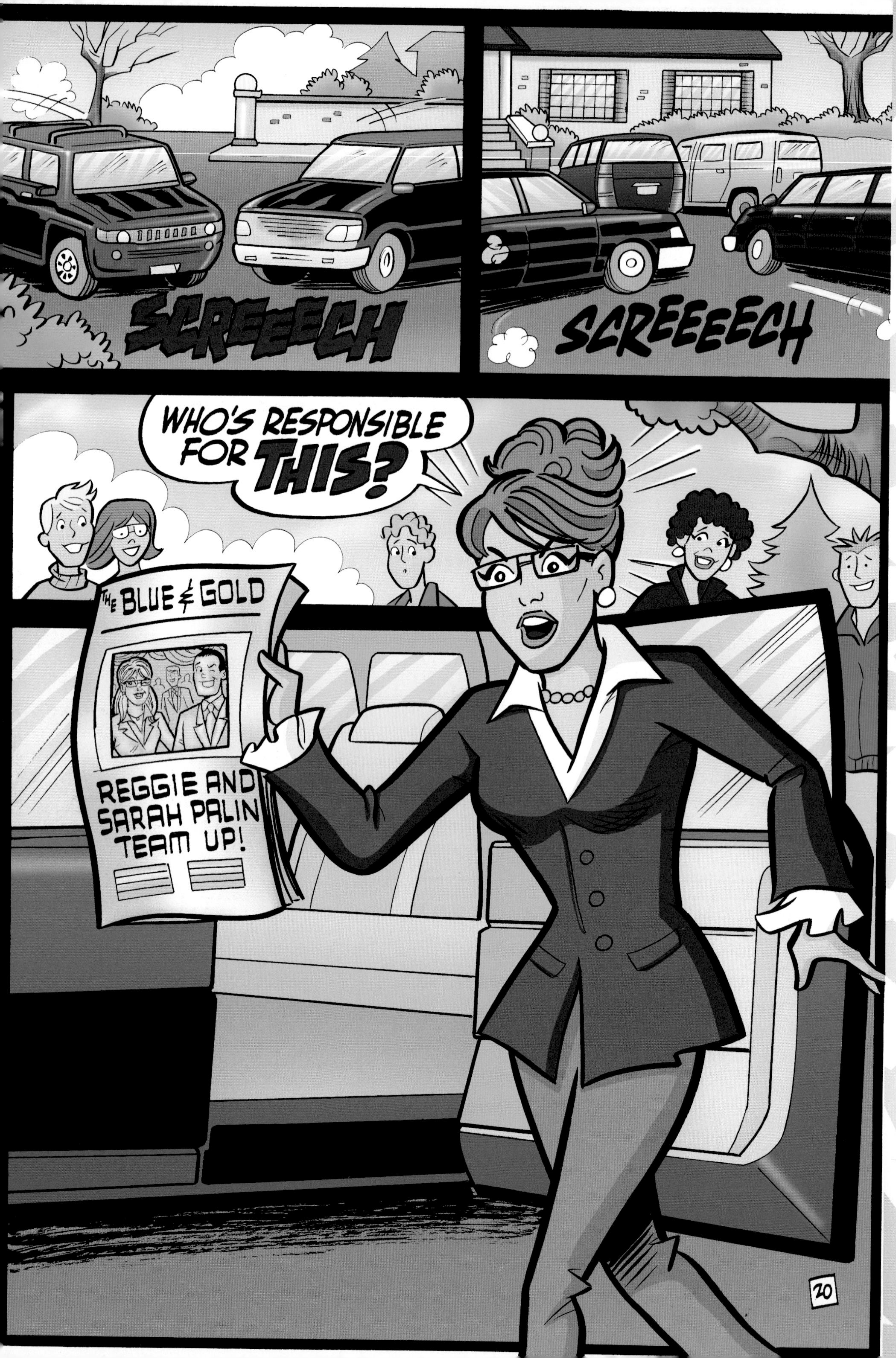
SCREEECH
SCREEEEECH
WHO'S RESPONSIBLE FOR THIS?
THE BLUE & GOLD
REGGIE AND SARAH PALIN TEAM UP!
20

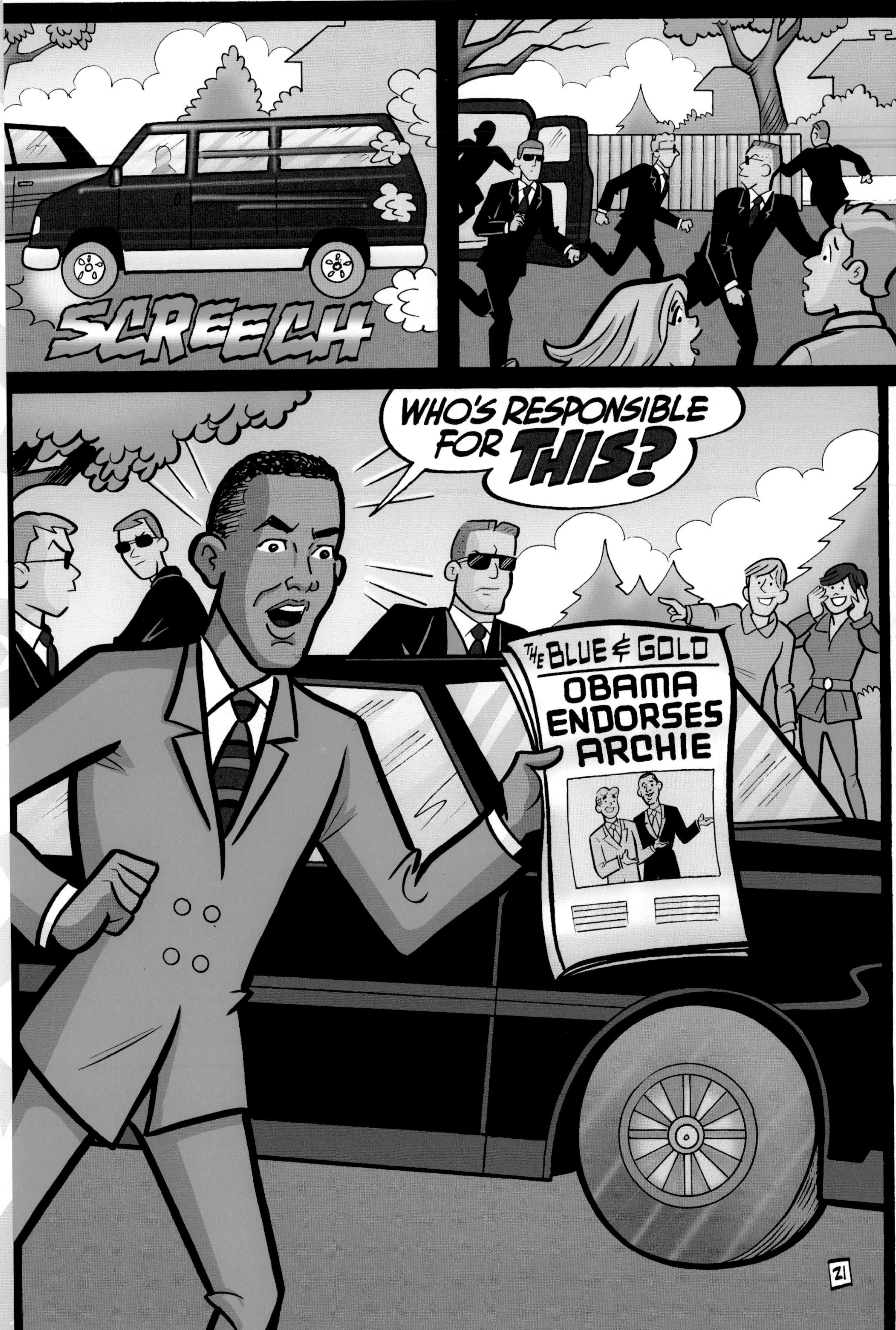
SCREECH
WHO'S RESPONSIBLE FOR THIS?
THE BLUE & GOLD
OBAMA ENDORSES ARCHIE

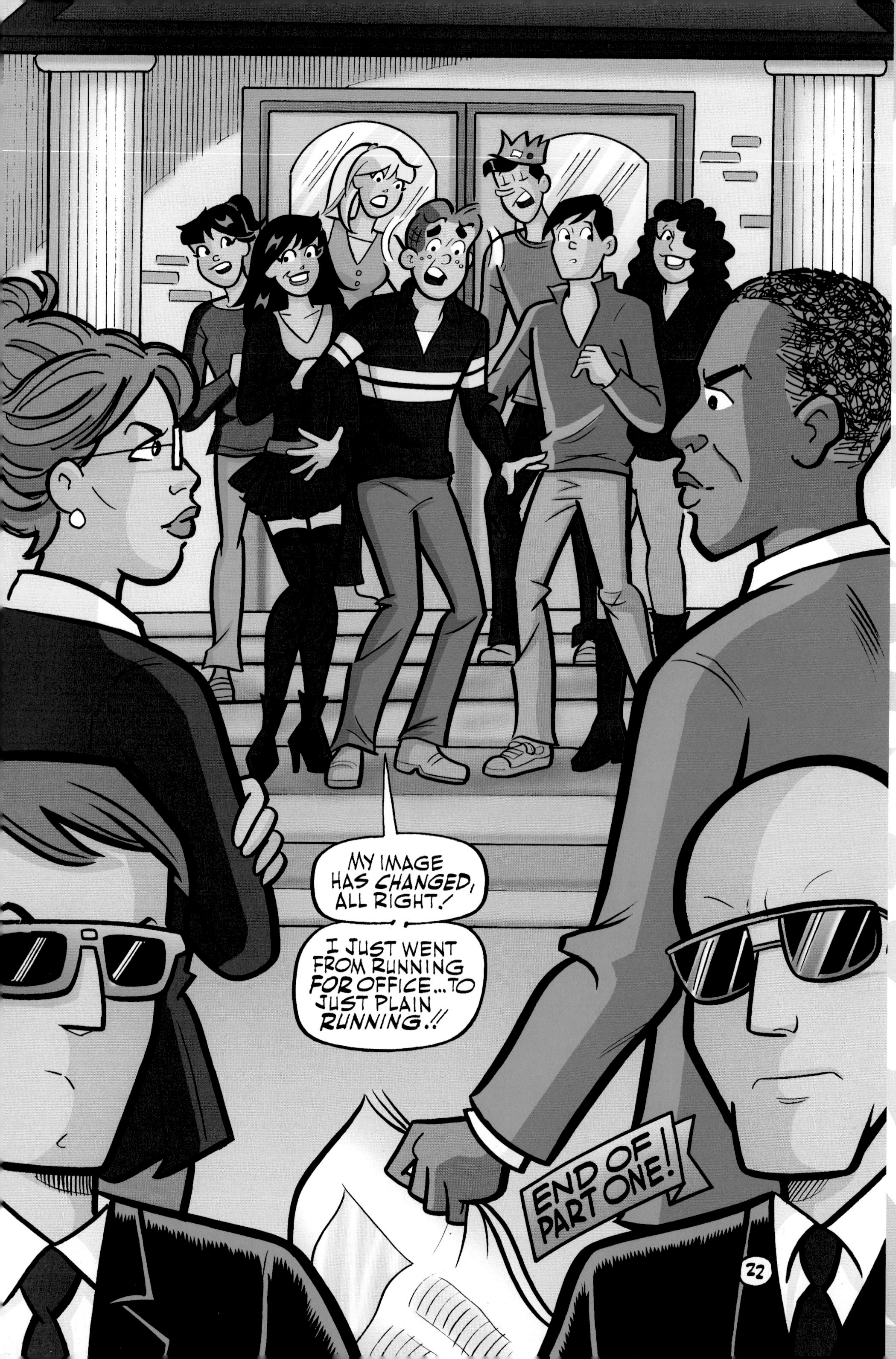
MY IMAGE HAS CHANGED, ALL RIGHT!
I JUST WENT FROM RUNNING FOR OFFICE... TO JUST PLAIN RUNNING.!!
END OF PART ONE!
22

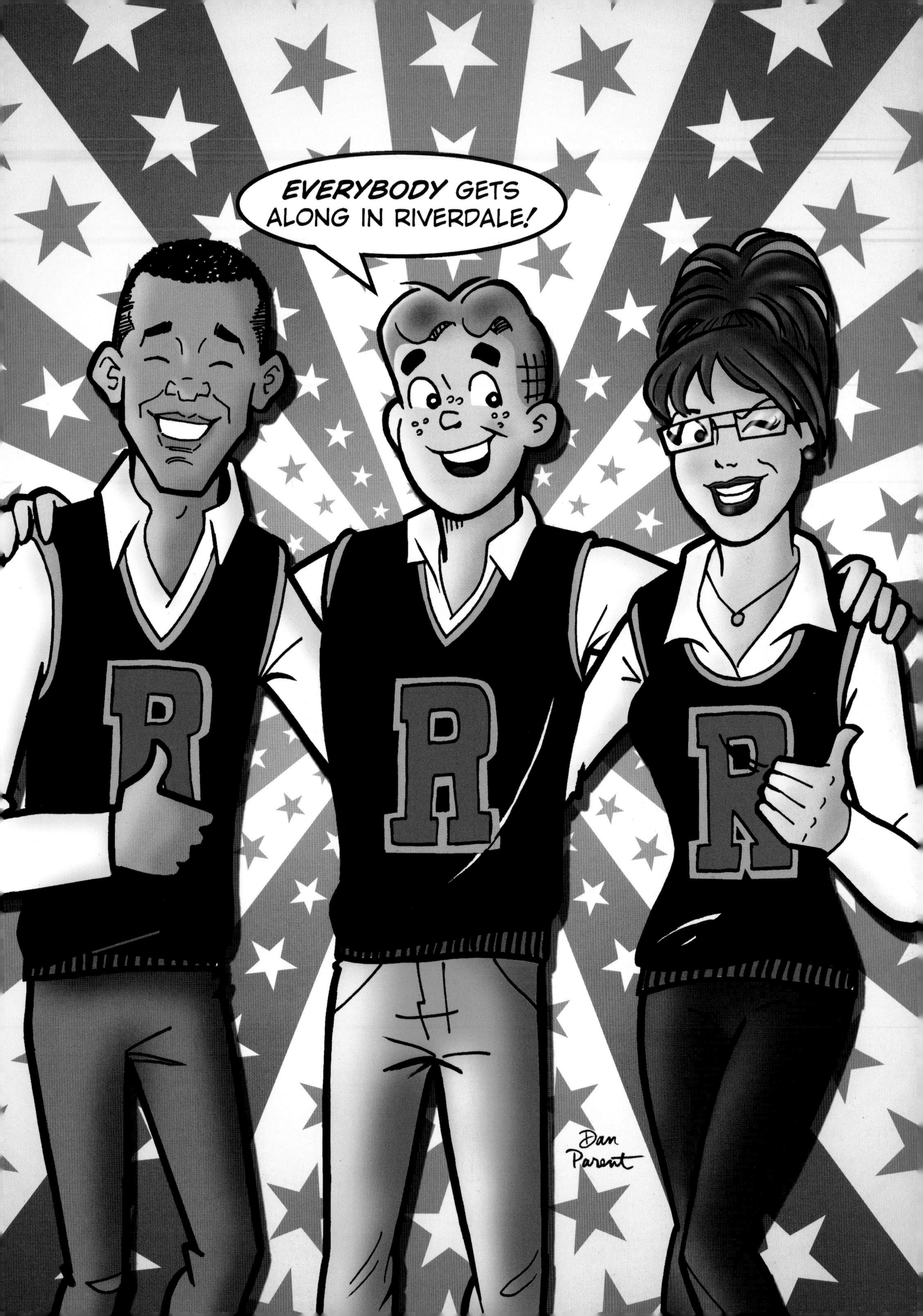
EVERYBODY GETS ALONG IN RIVERDALE!
Dan Parent

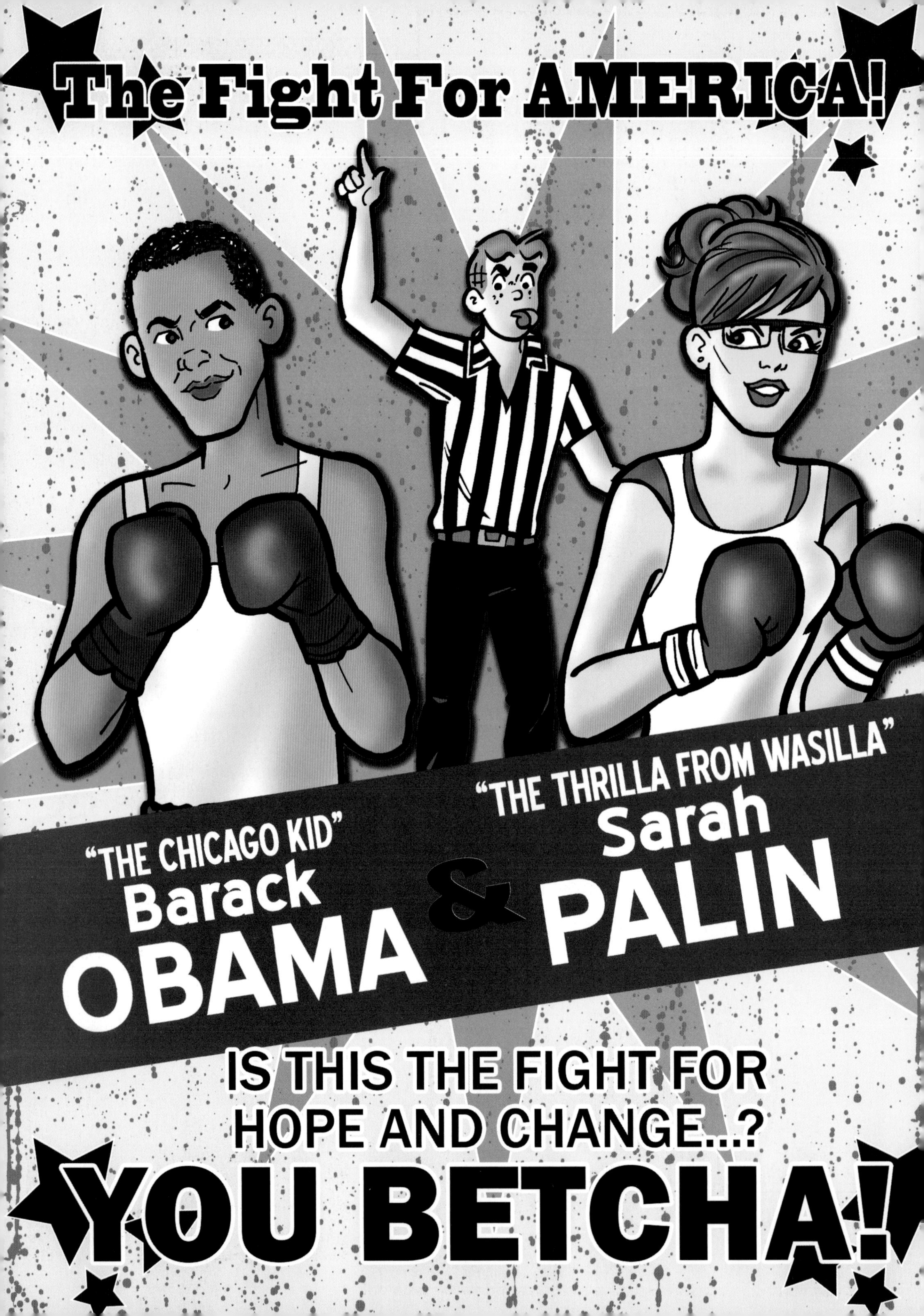

The Fight For AMERICA!
"THE CHICAGO KID"
Barack
OBAMA
&
"THE THRILLA FROM WASILLA"
Sarah
PALIN
IS THIS THE FIGHT FOR
HOPE AND CHANGE...?
YOU BETCHA!

RE-CAP

COME ON, ETHEL! WE HAVE TO MOVE WHILE THIS STORY IS *HOT!* WHAT HAVE WE GOT?

WELL, OKAY... HERE'S WHAT HAPPENED SO FAR...

ARCHIE HAS BEEN RUNNING AGAINST REGGIE FOR STUDENT BODY PRESIDENT!

AND REGGIE'S BEEN BEATING HIM IN THE POLLS LIKE A FAST FOOD OMELET!

BE KIND. SO VERONICA, AS ARCHIE'S PRESS AGENT, ARRANGES TO GET A PHOTO OF ARCHIE WITH THE PRESIDENT TO BOOST HIS REPUTATION!

BEING SEEN WITH ARCHIE WOULD BOOST *ANYBODY'S* REP!

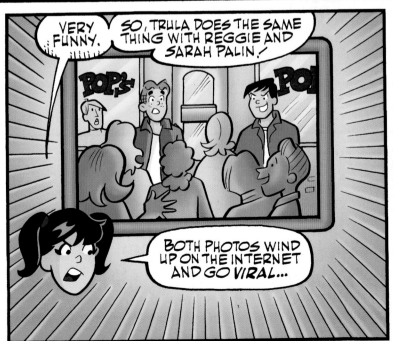

VERY FUNNY.

SO, TRULA DOES THE SAME THING WITH REGGIE AND SARAH PALIN!

POP'S!

POP'S

BOTH PHOTOS WIND UP ON THE INTERNET AND GO *VIRAL...*

...AND THE NATION GOES CRAZY IN *24 HOURS!*

GIVING US A SHOT AT THE HOTTEST STORY EVER TO HIT RIVERDALE, WHEN...

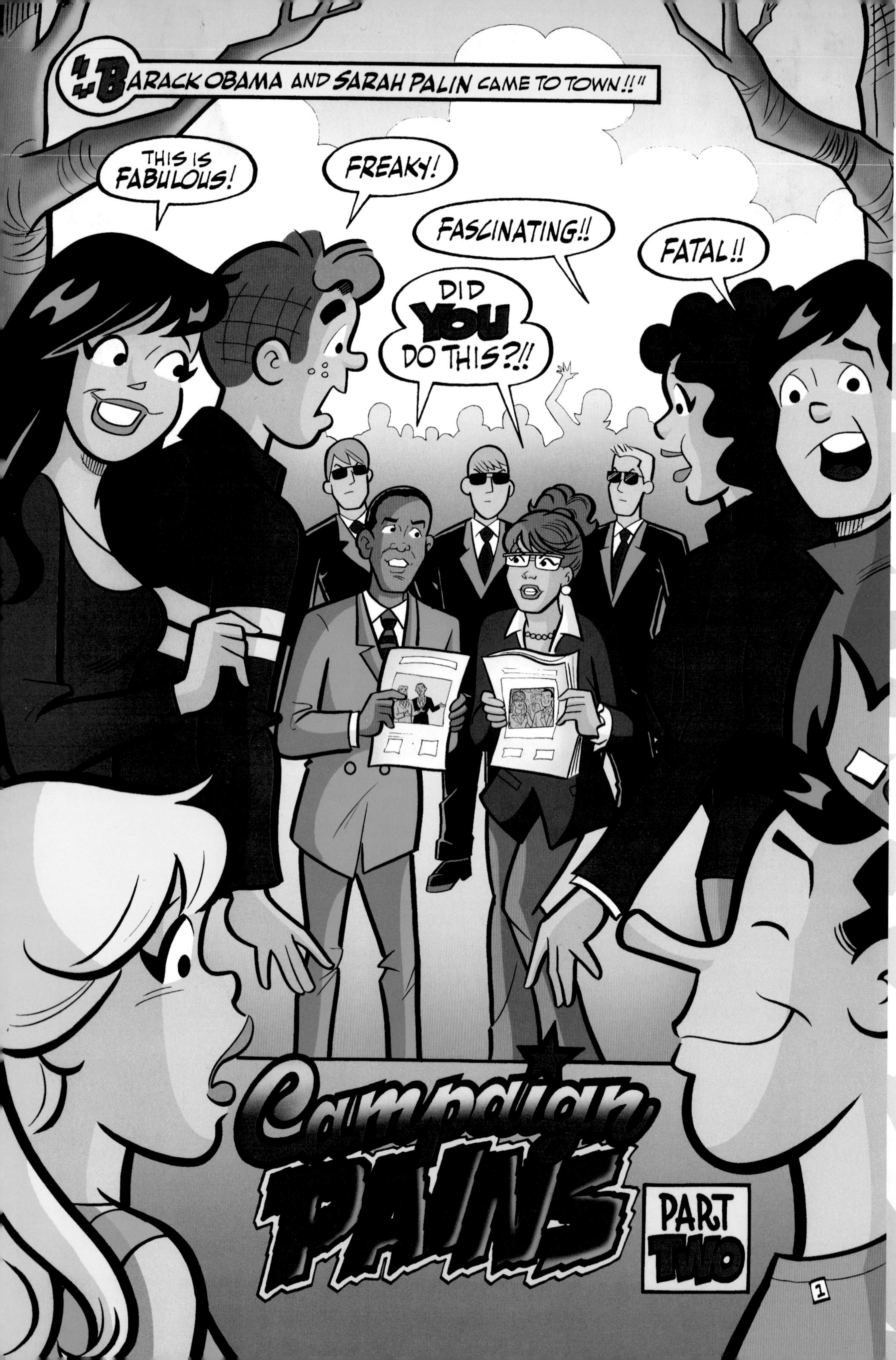

"BARACK OBAMA AND SARAH PALIN CAME TO TOWN!!"
THIS IS FABULOUS!
FREAKY!
FASCINATING!!
FATAL!!
DID YOU DO THIS?!!
Campaign PAINS
PART TWO

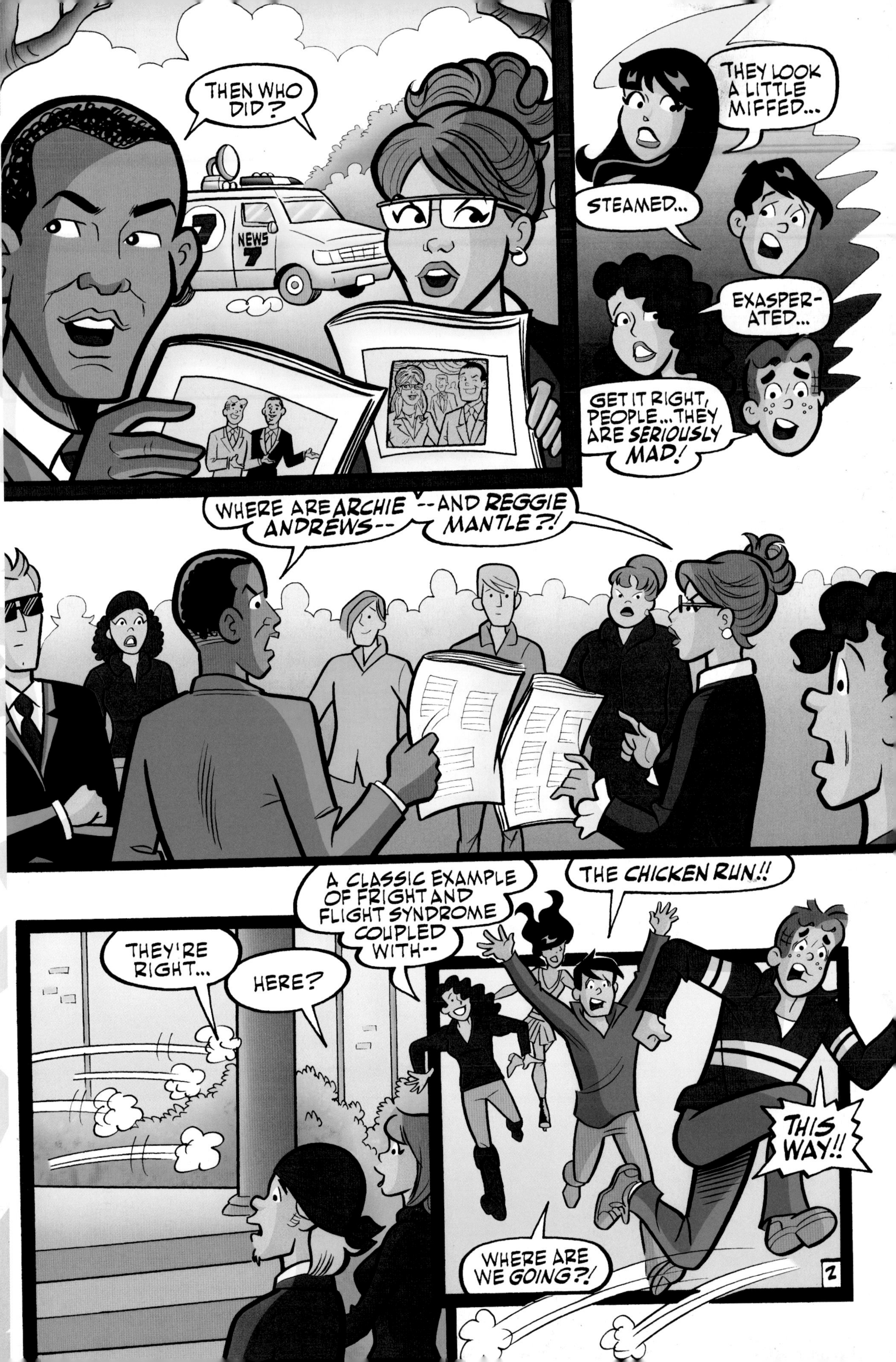
THEN WHO DID?
THEY LOOK A LITTLE MIFFED...
STEAMED...
EXASPERATED...
GET IT RIGHT, PEOPLE... THEY ARE SERIOUSLY MAD!
NEWS 7
WHERE ARE ARCHIE ANDREWS--
--AND REGGIE MANTLE?!
THEY'RE RIGHT...
HERE?
A CLASSIC EXAMPLE OF FRIGHT AND FLIGHT SYNDROME COUPLED WITH--
THE CHICKEN RUN!!
THIS WAY!!
WHERE ARE WE GOING?!
2

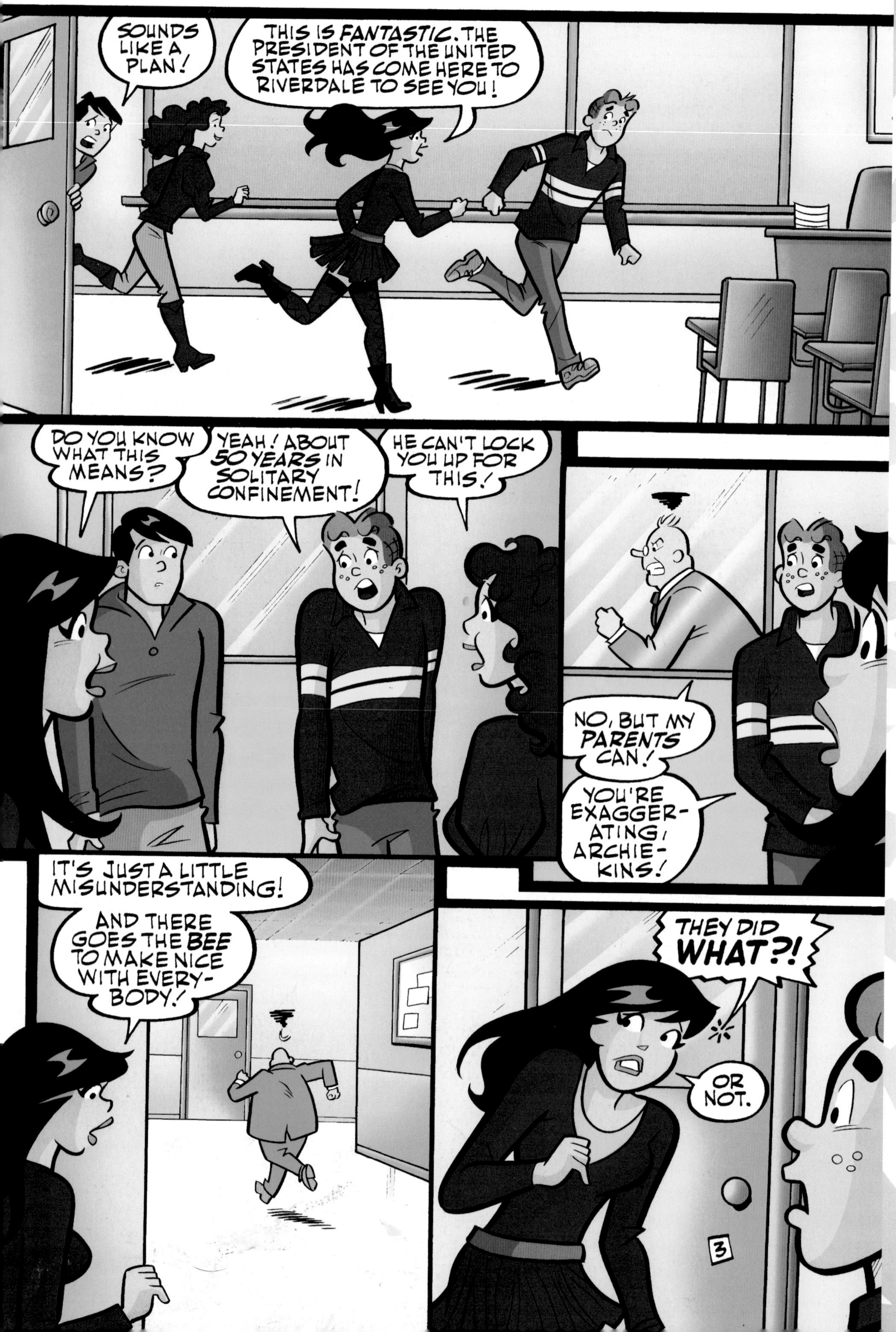
SOUNDS LIKE A PLAN!
THIS IS FANTASTIC. THE PRESIDENT OF THE UNITED STATES HAS COME HERE TO RIVERDALE TO SEE YOU!
DO YOU KNOW WHAT THIS MEANS?
YEAH! ABOUT 50 YEARS IN SOLITARY CONFINEMENT!
HE CAN'T LOCK YOU UP FOR THIS!
NO, BUT MY PARENTS CAN!
YOU'RE EXAGGER-ATING, ARCHIE-KINS!
IT'S JUST A LITTLE MISUNDERSTANDING!
AND THERE GOES THE BEE TO MAKE NICE WITH EVERY-BODY!
THEY DID WHAT?!
OR NOT.

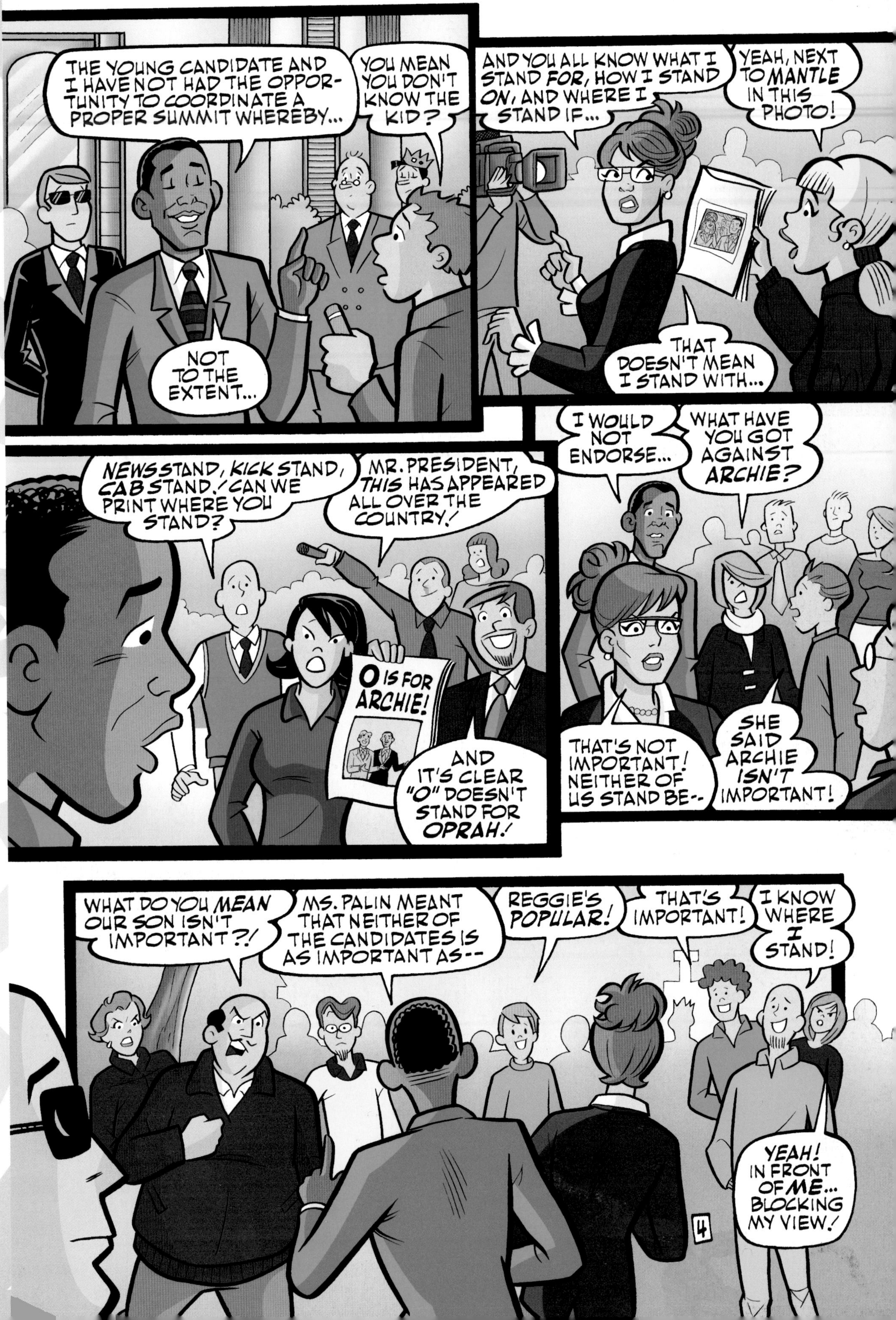

THE YOUNG CANDIDATE AND I HAVE NOT HAD THE OPPORTUNITY TO COORDINATE A PROPER SUMMIT WHEREBY...
YOU MEAN YOU DON'T KNOW THE KID?
NOT TO THE EXTENT...
AND YOU ALL KNOW WHAT I STAND FOR, HOW I STAND ON, AND WHERE I STAND IF...
YEAH, NEXT TO MANTLE IN THIS PHOTO!
THAT DOESN'T MEAN I STAND WITH...
NEWSSTAND, KICKSTAND, CABSTAND! CAN WE PRINT WHERE YOU STAND?
MR. PRESIDENT, THIS HAS APPEARED ALL OVER THE COUNTRY!
O IS FOR ARCHIE!
AND IT'S CLEAR "O" DOESN'T STAND FOR OPRAH!
I WOULD NOT ENDORSE...
WHAT HAVE YOU GOT AGAINST ARCHIE?
THAT'S NOT IMPORTANT! NEITHER OF US STAND BE--
SHE SAID ARCHIE ISN'T IMPORTANT!
WHAT DO YOU MEAN OUR SON ISN'T IMPORTANT?!
MS. PALIN MEANT THAT NEITHER OF THE CANDIDATES IS AS IMPORTANT AS--
REGGIE'S POPULAR!
THAT'S IMPORTANT!
I KNOW WHERE I STAND!
YEAH! IN FRONT OF ME... BLOCKING MY VIEW!
4

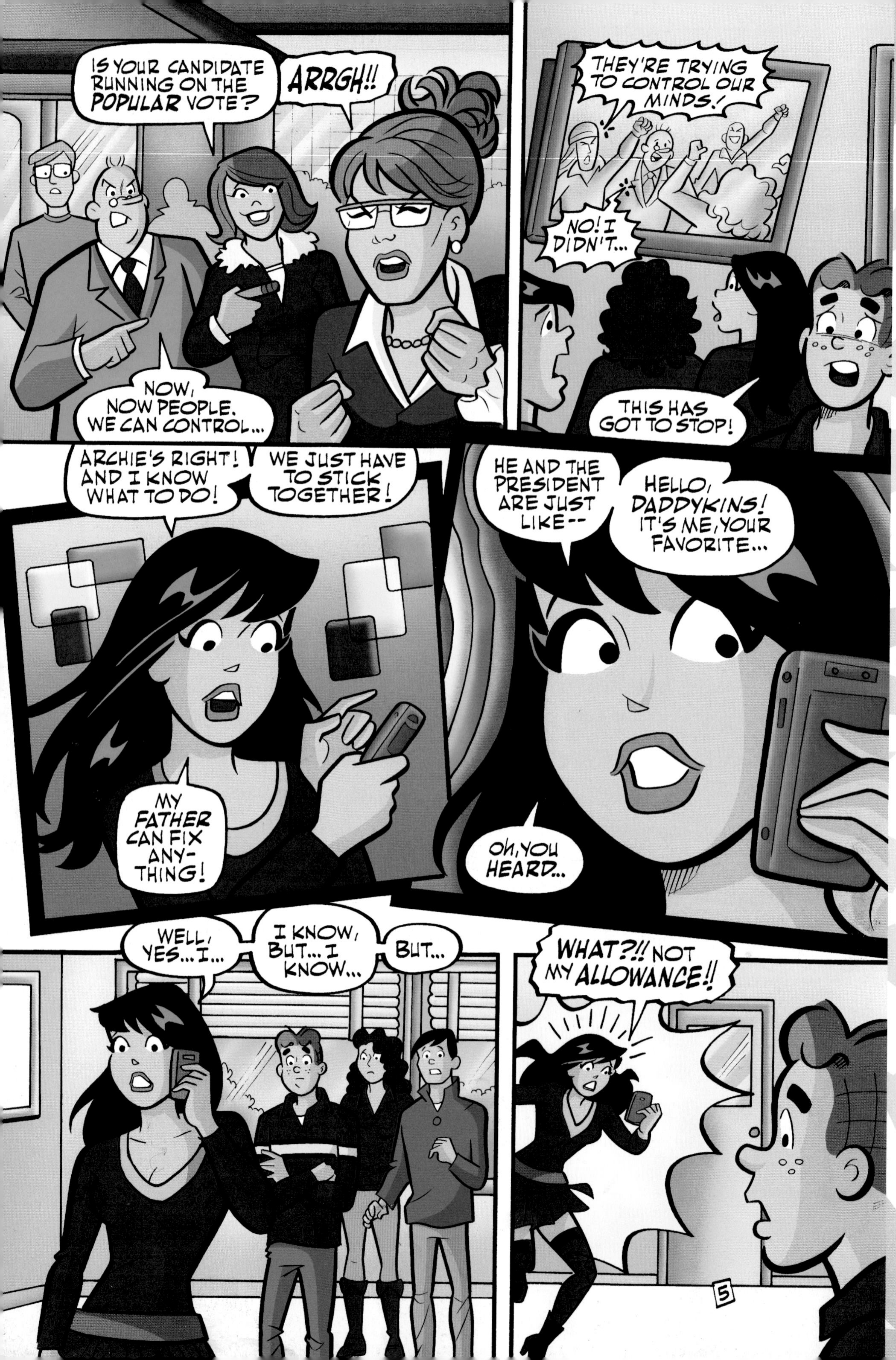
IS YOUR CANDIDATE RUNNING ON THE POPULAR VOTE?
ARRGH!!
NOW, NOW PEOPLE. WE CAN CONTROL...
THEY'RE TRYING TO CONTROL OUR MINDS!
NO! I DIDN'T...
THIS HAS GOT TO STOP!
ARCHIE'S RIGHT! AND I KNOW WHAT TO DO!
WE JUST HAVE TO STICK TOGETHER!
MY FATHER CAN FIX ANY-THING!
HE AND THE PRESIDENT ARE JUST LIKE--
HELLO, DADDYKINS! IT'S ME, YOUR FAVORITE...
OH, YOU HEARD..
WELL, YES... I...
I KNOW, BUT... I KNOW...
BUT...
WHAT?!! NOT MY ALLOWANCE!!
5

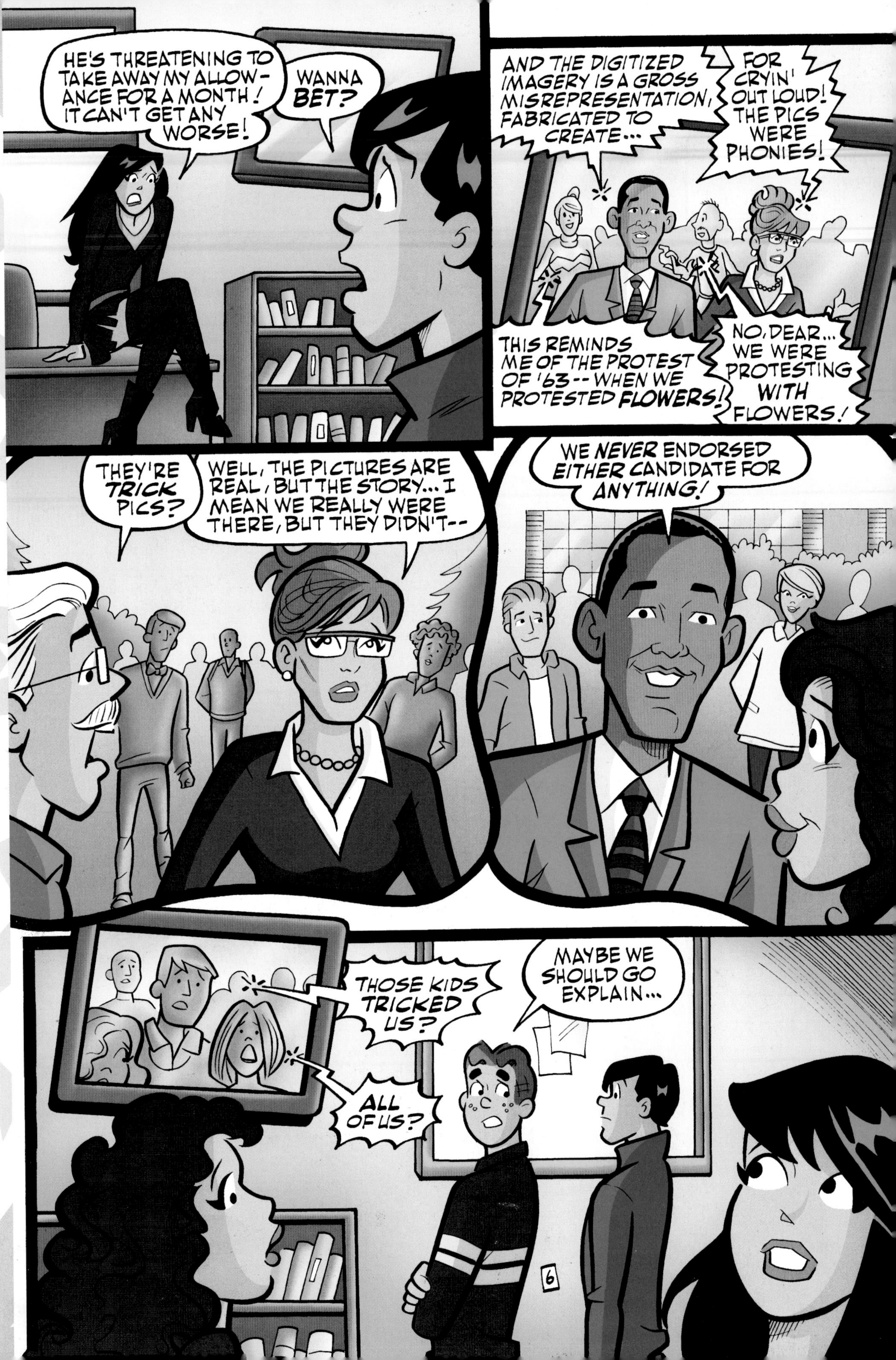
HE'S THREATENING TO TAKE AWAY MY ALLOW-ANCE FOR A MONTH! IT CAN'T GET ANY WORSE!
WANNA BET?
AND THE DIGITIZED IMAGERY IS A GROSS MISREPRESENTATION, FABRICATED TO CREATE...
FOR CRYIN' OUT LOUD! THE PICS WERE PHONIES!
THIS REMINDS ME OF THE PROTEST OF '63 -- WHEN WE PROTESTED FLOWERS!
NO, DEAR... WE WERE PROTESTING WITH FLOWERS!
THEY'RE TRICK PICS?
WELL, THE PICTURES ARE REAL, BUT THE STORY... I MEAN WE REALLY WERE THERE, BUT THEY DIDN'T--
WE NEVER ENDORSED EITHER CANDIDATE FOR ANYTHING!
THOSE KIDS TRICKED US?
ALL OF US?
MAYBE WE SHOULD GO EXPLAIN...
6

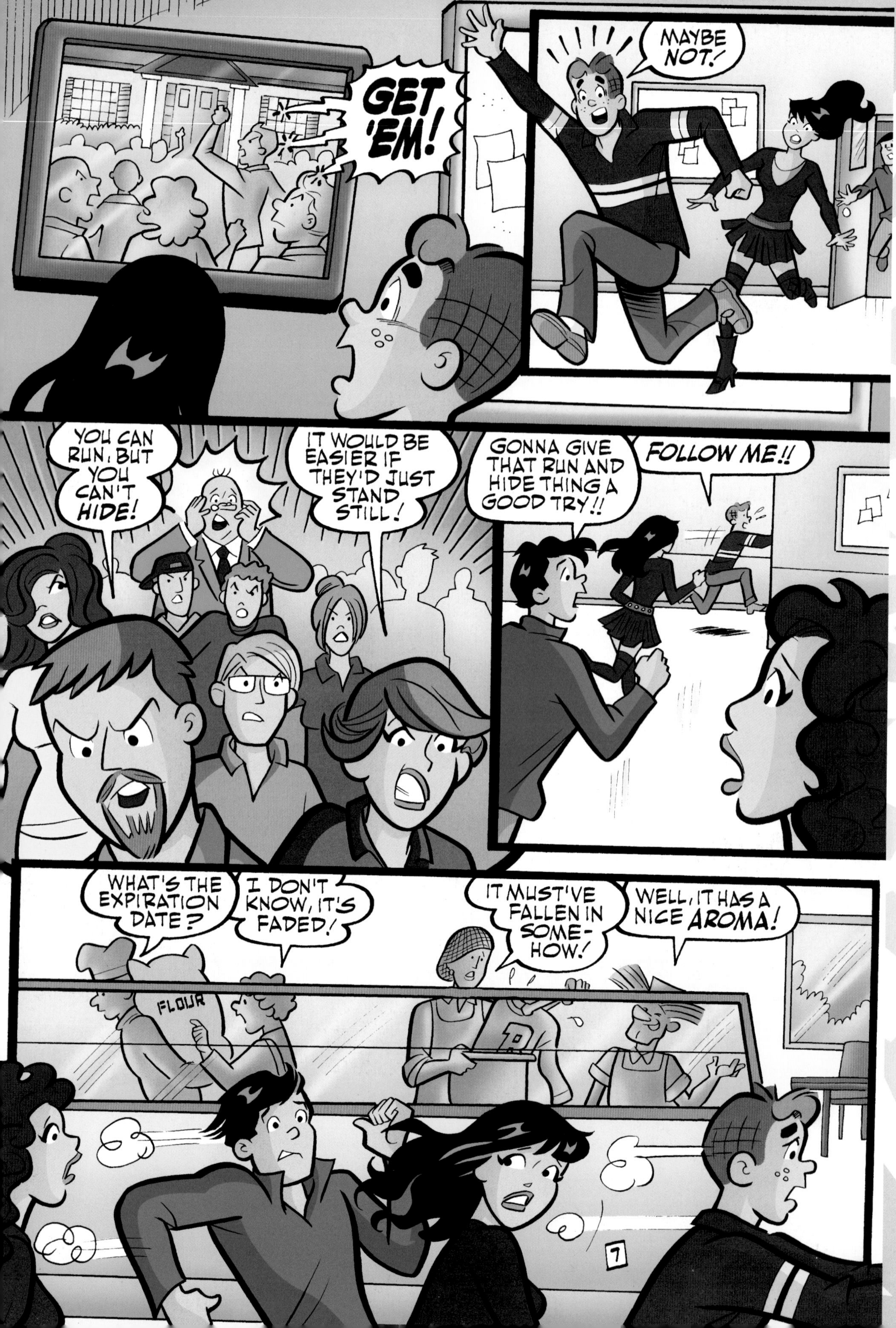
GET 'EM!
MAYBE NOT!
YOU CAN RUN, BUT YOU CAN'T HIDE!
IT WOULD BE EASIER IF THEY'D JUST STAND STILL!
GONNA GIVE THAT RUN AND HIDE THING A GOOD TRY!!
FOLLOW ME!!
WHAT'S THE EXPIRATION DATE?
I DON'T KNOW, IT'S FADED!
IT MUST'VE FALLEN IN SOME-HOW!
WELL, IT HAS A NICE AROMA!
FLOUR

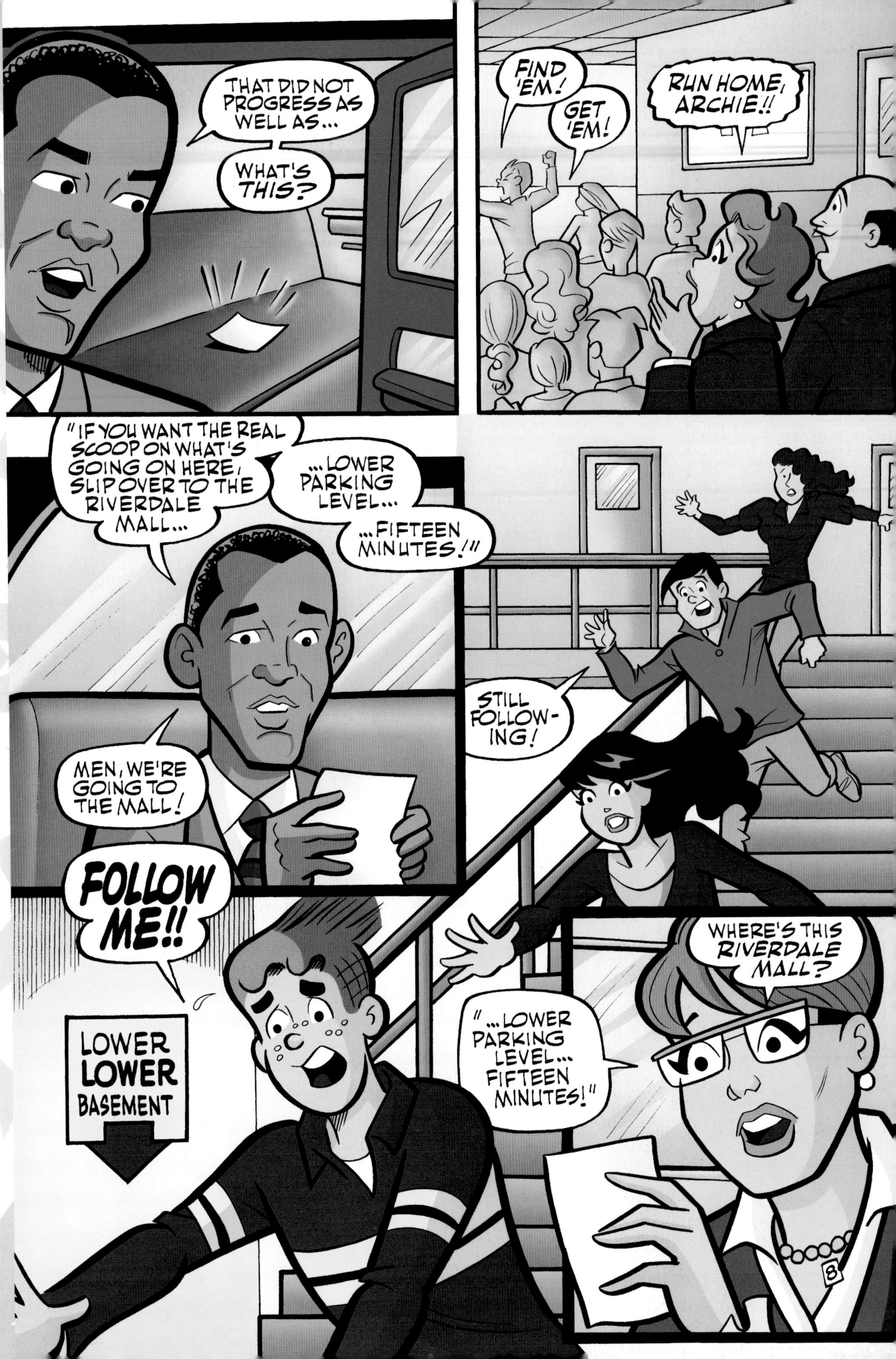
THAT DID NOT PROGRESS AS WELL AS...
WHAT'S THIS?
FIND 'EM!
GET 'EM!
RUN HOME, ARCHIE!!
"IF YOU WANT THE REAL SCOOP ON WHAT'S GOING ON HERE, SLIP OVER TO THE RIVERDALE MALL...
...LOWER PARKING LEVEL...
...FIFTEEN MINUTES!"
MEN, WE'RE GOING TO THE MALL!
FOLLOW ME!!
STILL FOLLOW-ING!
LOWER LOWER BASEMENT
WHERE'S THIS RIVERDALE MALL?
"...LOWER PARKING LEVEL... FIFTEEN MINUTES!"
8

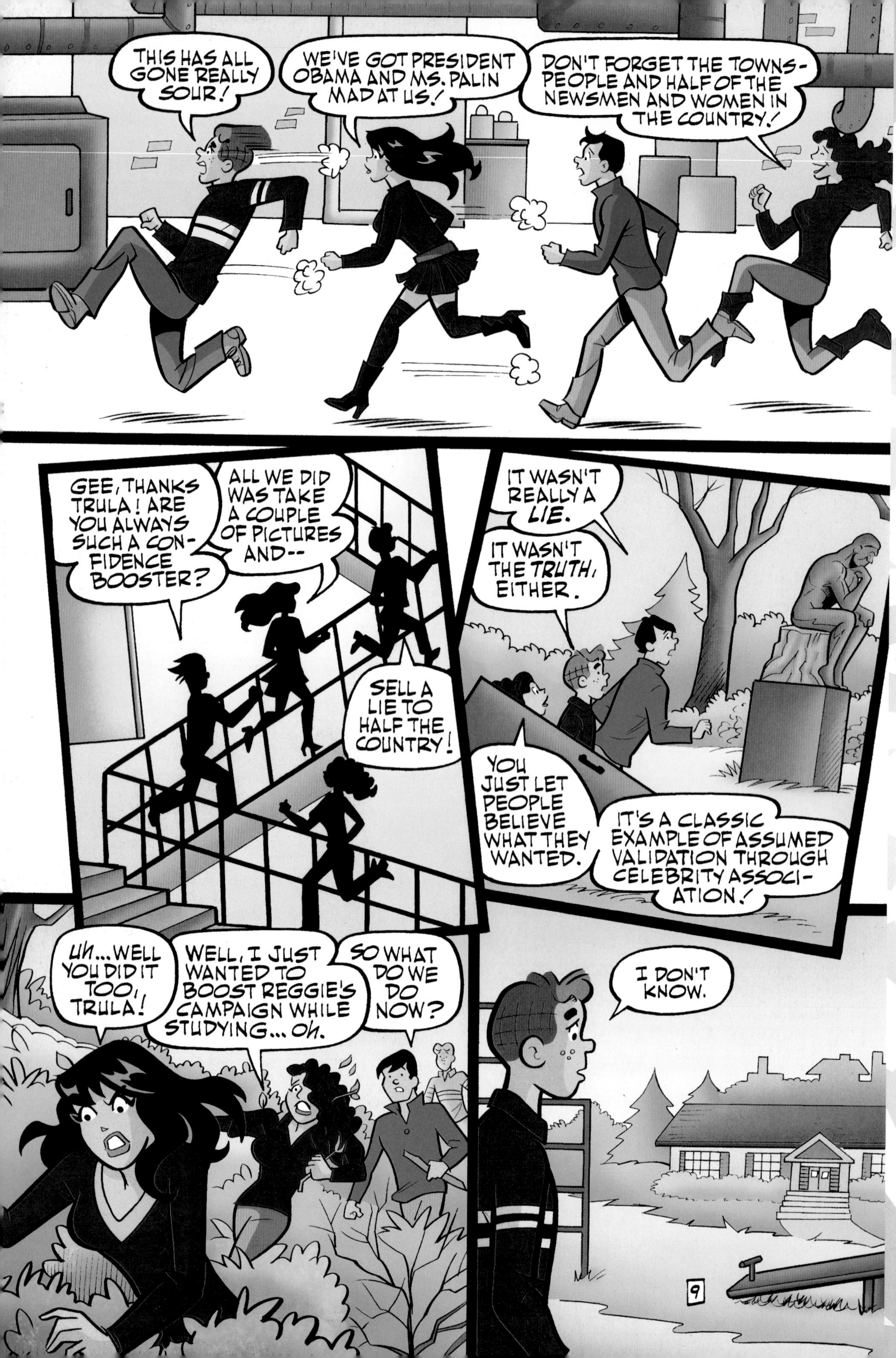
THIS HAS ALL GONE REALLY SOUR!
WE'VE GOT PRESIDENT OBAMA AND MS. PALIN MAD AT US!
DON'T FORGET THE TOWNSPEOPLE AND HALF OF THE NEWSMEN AND WOMEN IN THE COUNTRY!
GEE, THANKS TRULA! ARE YOU ALWAYS SUCH A CONFIDENCE BOOSTER?
ALL WE DID WAS TAKE A COUPLE OF PICTURES AND--
SELL A LIE TO HALF THE COUNTRY!
IT WASN'T REALLY A LIE.
IT WASN'T THE TRUTH, EITHER.
YOU JUST LET PEOPLE BELIEVE WHAT THEY WANTED.
IT'S A CLASSIC EXAMPLE OF ASSUMED VALIDATION THROUGH CELEBRITY ASSOCIATION!
UH... WELL YOU DID IT TOO, TRULA!
WELL, I JUST WANTED TO BOOST REGGIE'S CAMPAIGN WHILE STUDYING... OH.
SO WHAT DO WE DO NOW?
I DON'T KNOW.
9

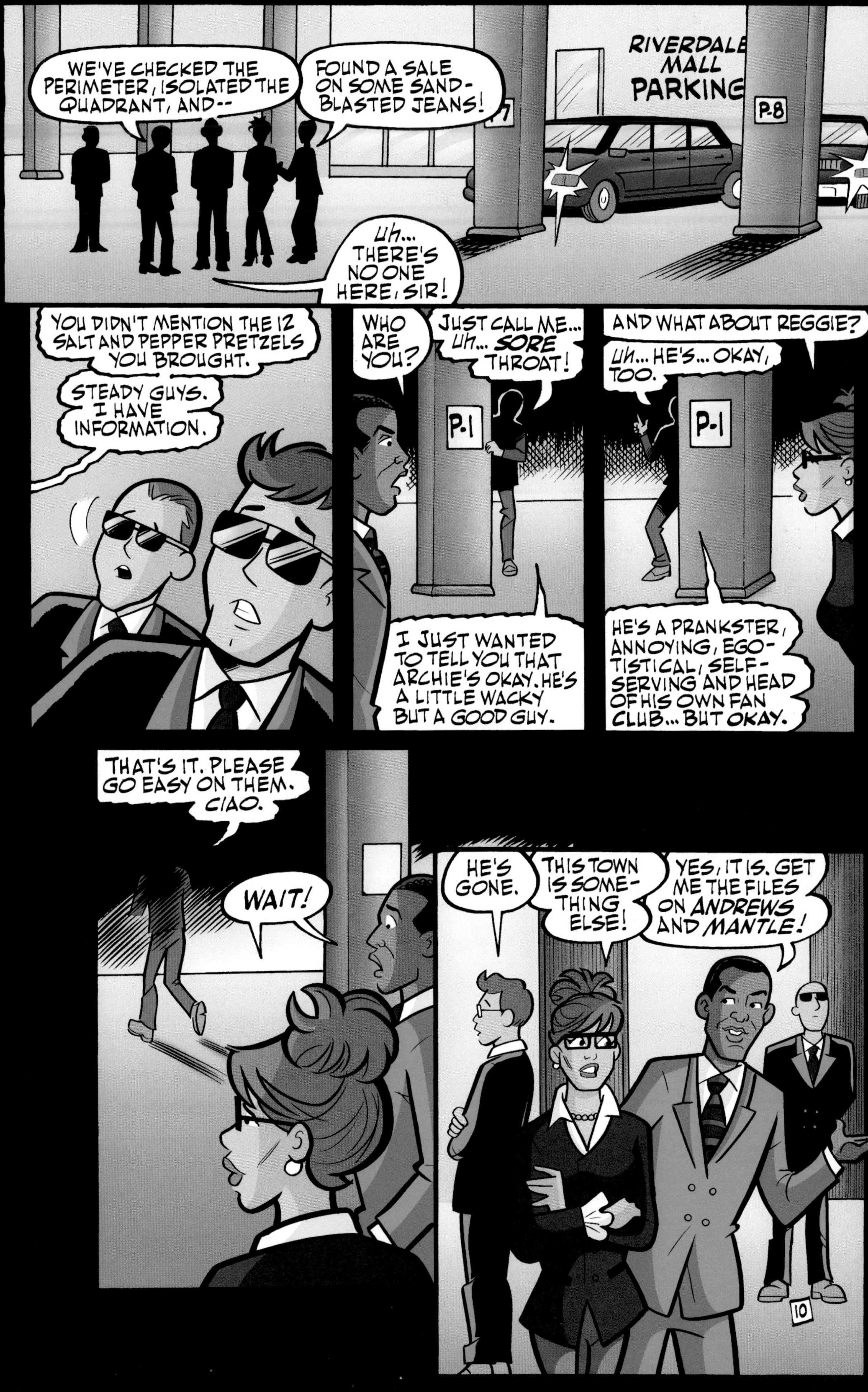
RIVERDALE MALL PARKING
P-7
P-8
WE'VE CHECKED THE PERIMETER, ISOLATED THE QUADRANT, AND--
FOUND A SALE ON SOME SAND-BLASTED JEANS!
UH... THERE'S NO ONE HERE, SIR!
YOU DIDN'T MENTION THE 12 SALT AND PEPPER PRETZELS YOU BROUGHT.
STEADY GUYS. I HAVE INFORMATION.
WHO ARE YOU?
JUST CALL ME... UH... SORE THROAT!
P-1
I JUST WANTED TO TELL YOU THAT ARCHIE'S OKAY. HE'S A LITTLE WACKY BUT A GOOD GUY.
AND WHAT ABOUT REGGIE?
UH... HE'S... OKAY, TOO.
P-1
HE'S A PRANKSTER, ANNOYING, EGO-TISTICAL, SELF-SERVING AND HEAD OF HIS OWN FAN CLUB... BUT OKAY.
THAT'S IT. PLEASE GO EASY ON THEM. CIAO.
WAIT!
HE'S GONE.
THIS TOWN IS SOME-THING ELSE!
YES, IT IS. GET ME THE FILES ON ANDREWS AND MANTLE!
10

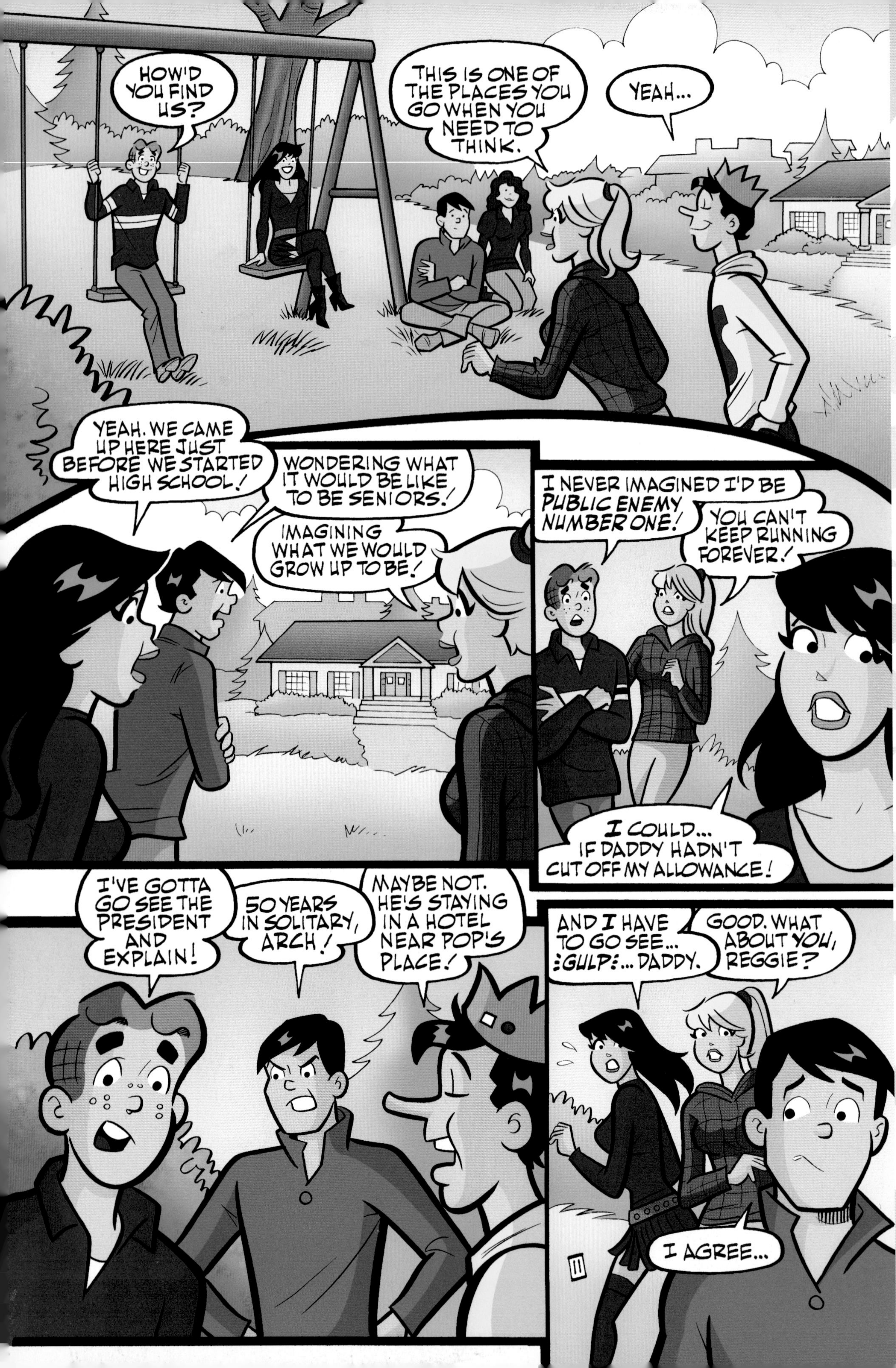
HOW'D YOU FIND US?
THIS IS ONE OF THE PLACES YOU GO WHEN YOU NEED TO THINK.
YEAH...
YEAH. WE CAME UP HERE JUST BEFORE WE STARTED HIGH SCHOOL!
WONDERING WHAT IT WOULD BE LIKE TO BE SENIORS!
IMAGINING WHAT WE WOULD GROW UP TO BE!
I NEVER IMAGINED I'D BE PUBLIC ENEMY NUMBER ONE!
YOU CAN'T KEEP RUNNING FOREVER!
I COULD... IF DADDY HADN'T CUT OFF MY ALLOWANCE!
I'VE GOTTA GO SEE THE PRESIDENT AND EXPLAIN!
50 YEARS IN SOLITARY, ARCH!
MAYBE NOT. HE'S STAYING IN A HOTEL NEAR POP'S PLACE!
AND I HAVE TO GO SEE... :GULP: ... DADDY.
GOOD. WHAT ABOUT YOU, REGGIE?
I AGREE...
11

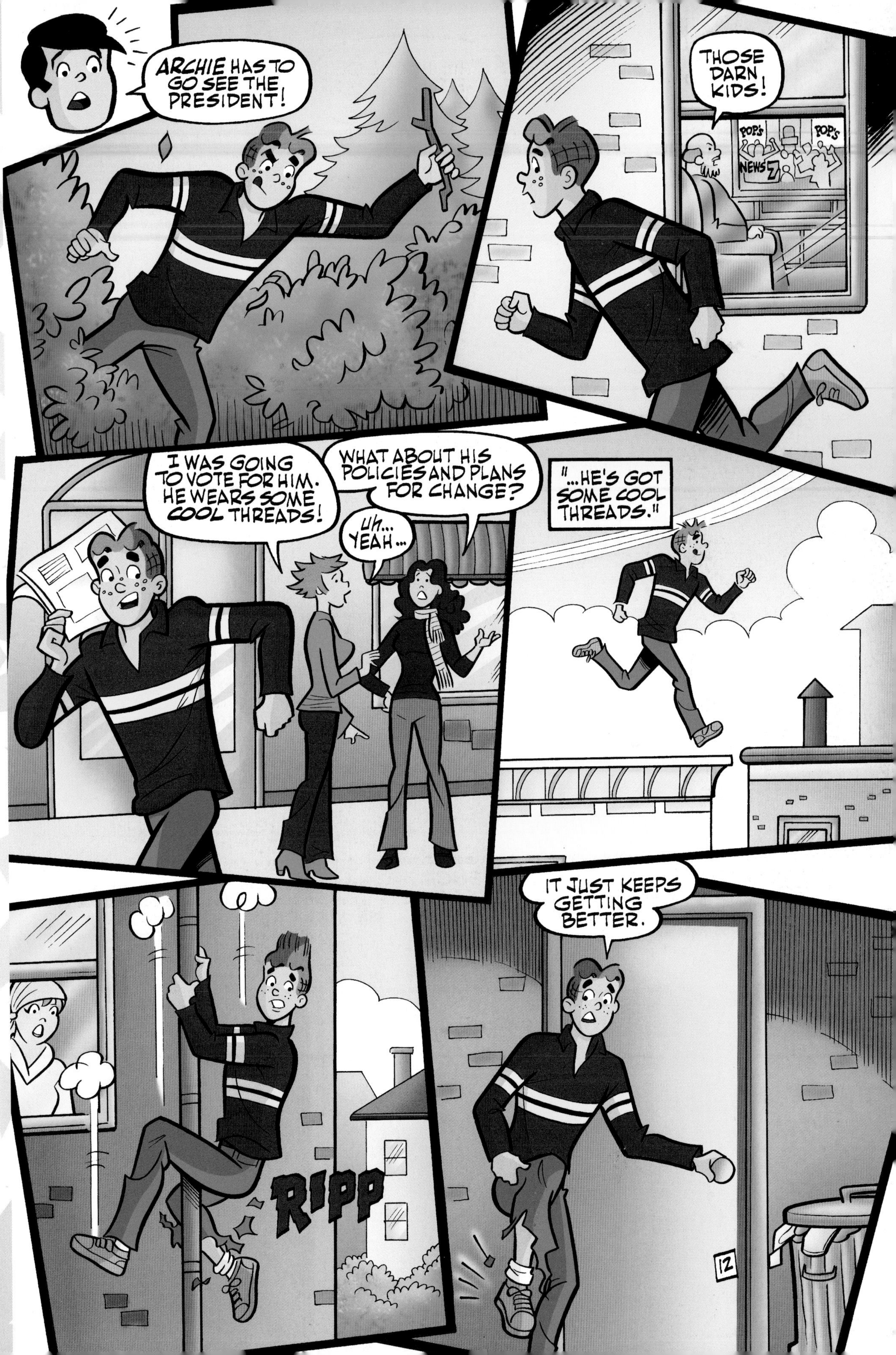
ARCHIE HAS TO GO SEE THE PRESIDENT!
THOSE DARN KIDS!
POP'S
NEWS 7
I WAS GOING TO VOTE FOR HIM. HE WEARS SOME COOL THREADS!
WHAT ABOUT HIS POLICIES AND PLANS FOR CHANGE?
UH... YEAH...
"...HE'S GOT SOME COOL THREADS."
RIPP
IT JUST KEEPS GETTING BETTER.
12

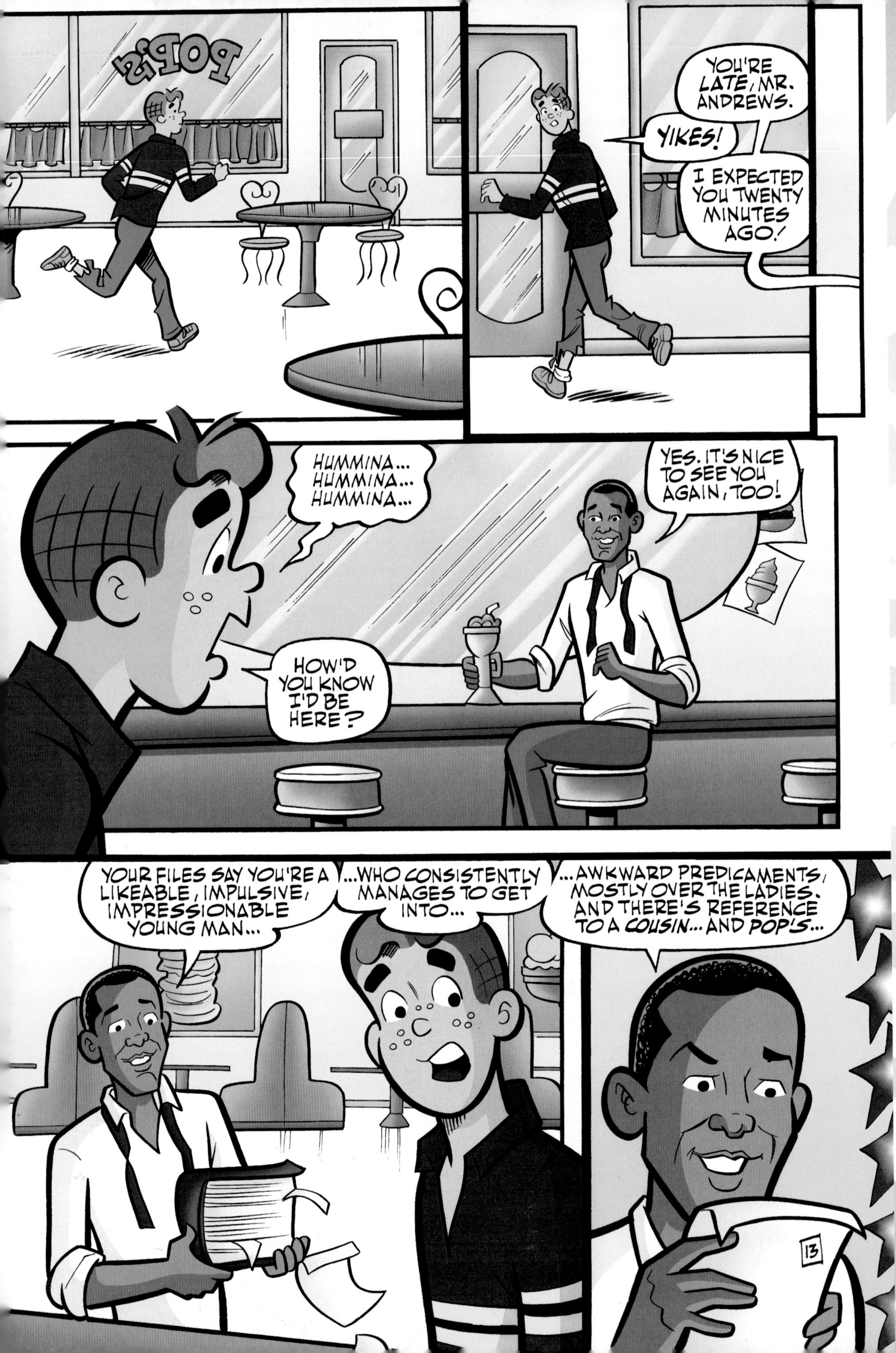
YOU'RE LATE, MR. ANDREWS.
YIKES!
I EXPECTED YOU TWENTY MINUTES AGO!
HUMMINA... HUMMINA... HUMMINA...
YES. IT'S NICE TO SEE YOU AGAIN, TOO!
HOW'D YOU KNOW I'D BE HERE?
YOUR FILES SAY YOU'RE A LIKEABLE, IMPULSIVE, IMPRESSIONABLE YOUNG MAN...
...WHO CONSISTENTLY MANAGES TO GET INTO...
...AWKWARD PREDICAMENTS, MOSTLY OVER THE LADIES. AND THERE'S REFERENCE TO A COUSIN... AND POP'S...
13

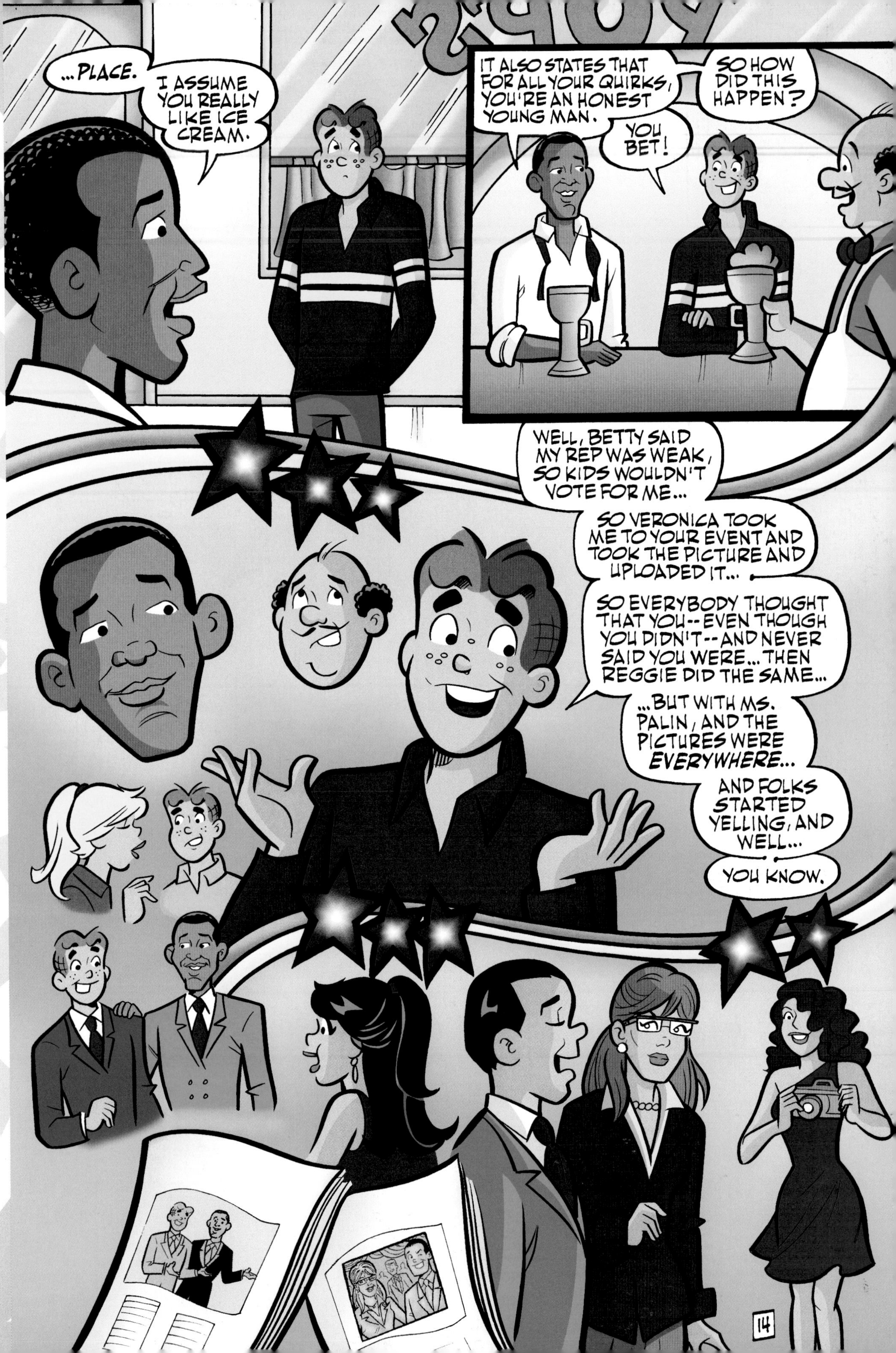

...PLACE.
I ASSUME YOU REALLY LIKE ICE CREAM.
IT ALSO STATES THAT FOR ALL YOUR QUIRKS, YOU'RE AN HONEST YOUNG MAN.
YOU BET!
SO HOW DID THIS HAPPEN?
WELL, BETTY SAID MY REP WAS WEAK, SO KIDS WOULDN'T VOTE FOR ME...
SO VERONICA TOOK ME TO YOUR EVENT AND TOOK THE PICTURE AND UPLOADED IT...
SO EVERYBODY THOUGHT THAT YOU-- EVEN THOUGH YOU DIDN'T--AND NEVER SAID YOU WERE... THEN REGGIE DID THE SAME...
...BUT WITH MS. PALIN, AND THE PICTURES WERE EVERYWHERE...
AND FOLKS STARTED YELLING, AND WELL...
YOU KNOW.

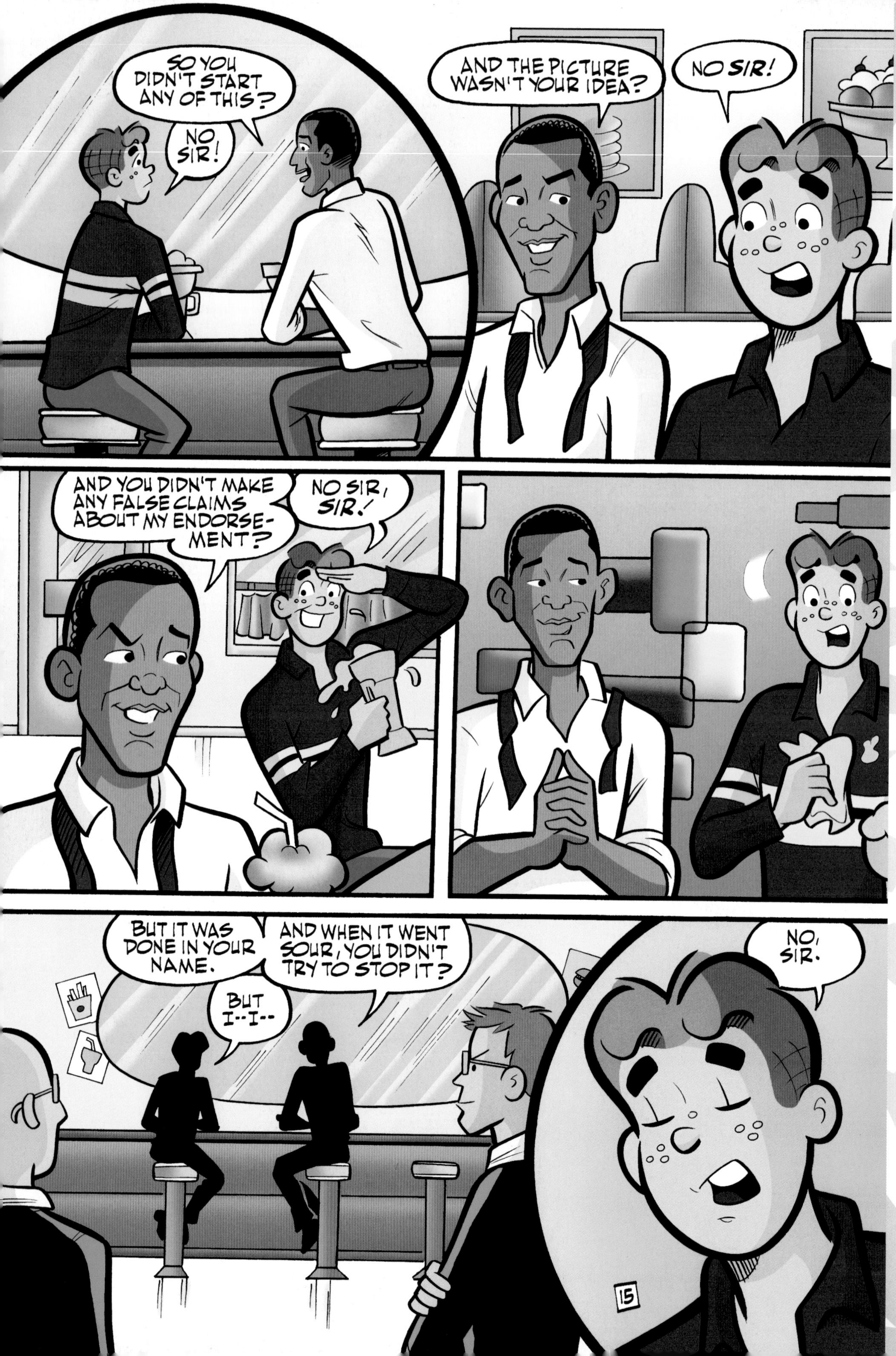
SO YOU DIDN'T START ANY OF THIS?
NO SIR!
AND THE PICTURE WASN'T YOUR IDEA?
NO SIR!
AND YOU DIDN'T MAKE ANY FALSE CLAIMS ABOUT MY ENDORSEMENT?
NO SIR, SIR!
BUT IT WAS DONE IN YOUR NAME.
BUT I--I--
AND WHEN IT WENT SOUR, YOU DIDN'T TRY TO STOP IT?
NO, SIR.
15

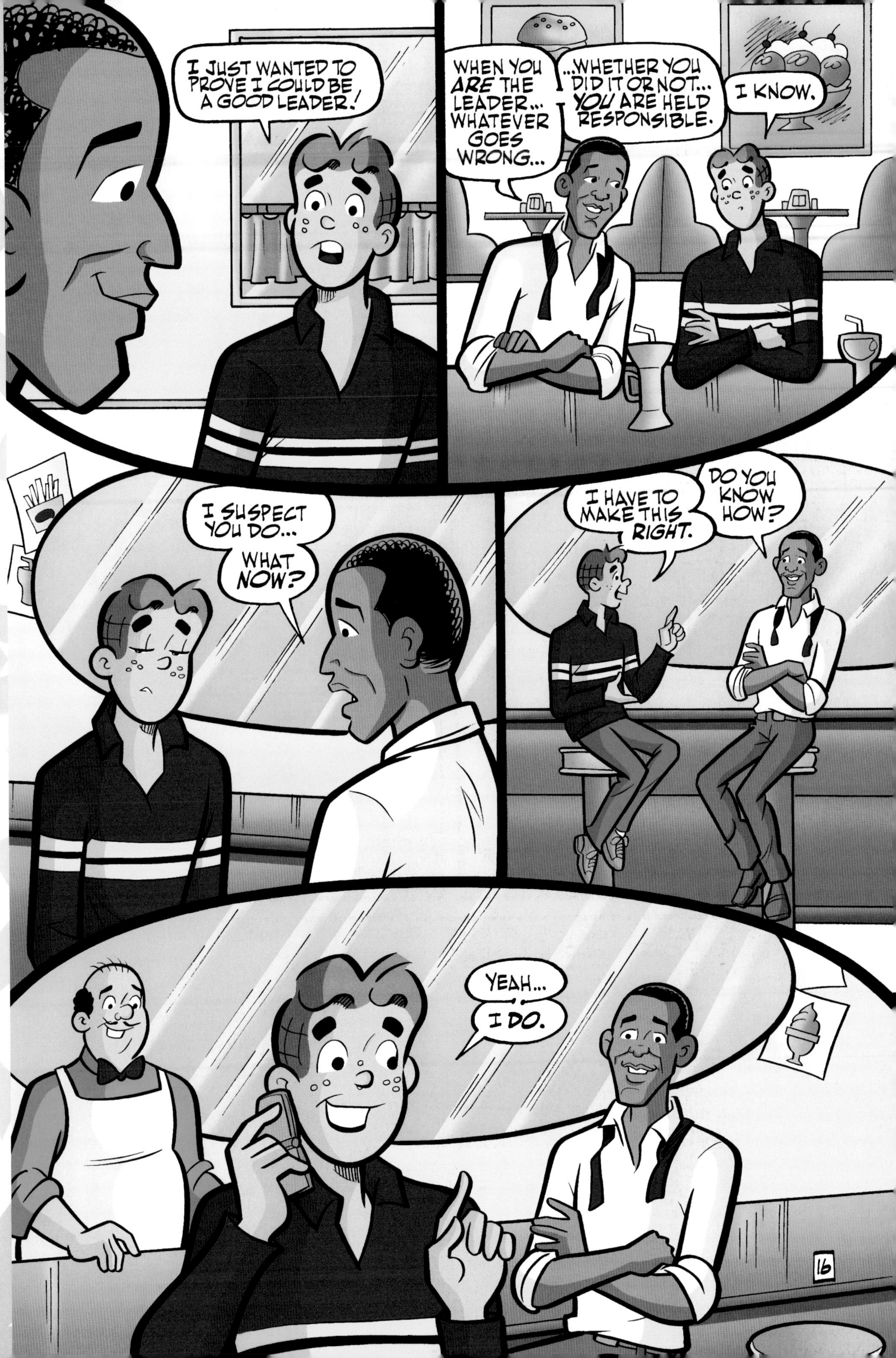
I JUST WANTED TO PROVE I COULD BE A GOOD LEADER!
WHEN YOU ARE THE LEADER... WHATEVER GOES WRONG...
...WHETHER YOU DID IT OR NOT... YOU ARE HELD RESPONSIBLE.
I KNOW.
I SUSPECT YOU DO...
WHAT NOW?
I HAVE TO MAKE THIS RIGHT.
DO YOU KNOW HOW?
YEAH...
I DO.
16

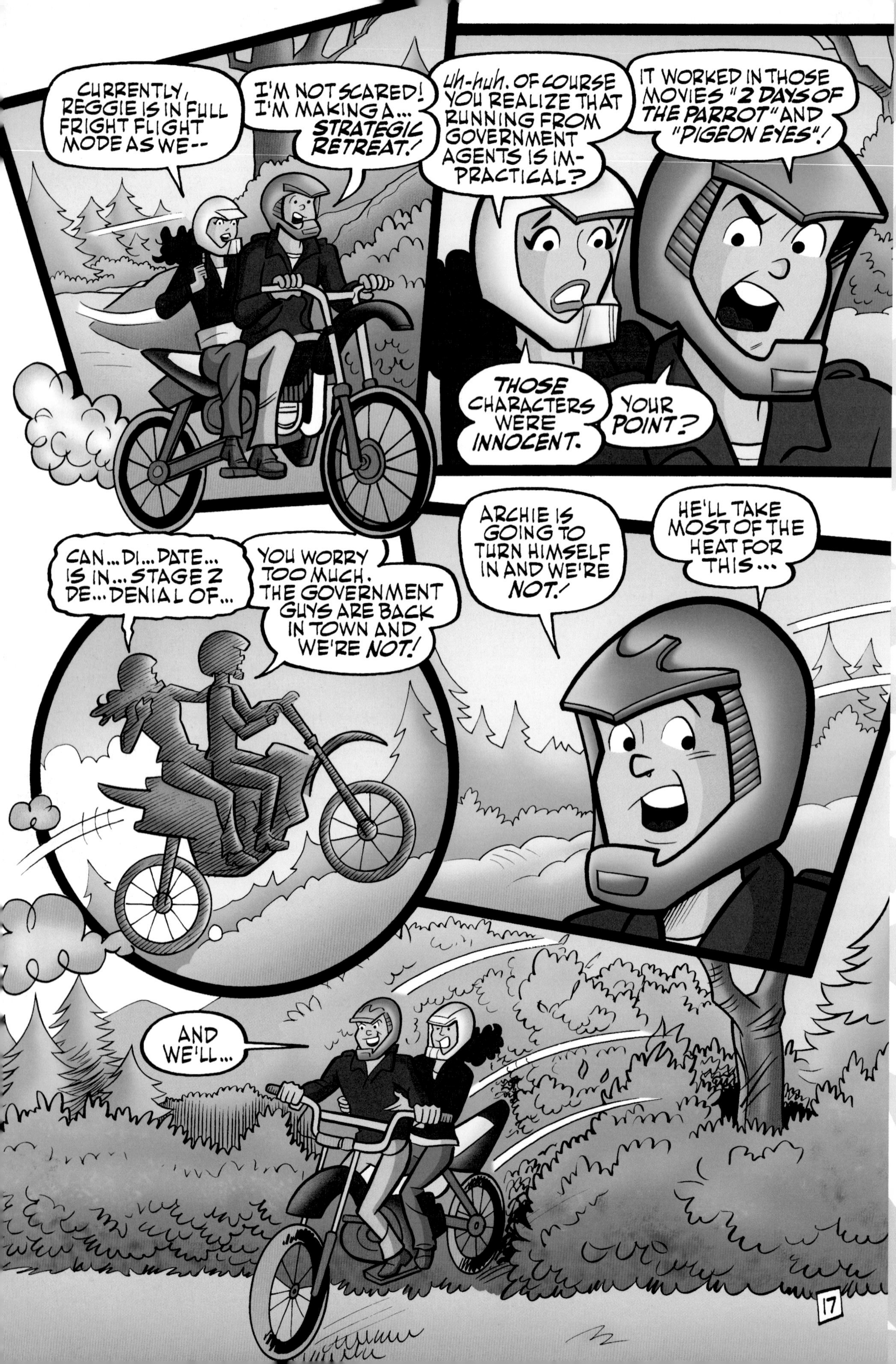

CURRENTLY, REGGIE IS IN FULL FRIGHT FLIGHT MODE AS WE--
I'M NOT SCARED! I'M MAKING A... STRATEGIC RETREAT!
uh-huh. OF COURSE YOU REALIZE THAT RUNNING FROM GOVERNMENT AGENTS IS IM-PRACTICAL?
IT WORKED IN THOSE MOVIES "2 DAYS OF THE PARROT" AND "PIGEON EYES"!
THOSE CHARACTERS WERE INNOCENT.
YOUR POINT?
CAN... DI... DATE... IS IN... STAGE 2 DE... DENIAL OF...
YOU WORRY TOO MUCH. THE GOVERNMENT GUYS ARE BACK IN TOWN AND WE'RE NOT!
ARCHIE IS GOING TO TURN HIMSELF IN AND WE'RE NOT!
HE'LL TAKE MOST OF THE HEAT FOR THIS...
AND WE'LL...

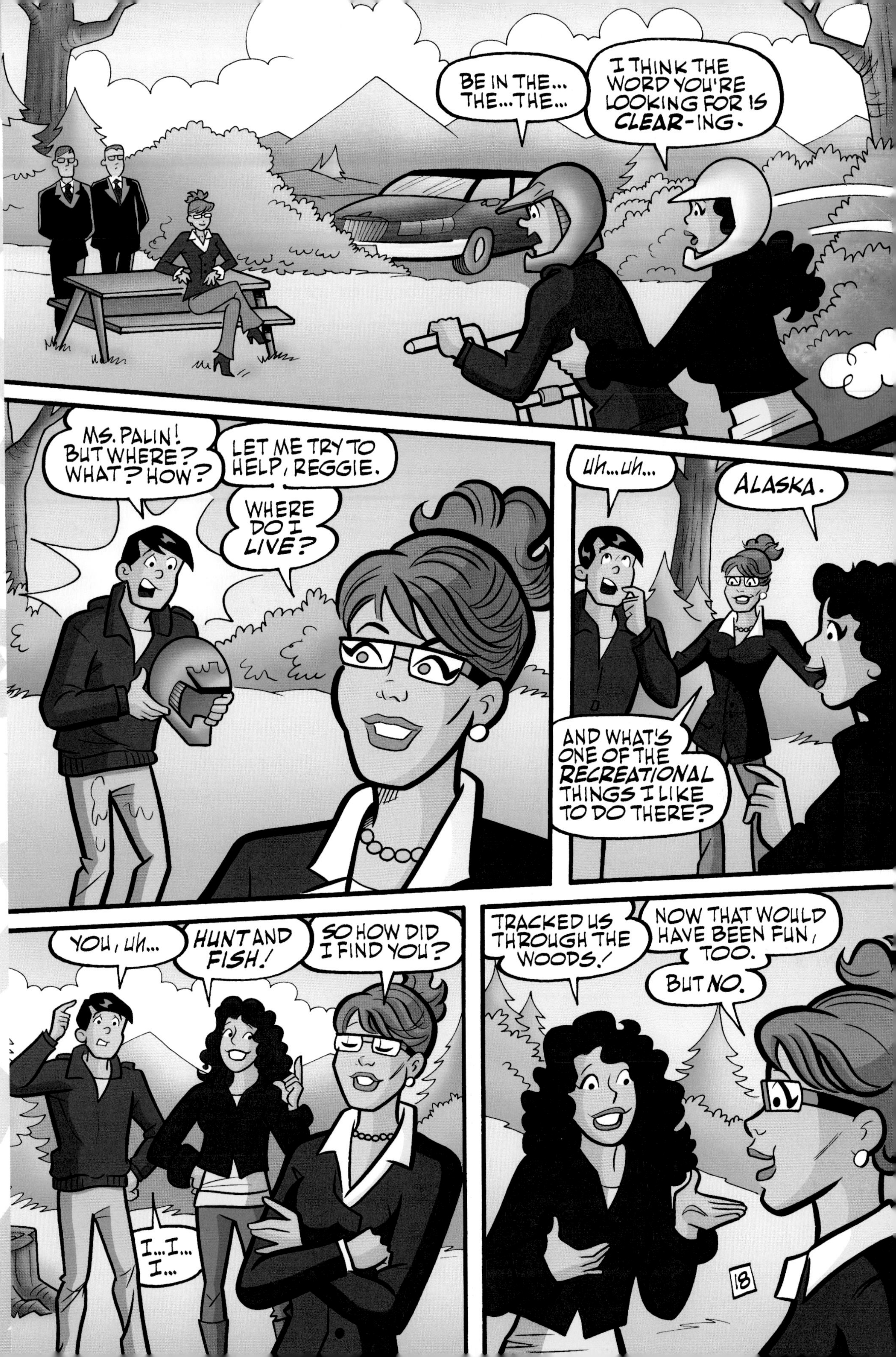
BE IN THE... THE...THE...
I THINK THE WORD YOU'RE LOOKING FOR IS CLEAR-ING.
MS. PALIN! BUT WHERE? WHAT? HOW?
LET ME TRY TO HELP, REGGIE.
WHERE DO I LIVE?
UH...UH...
ALASKA.
AND WHAT'S ONE OF THE RECREATIONAL THINGS I LIKE TO DO THERE?
YOU, UH...
HUNT AND FISH!
SO HOW DID I FIND YOU?
I...I... I... I...
TRACKED US THROUGH THE WOODS!
NOW THAT WOULD HAVE BEEN FUN, TOO.
BUT NO.
18

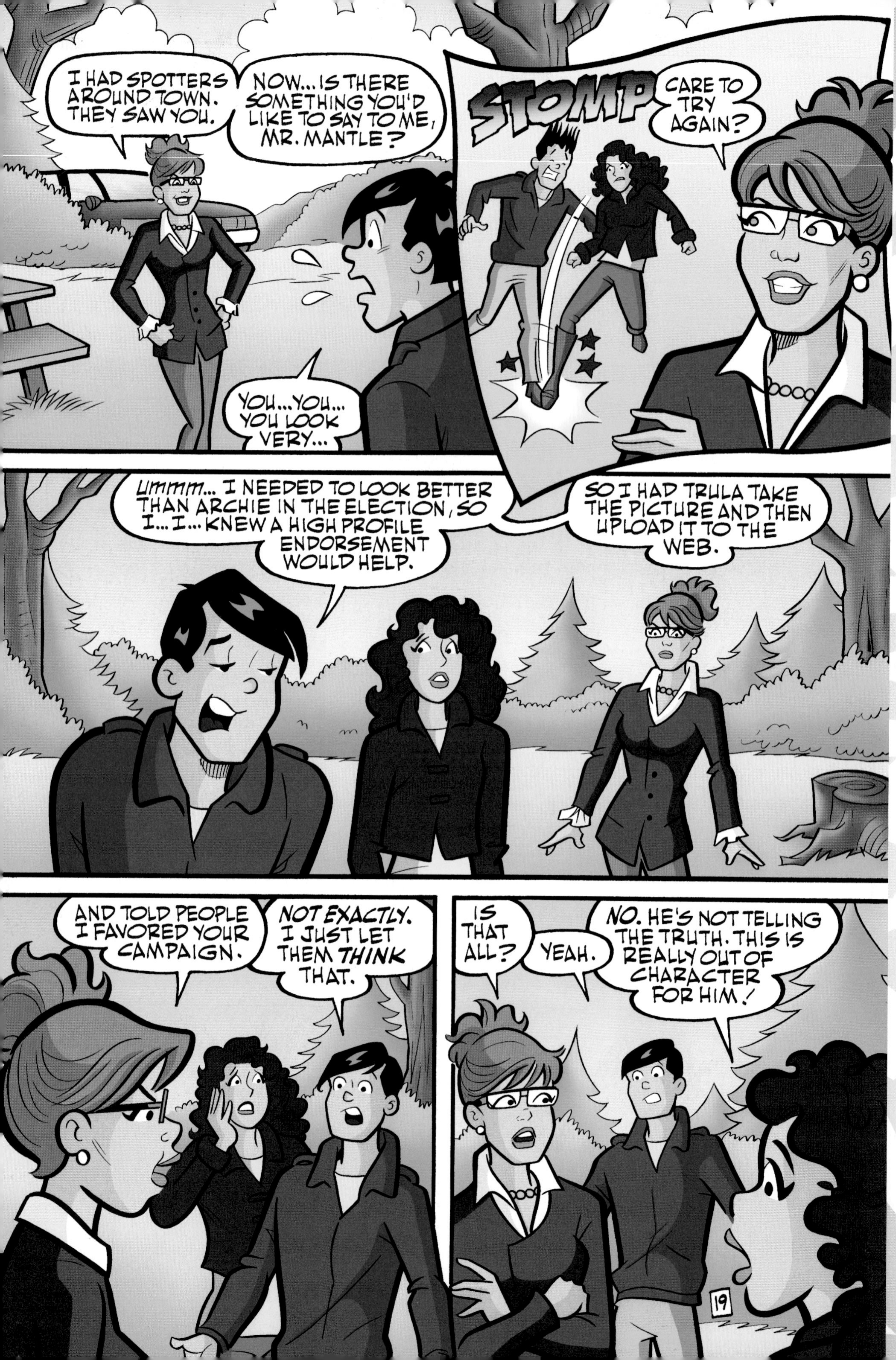
I HAD SPOTTERS AROUND TOWN. THEY SAW YOU.
NOW... IS THERE SOMETHING YOU'D LIKE TO SAY TO ME, MR. MANTLE?
YOU... YOU... YOU LOOK VERY...
STOMP
CARE TO TRY AGAIN?
UMMMM... I NEEDED TO LOOK BETTER THAN ARCHIE IN THE ELECTION, SO I... I... KNEW A HIGH PROFILE ENDORSEMENT WOULD HELP.
SO I HAD TRULA TAKE THE PICTURE AND THEN UPLOAD IT TO THE WEB.
AND TOLD PEOPLE I FAVORED YOUR CAMPAIGN.
NOT EXACTLY. I JUST LET THEM THINK THAT.
IS THAT ALL?
YEAH.
NO. HE'S NOT TELLING THE TRUTH. THIS IS REALLY OUT OF CHARACTER FOR HIM!
19

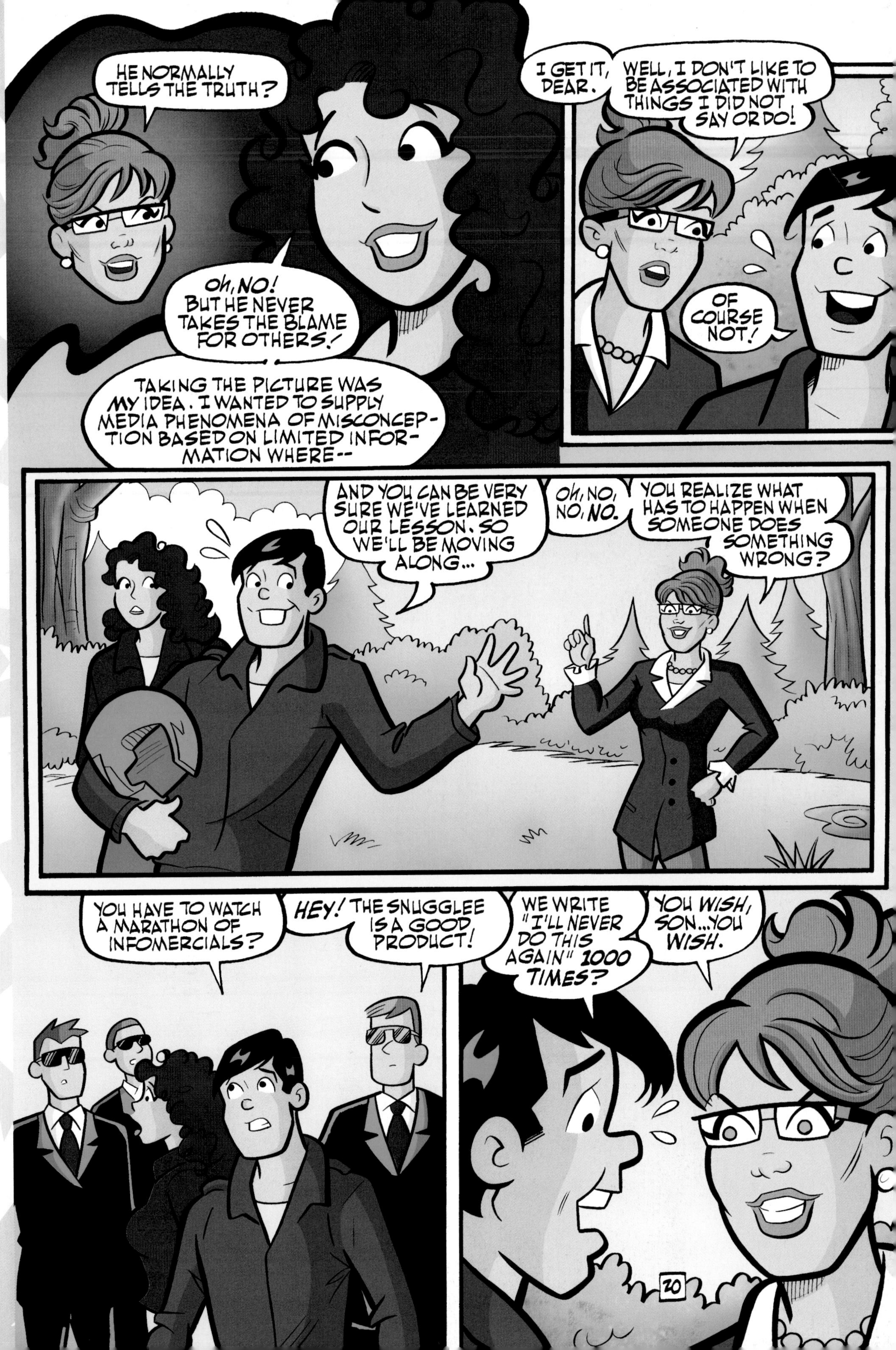
HE NORMALLY TELLS THE TRUTH?
Oh, NO! BUT HE NEVER TAKES THE BLAME FOR OTHERS!
TAKING THE PICTURE WAS MY IDEA. I WANTED TO SUPPLY MEDIA PHENOMENA OF MISCONCEPTION BASED ON LIMITED INFORMATION WHERE--
I GET IT, DEAR.
WELL, I DON'T LIKE TO BE ASSOCIATED WITH THINGS I DID NOT SAY OR DO!
OF COURSE NOT!
AND YOU CAN BE VERY SURE WE'VE LEARNED OUR LESSON. SO WE'LL BE MOVING ALONG...
Oh, NO, NO, NO.
YOU REALIZE WHAT HAS TO HAPPEN WHEN SOMEONE DOES SOMETHING WRONG?
YOU HAVE TO WATCH A MARATHON OF INFOMERCIALS?
HEY! THE SNUGGLEE IS A GOOD PRODUCT!
WE WRITE "I'LL NEVER DO THIS AGAIN" 1000 TIMES?
YOU WISH, SON...YOU WISH.
20

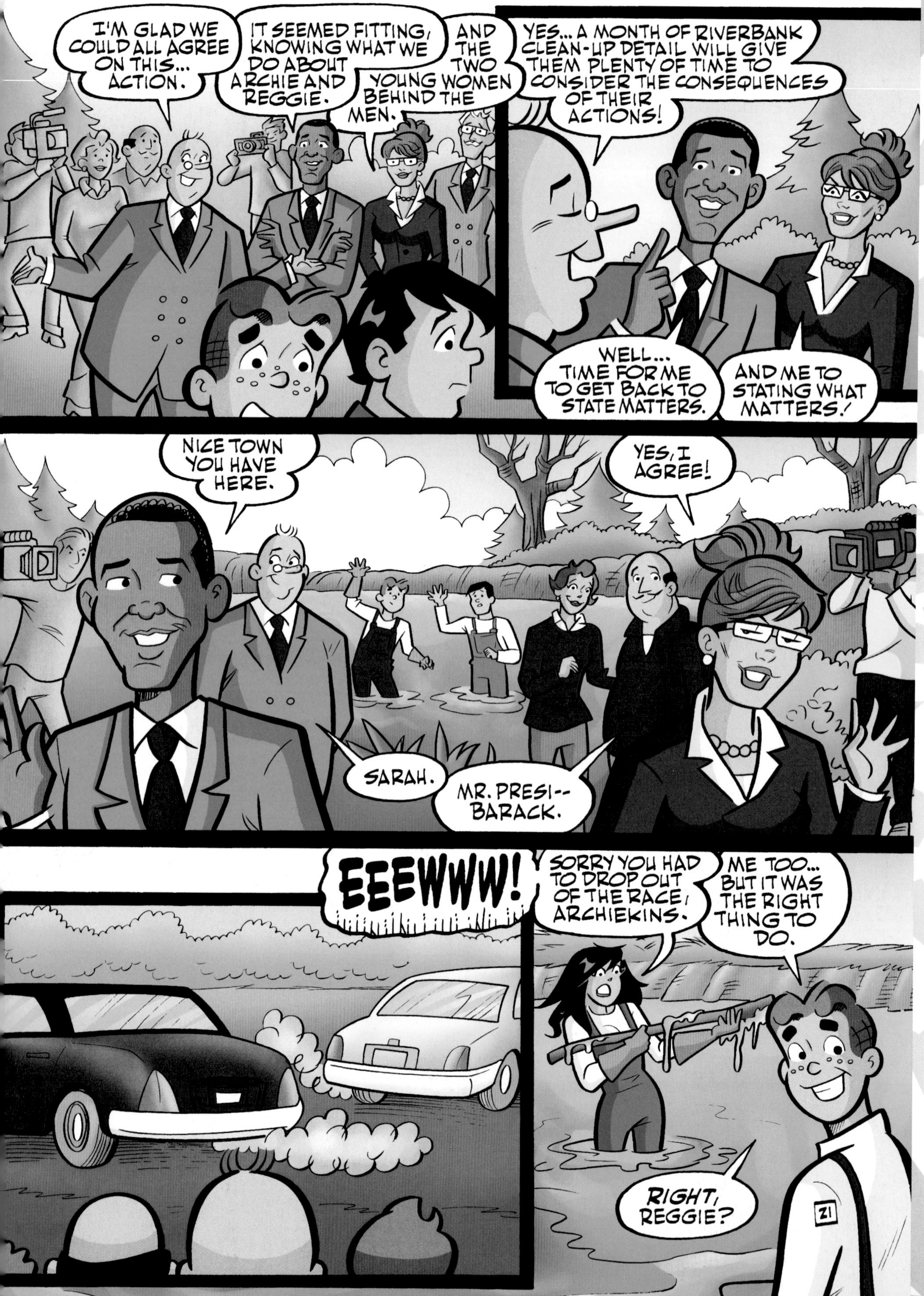

I'M GLAD WE COULD ALL AGREE ON THIS... ACTION.
IT SEEMED FITTING, KNOWING WHAT WE DO ABOUT ARCHIE AND REGGIE.
AND THE TWO YOUNG WOMEN BEHIND THE MEN.
YES... A MONTH OF RIVERBANK CLEAN-UP DETAIL WILL GIVE THEM PLENTY OF TIME TO CONSIDER THE CONSEQUENCES OF THEIR ACTIONS!
WELL... TIME FOR ME TO GET BACK TO STATE MATTERS.
AND ME TO STATING WHAT MATTERS!
NICE TOWN YOU HAVE HERE.
YES, I AGREE!
SARAH.
MR. PRESI-- BARACK.
EEEWWW!
SORRY YOU HAD TO DROP OUT OF THE RACE, ARCHIEKINS.
ME TOO... BUT IT WAS THE RIGHT THING TO DO.
RIGHT, REGGIE?
21

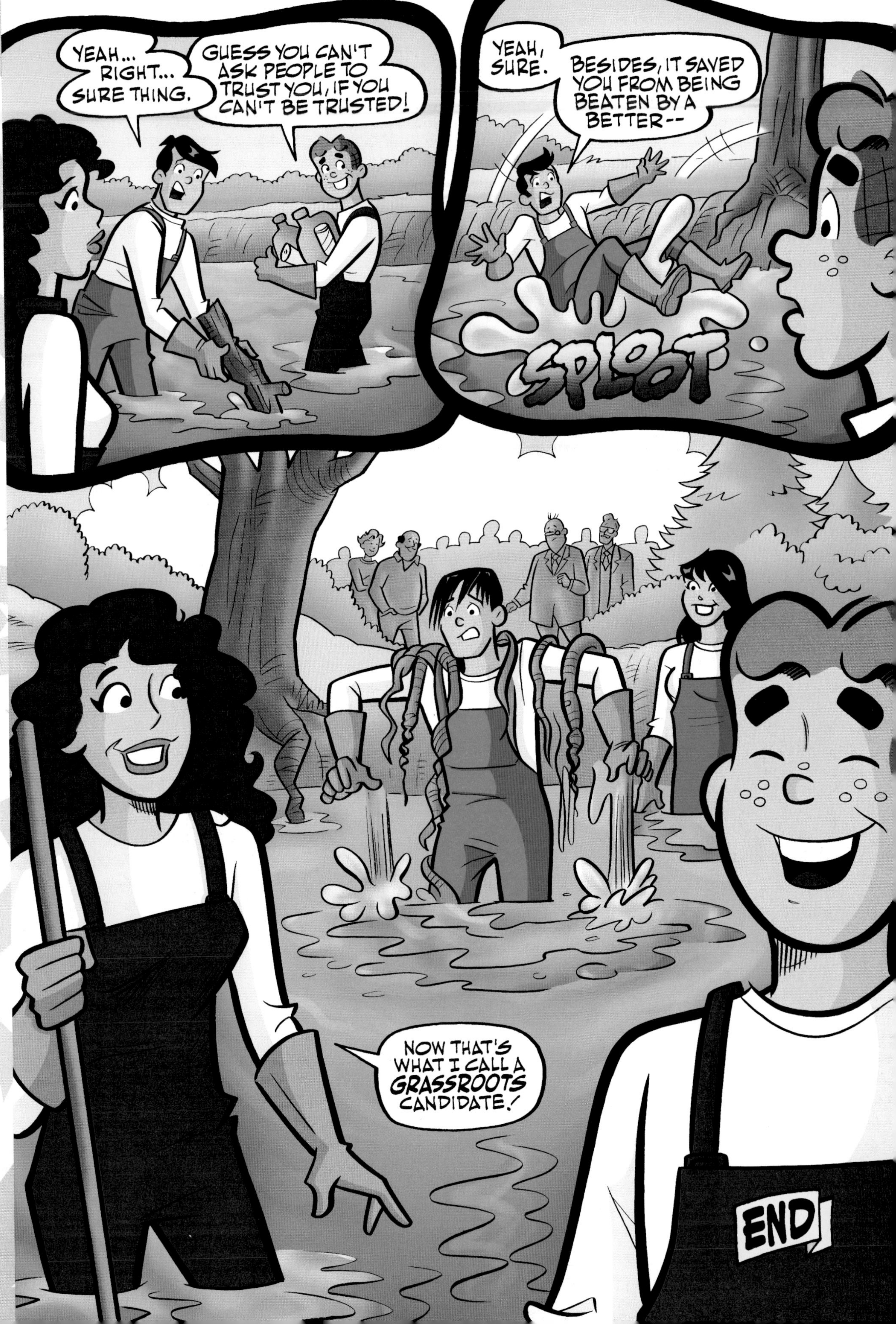
YEAH... RIGHT... SURE THING.
GUESS YOU CAN'T ASK PEOPLE TO TRUST YOU, IF YOU CAN'T BE TRUSTED!
YEAH, SURE.
BESIDES, IT SAVED YOU FROM BEING BEATEN BY A BETTER--
SPLOOT
NOW THAT'S WHAT I CALL A GRASSROOTS CANDIDATE!
END

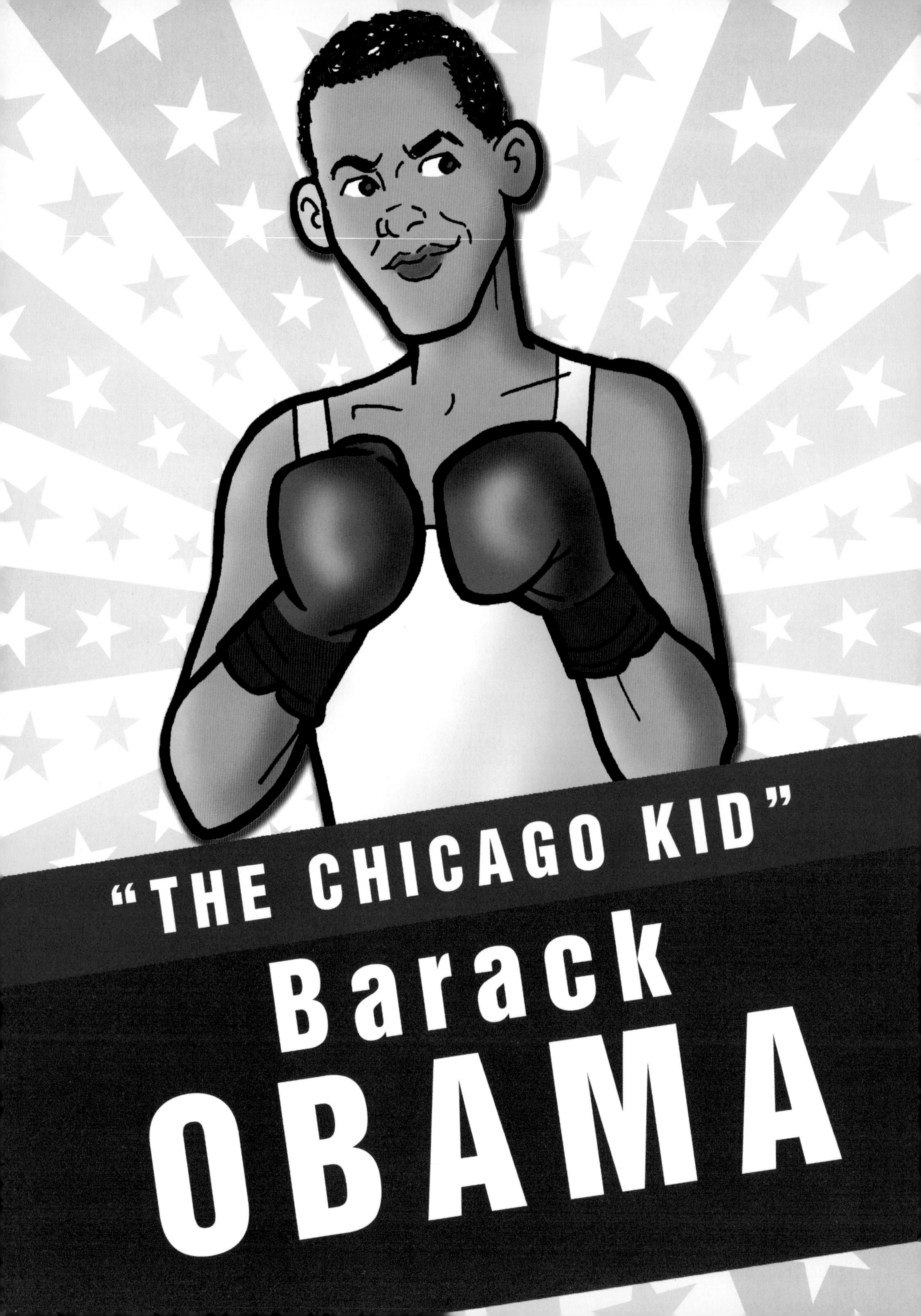
"THE CHICAGO KID"
Barack
OBAMA

Did You Know...

The **44th president, Barack Obama** is the **first African-American** to hold office. **President Obama** doesn't like ice cream or mayonnaise, but **loves** chili? He loves playing Scrabble®! His favorite books include *Moby Dick* and *The Bible*. He likes to **collects comics**. His favorite musicians include Bob Dylan, Stevie Wonder and The Fugees and he has even **won two Grammy® Awards** for the audio versions of his best-selling books.

Did You Know...

In high school, **Governor Palin** was known as **"Sarah Barracuda"** on her basketball team due to her ferociousness on the court. In 1984 she won the **Miss Wasilla pageant** as well as placed second in the **Miss Alaska pageant**, where she won the **"Miss Congeniality"** award and a college scholarship! She was the second major party female vice presidential candidate (*after Geraldine Ferraro in 1984*) and the **first Alaskan** on a national ticket. She was also the **first female vice presidential nominee** of the Republican Party!

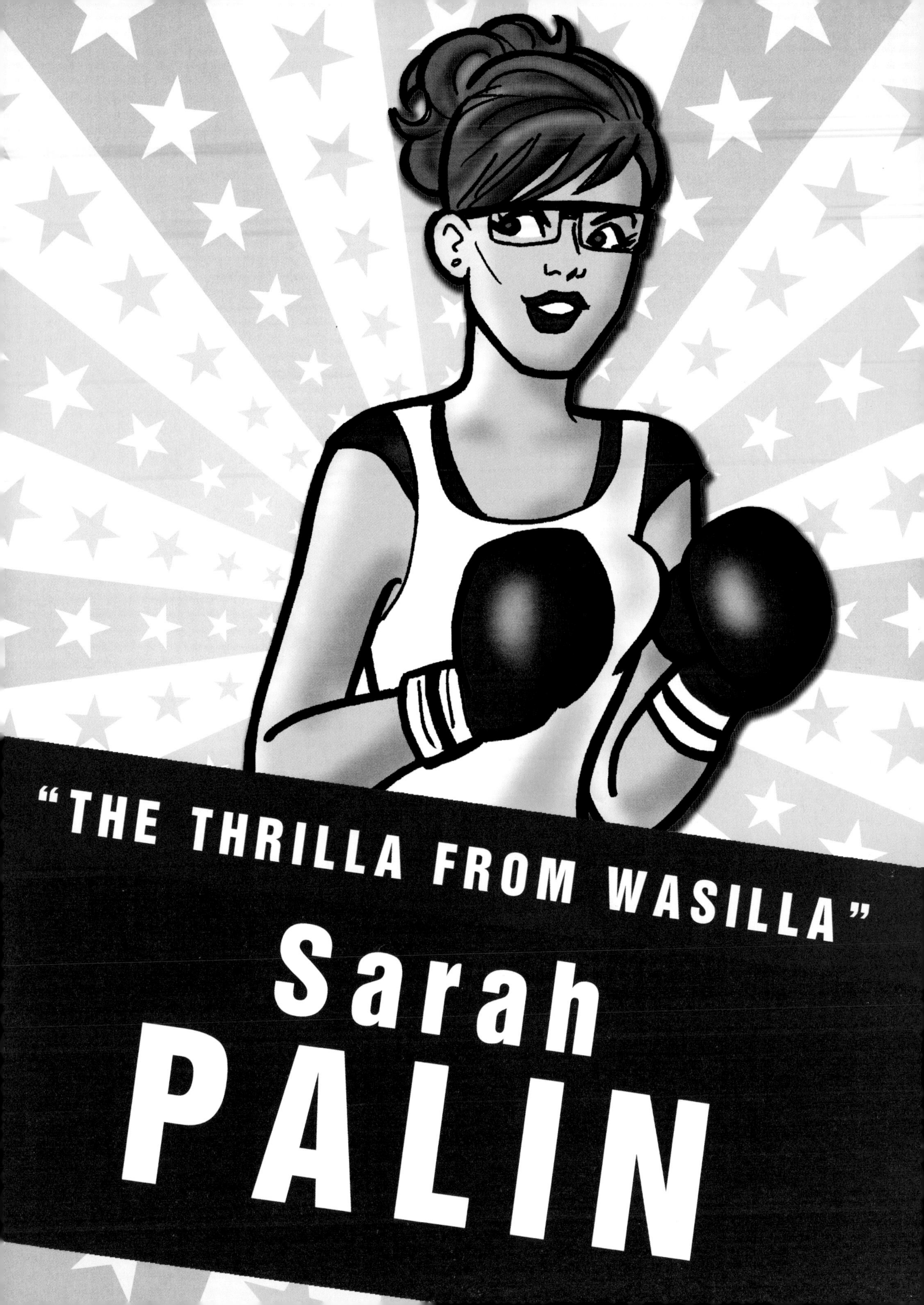
"THE THRILLA FROM WASILLA"
Sarah
PALIN

Did You Know...

Before arriving in America's favorite town and facing off with **Governor Sarah Palin**, **President Barack Obama** received a visit from Riverdale's resident socialite, **Veronica Lodge**, in a two-part story entitled, **"Ms. Lodge Goes to Washington."**

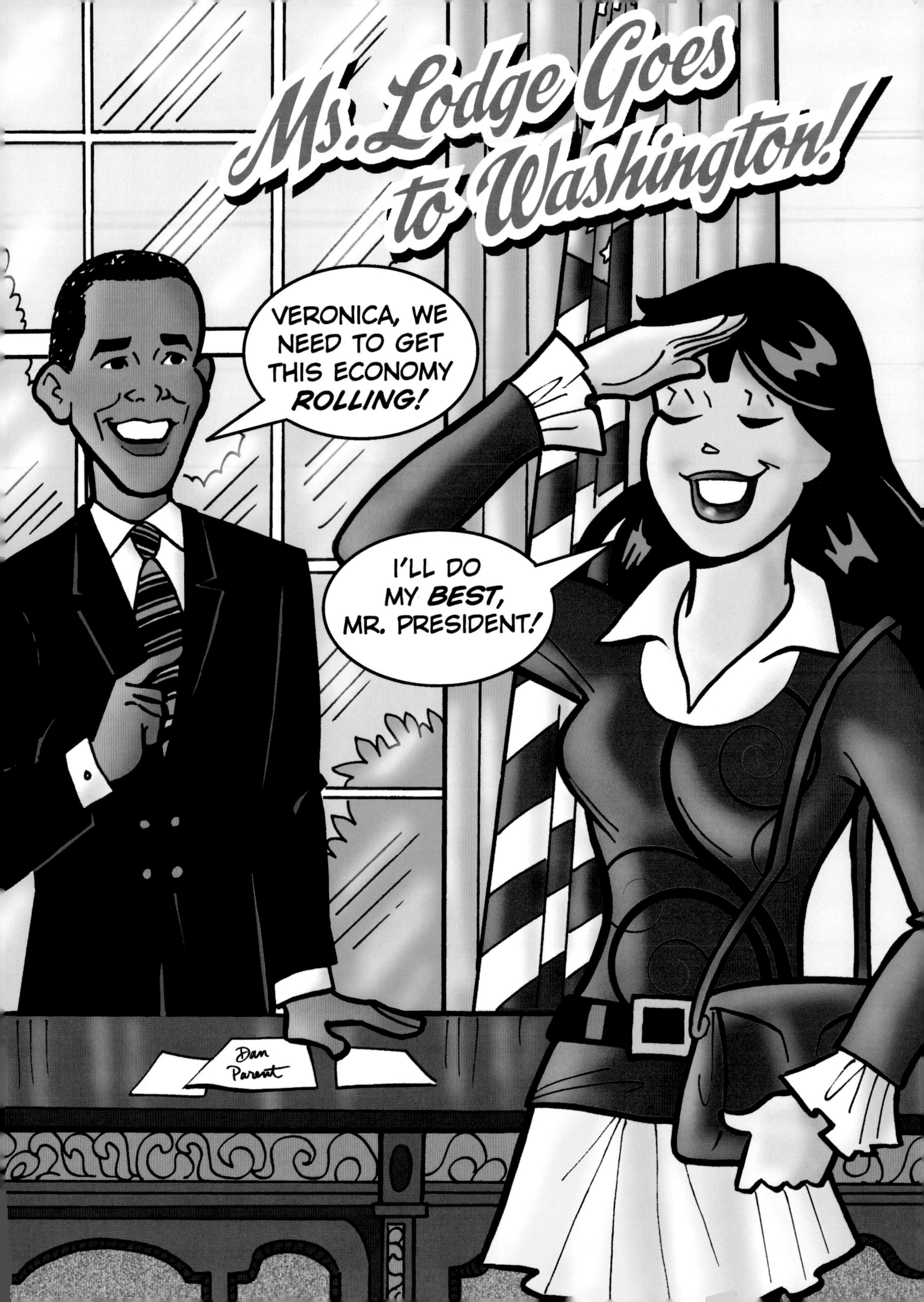
Ms. Lodge Goes to Washington!
VERONICA, WE NEED TO GET THIS ECONOMY ROLLING!
I'LL DO MY BEST, MR. PRESIDENT!
Dan Parent

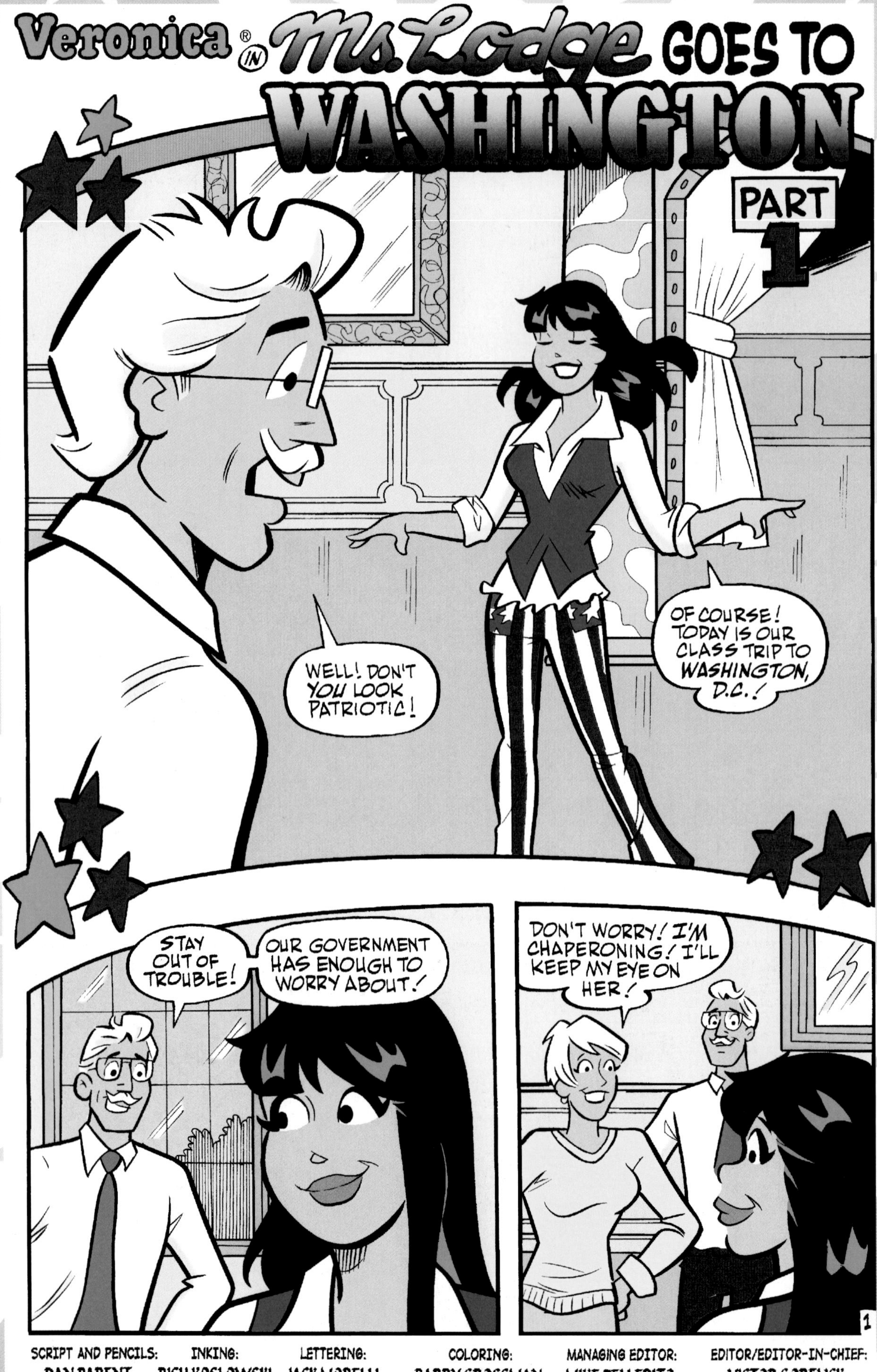
Veronica® IN Ms. Lodge GOES TO WASHINGTON
PART 1
WELL! DON'T YOU LOOK PATRIOTIC!
OF COURSE! TODAY IS OUR CLASS TRIP TO WASHINGTON, D.C.!
STAY OUT OF TROUBLE!
OUR GOVERNMENT HAS ENOUGH TO WORRY ABOUT!
DON'T WORRY! I'M CHAPERONING! I'LL KEEP MY EYE ON HER!
1

SCRIPT AND PENCILS: DAN PARENT INKING: RICH KOSLOWSKI LETTERING: JACK MORELLI COLORING: BARRY GROSSMAN MANAGING EDITOR: MIKE PELLERITO EDITOR/EDITOR-IN-CHIEF: VICTOR GORELICK

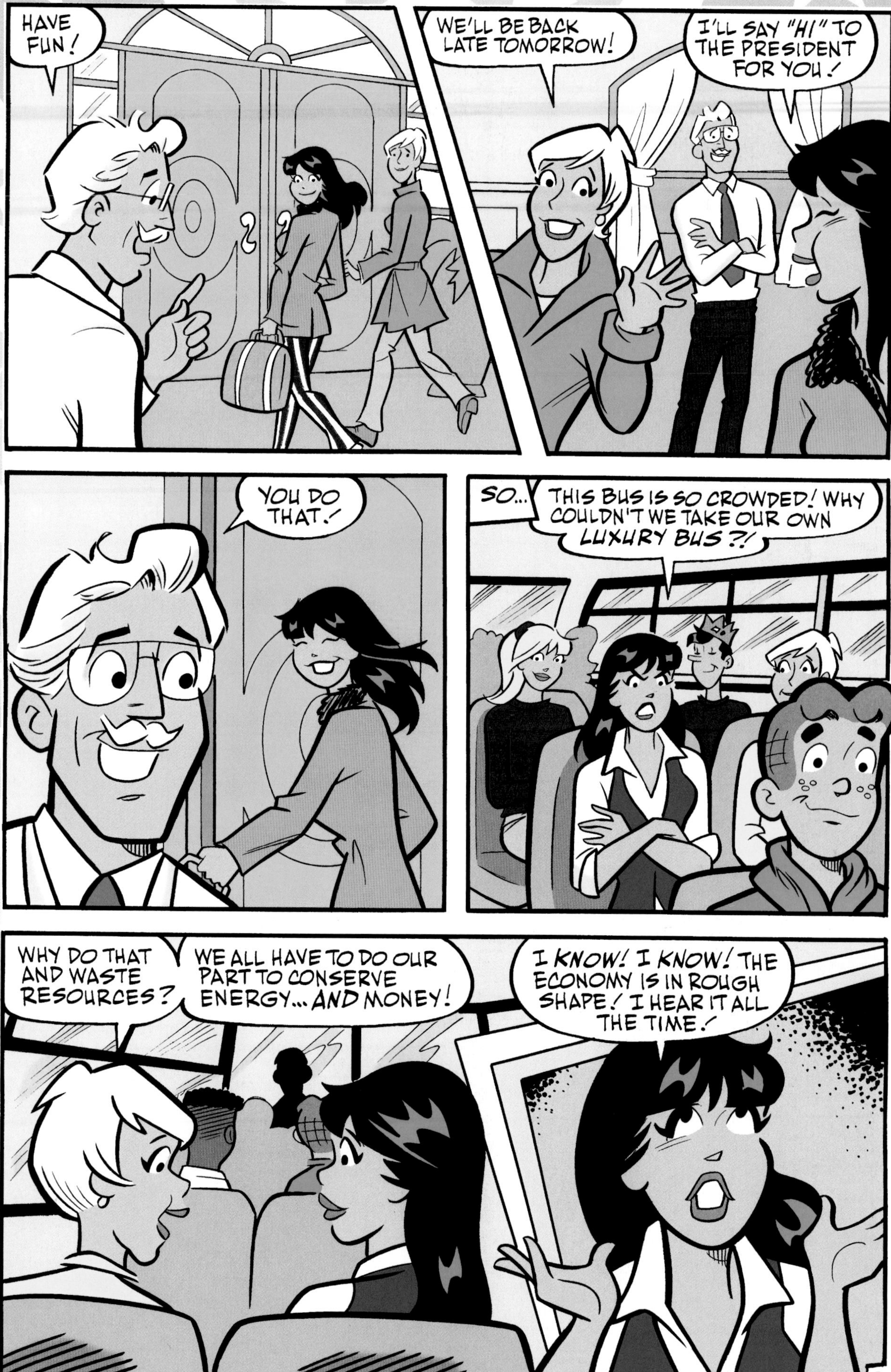
HAVE FUN!
WE'LL BE BACK LATE TOMORROW!
I'LL SAY "HI" TO THE PRESIDENT FOR YOU!
YOU DO THAT!
SO...
THIS BUS IS SO CROWDED! WHY COULDN'T WE TAKE OUR OWN LUXURY BUS?!
WHY DO THAT AND WASTE RESOURCES?
WE ALL HAVE TO DO OUR PART TO CONSERVE ENERGY... AND MONEY!
I KNOW! I KNOW! THE ECONOMY IS IN ROUGH SHAPE! I HEAR IT ALL THE TIME!
2

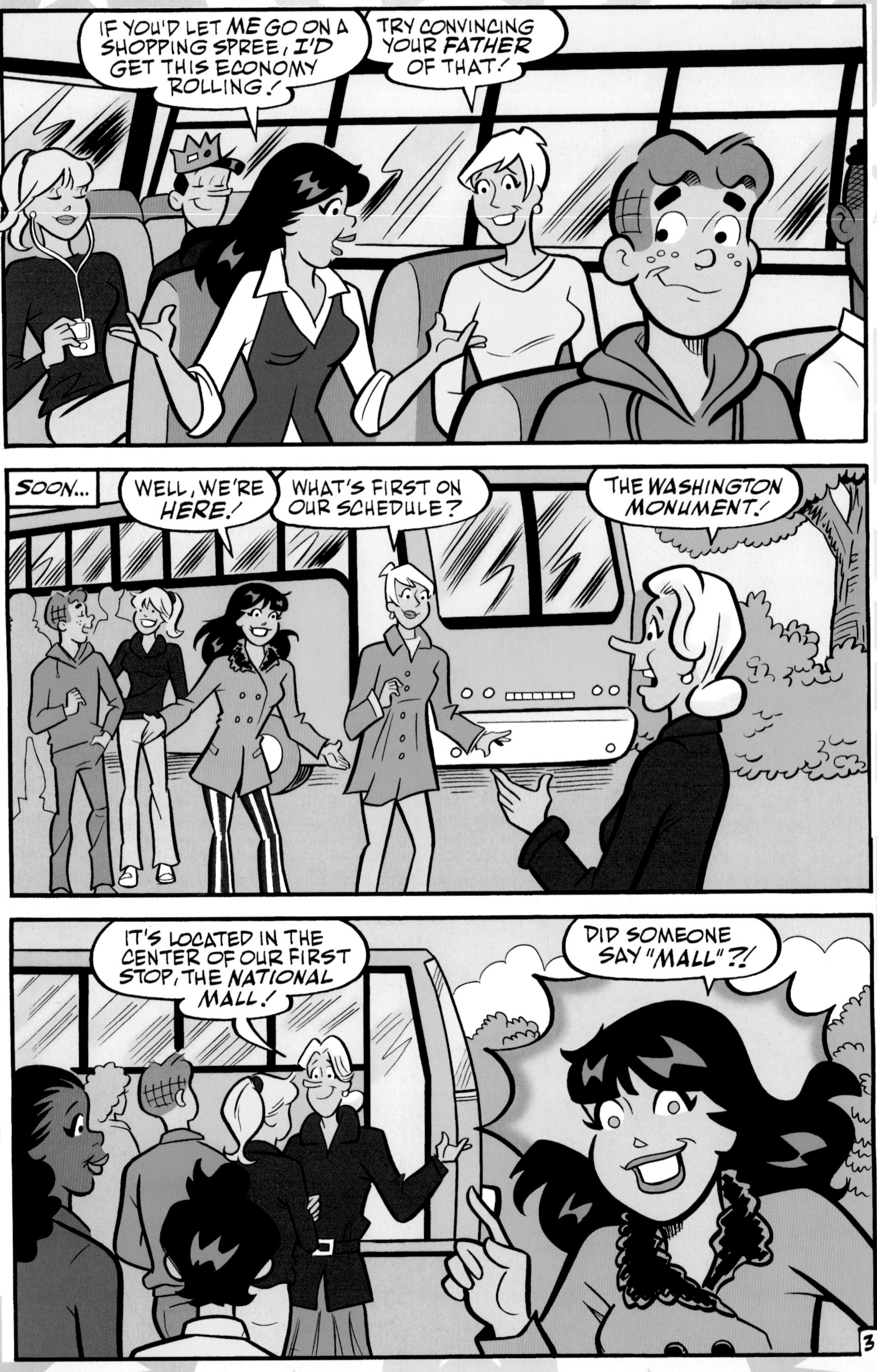
IF YOU'D LET ME GO ON A SHOPPING SPREE, I'D GET THIS ECONOMY ROLLING!
TRY CONVINCING YOUR FATHER OF THAT!
SOON...
WELL, WE'RE HERE!
WHAT'S FIRST ON OUR SCHEDULE?
THE WASHINGTON MONUMENT!
IT'S LOCATED IN THE CENTER OF OUR FIRST STOP, THE NATIONAL MALL!
DID SOMEONE SAY "MALL"?!

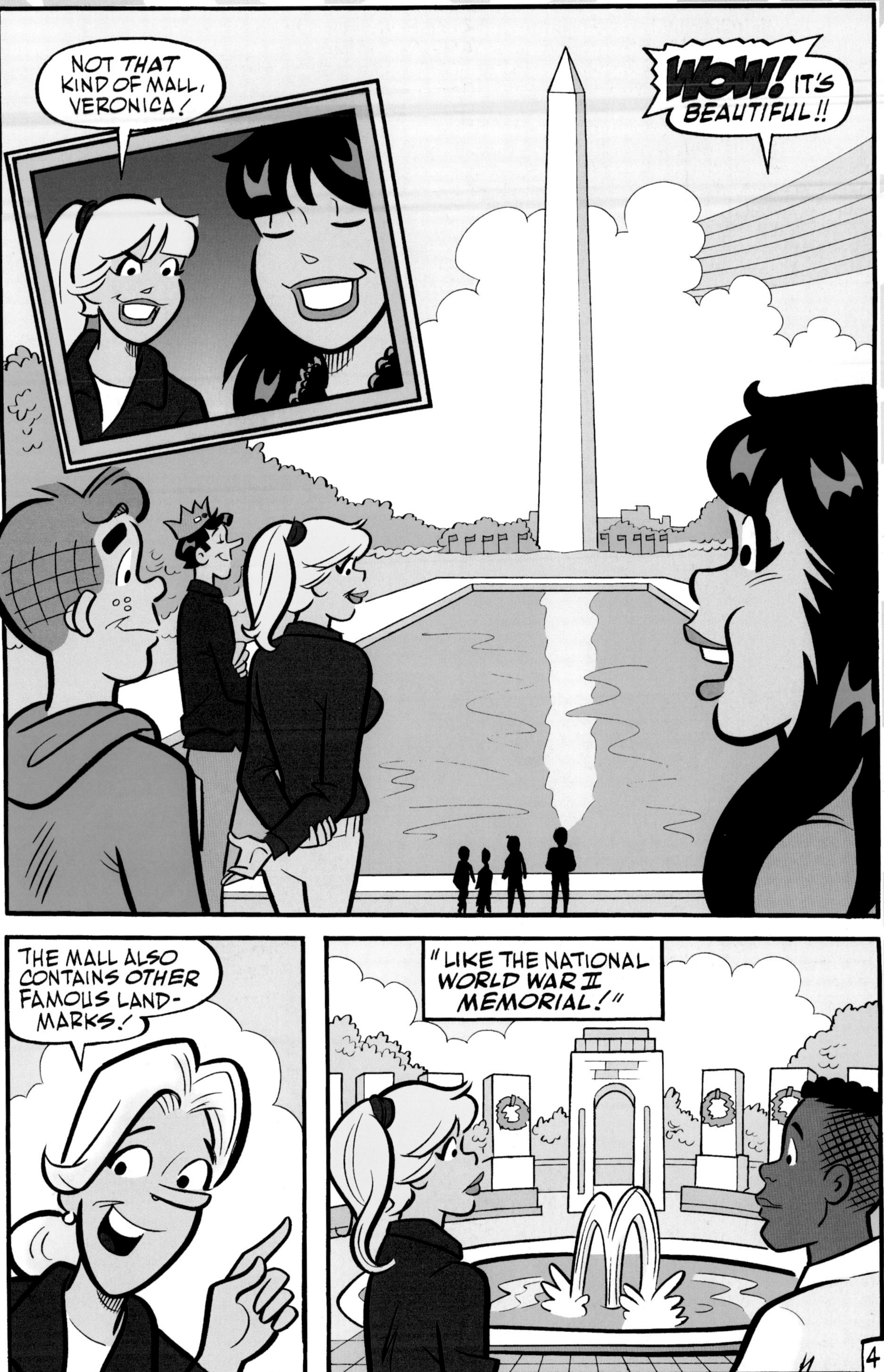
NOT THAT KIND OF MALL, VERONICA!
WOW! IT'S BEAUTIFUL!!
THE MALL ALSO CONTAINS OTHER FAMOUS LAND-MARKS!
"LIKE THE NATIONAL WORLD WAR II MEMORIAL!"
4

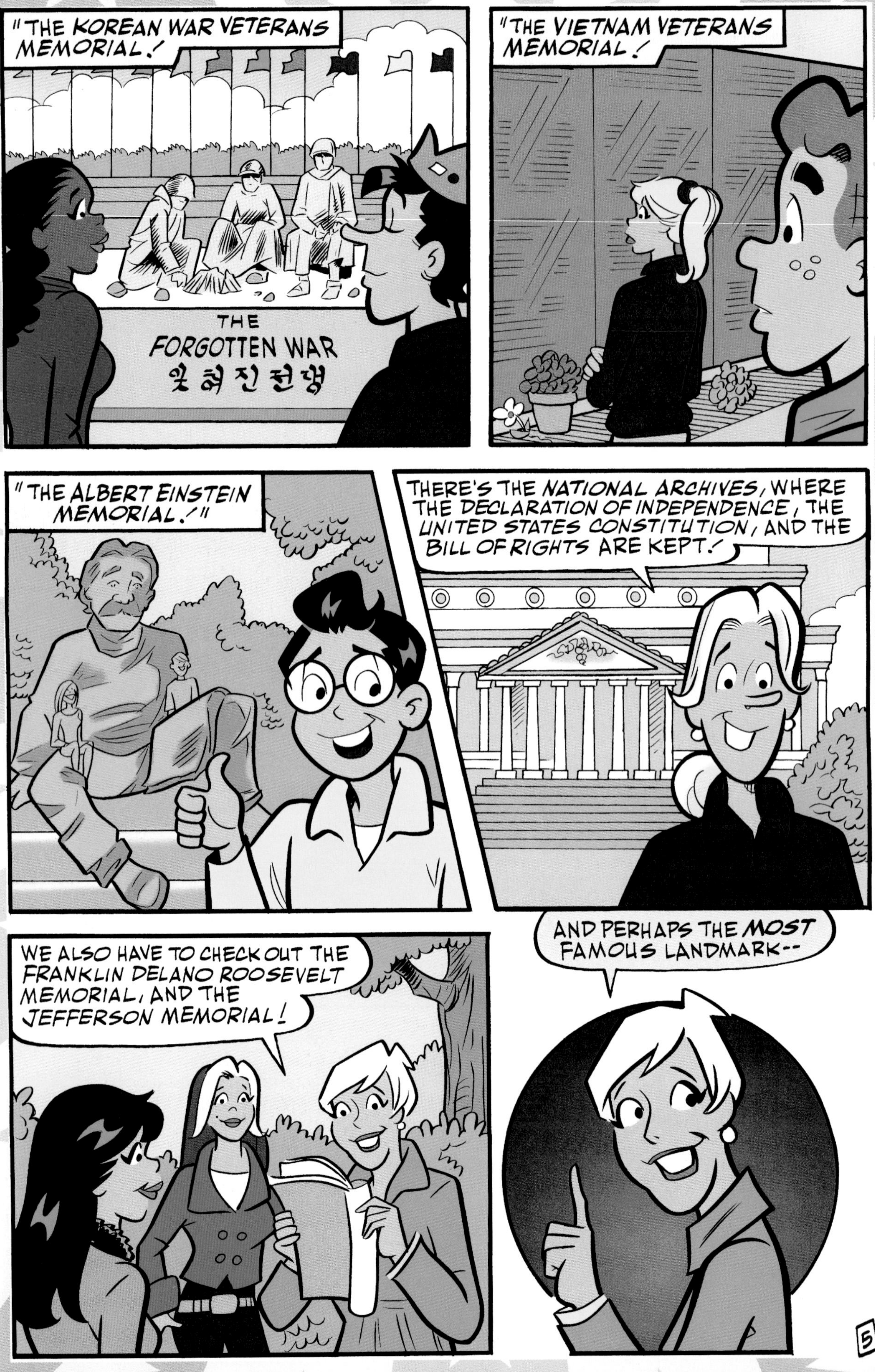
"THE KOREAN WAR VETERANS MEMORIAL!
THE FORGOTTEN WAR
잊혀진전쟁
"THE VIETNAM VETERANS MEMORIAL!
"THE ALBERT EINSTEIN MEMORIAL!"
THERE'S THE NATIONAL ARCHIVES, WHERE THE DECLARATION OF INDEPENDENCE, THE UNITED STATES CONSTITUTION, AND THE BILL OF RIGHTS ARE KEPT!
WE ALSO HAVE TO CHECK OUT THE FRANKLIN DELANO ROOSEVELT MEMORIAL, AND THE JEFFERSON MEMORIAL!
AND PERHAPS THE MOST FAMOUS LANDMARK--

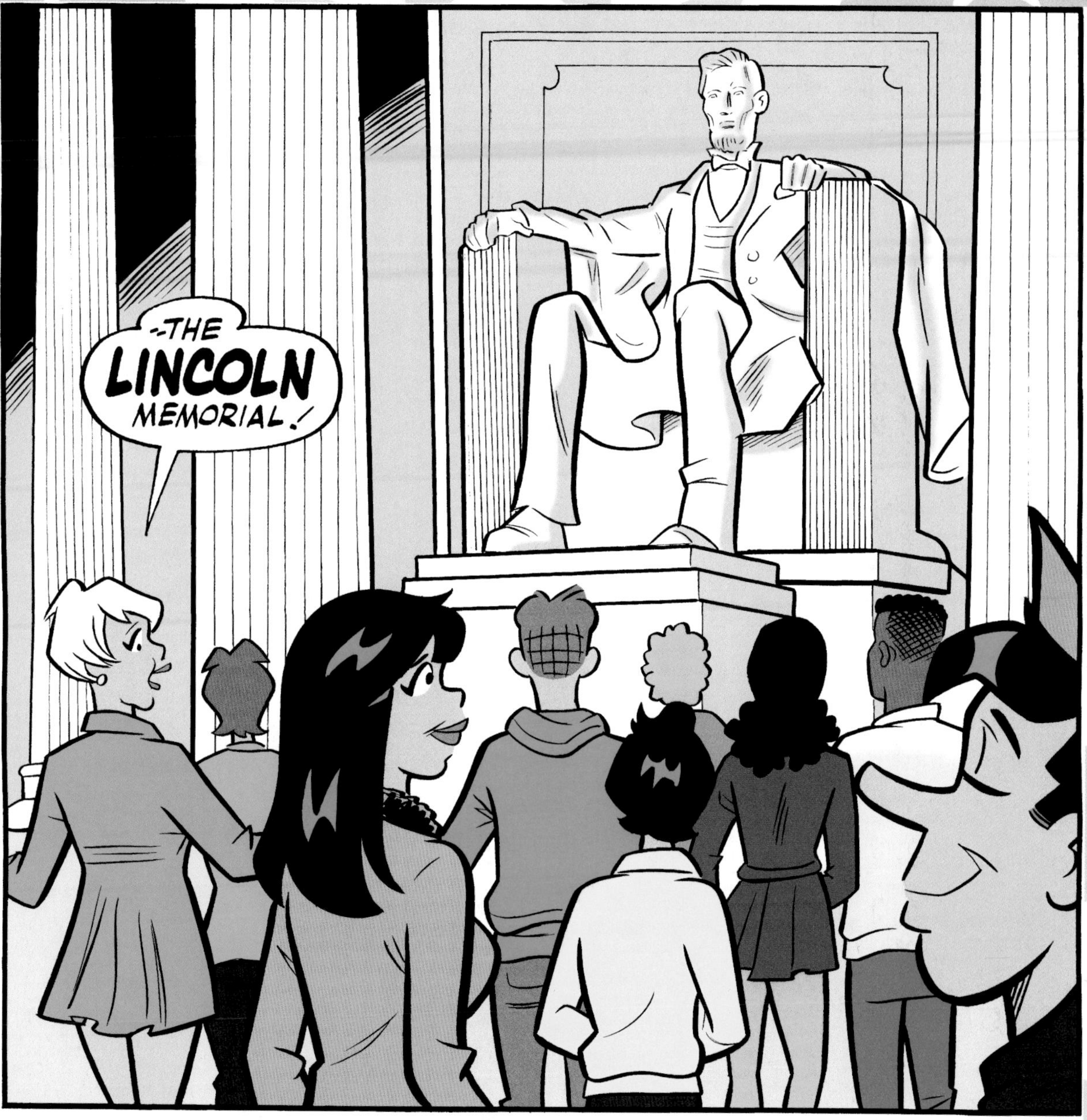
-THE LINCOLN MEMORIAL!

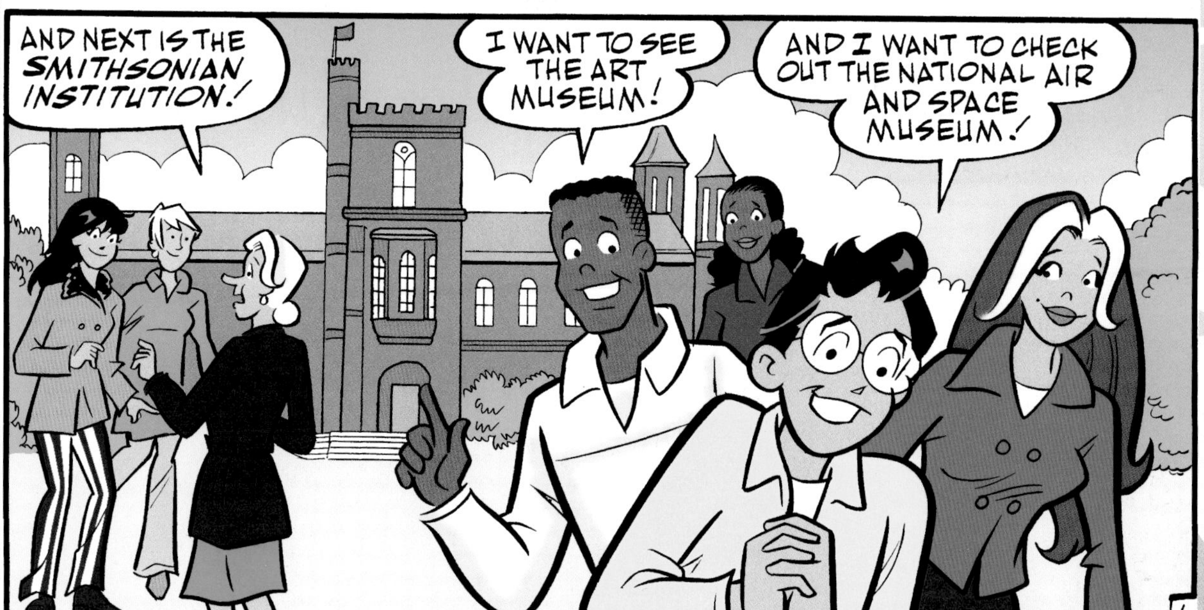
AND NEXT IS THE SMITHSONIAN INSTITUTION!
I WANT TO SEE THE ART MUSEUM!
AND I WANT TO CHECK OUT THE NATIONAL AIR AND SPACE MUSEUM!

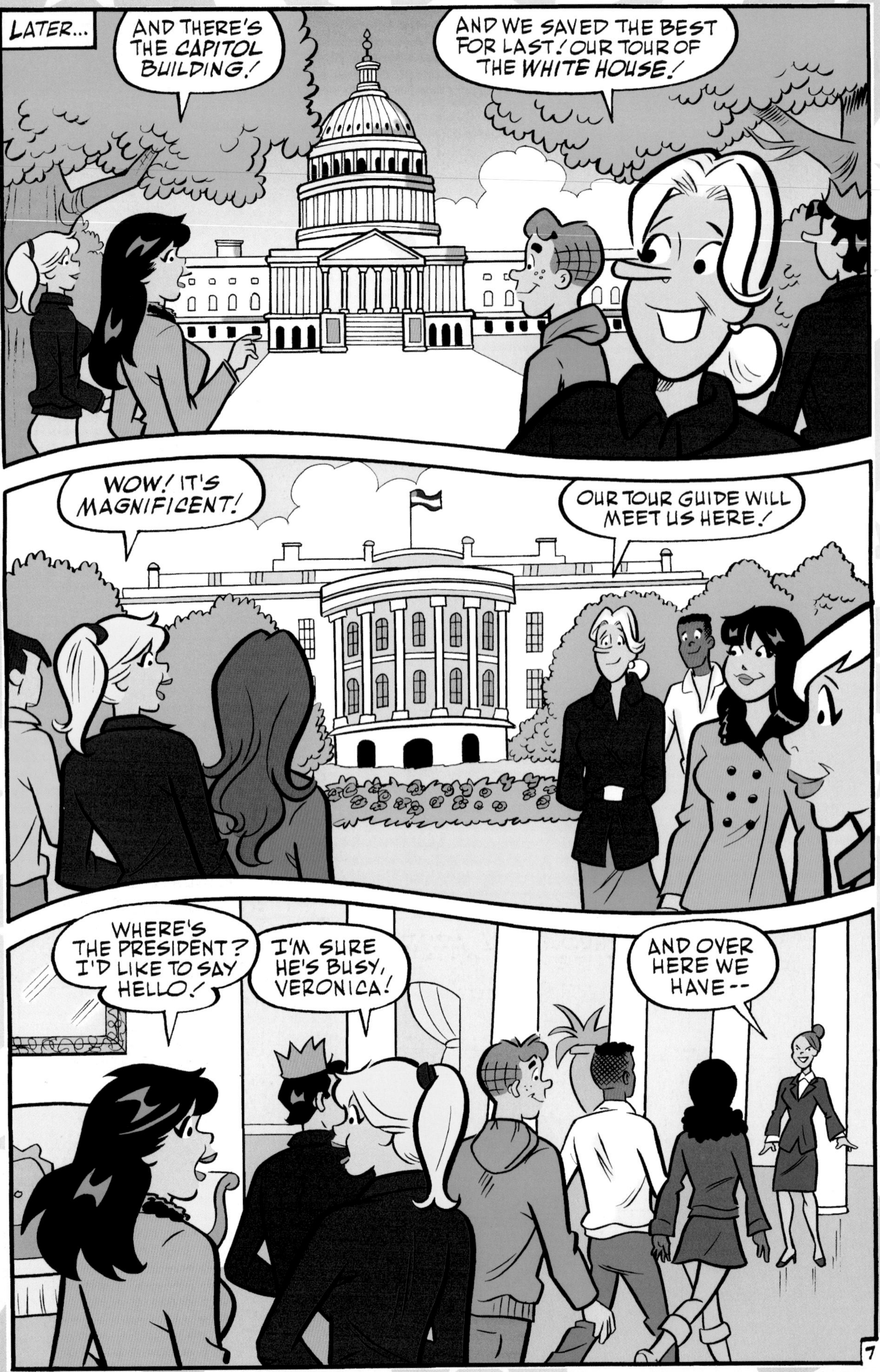
LATER...
AND THERE'S THE CAPITOL BUILDING!
AND WE SAVED THE BEST FOR LAST! OUR TOUR OF THE WHITE HOUSE!
WOW! IT'S MAGNIFICENT!
OUR TOUR GUIDE WILL MEET US HERE!
WHERE'S THE PRESIDENT? I'D LIKE TO SAY HELLO!
I'M SURE HE'S BUSY, VERONICA!
AND OVER HERE WE HAVE--

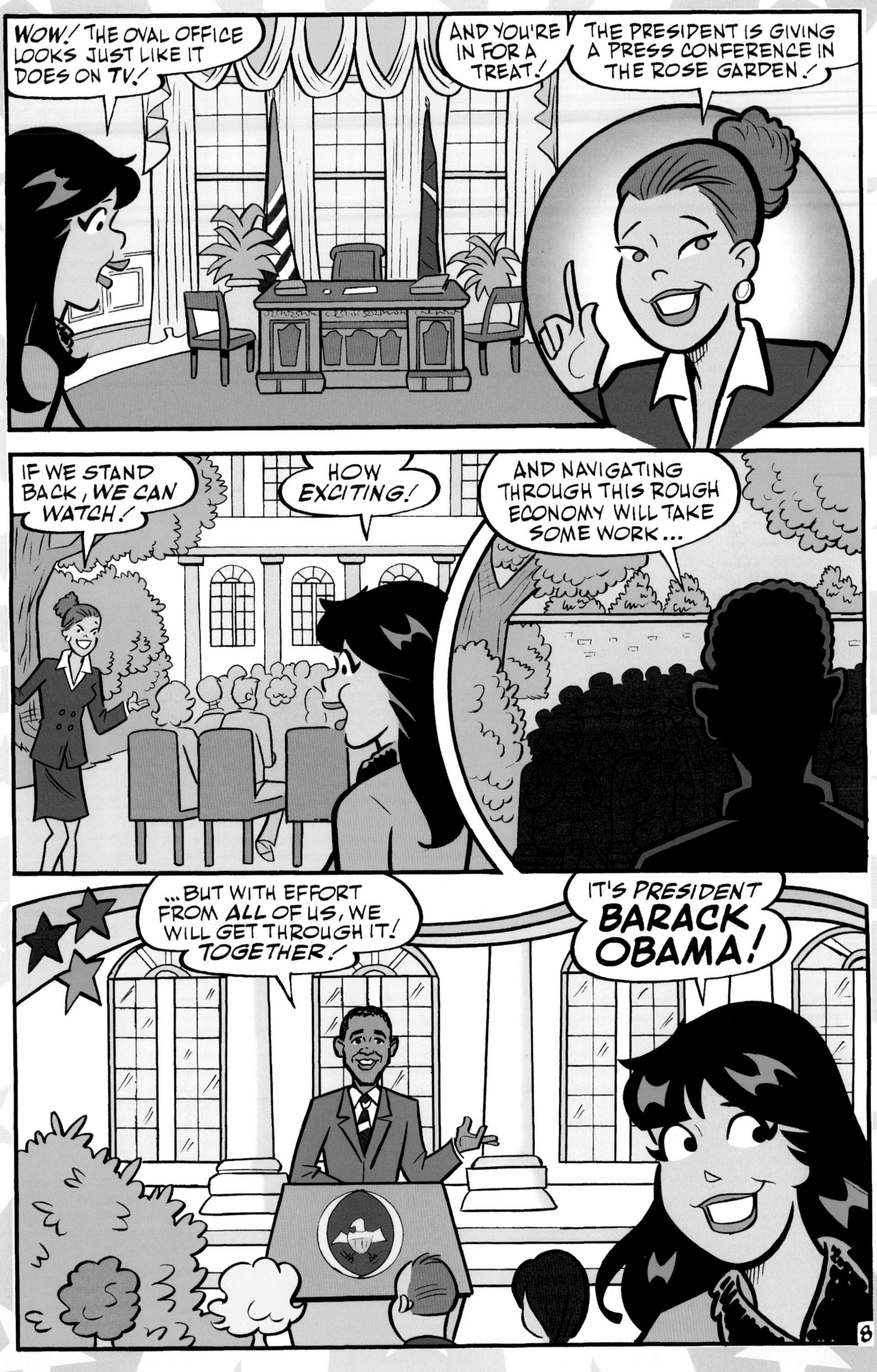
WOW! THE OVAL OFFICE LOOKS JUST LIKE IT DOES ON TV!
AND YOU'RE IN FOR A TREAT!
THE PRESIDENT IS GIVING A PRESS CONFERENCE IN THE ROSE GARDEN!
IF WE STAND BACK, WE CAN WATCH!
HOW EXCITING!
AND NAVIGATING THROUGH THIS ROUGH ECONOMY WILL TAKE SOME WORK...
...BUT WITH EFFORT FROM ALL OF US, WE WILL GET THROUGH IT! TOGETHER!
IT'S PRESIDENT BARACK OBAMA!

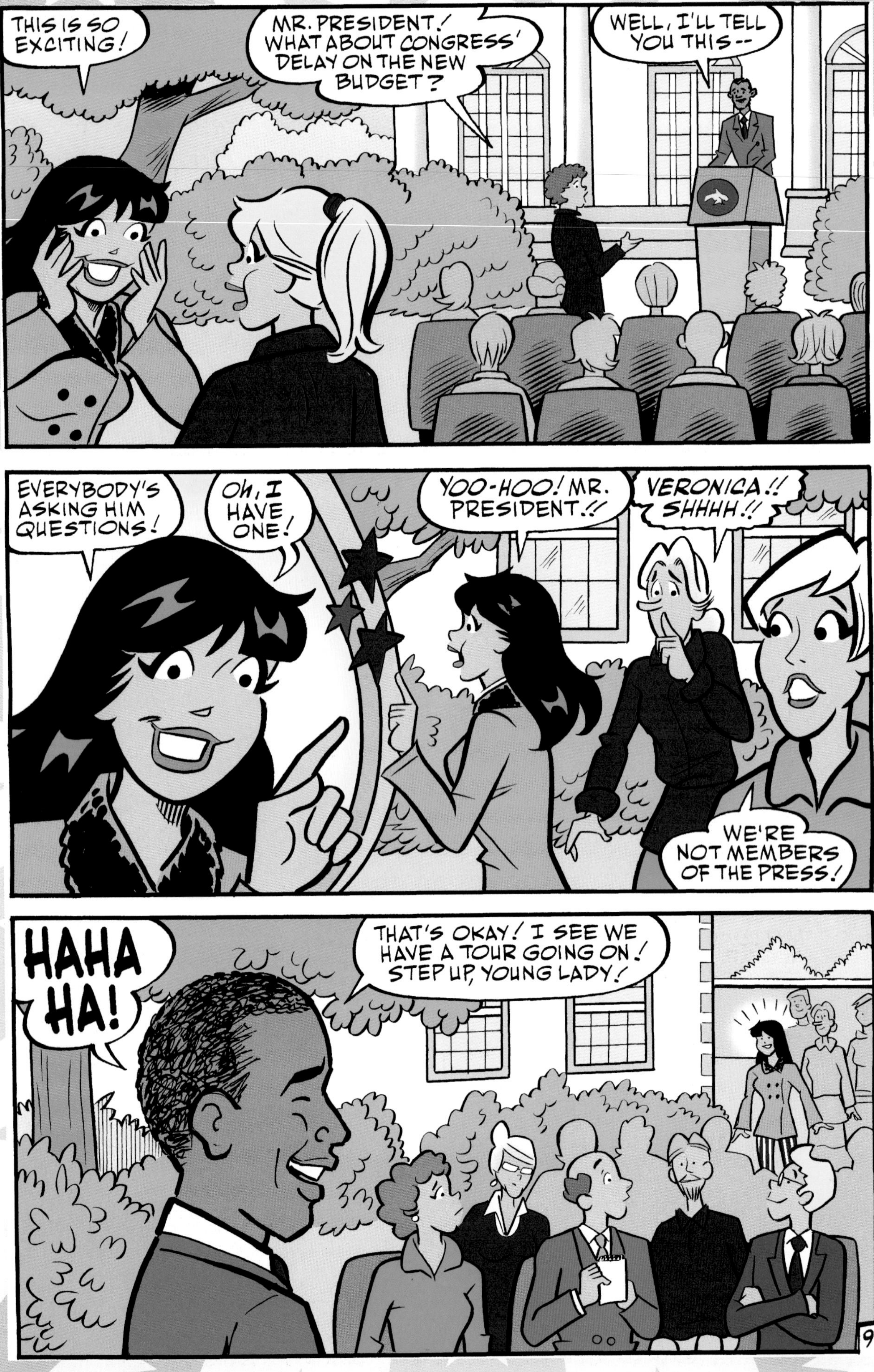
THIS IS SO EXCITING!
MR. PRESIDENT! WHAT ABOUT CONGRESS' DELAY ON THE NEW BUDGET?
WELL, I'LL TELL YOU THIS --
EVERYBODY'S ASKING HIM QUESTIONS!
Oh, I HAVE ONE!
YOO-HOO! MR. PRESIDENT!!
VERONICA!! SHHHH!!
WE'RE NOT MEMBERS OF THE PRESS!
HAHA HA!
THAT'S OKAY! I SEE WE HAVE A TOUR GOING ON! STEP UP, YOUNG LADY!

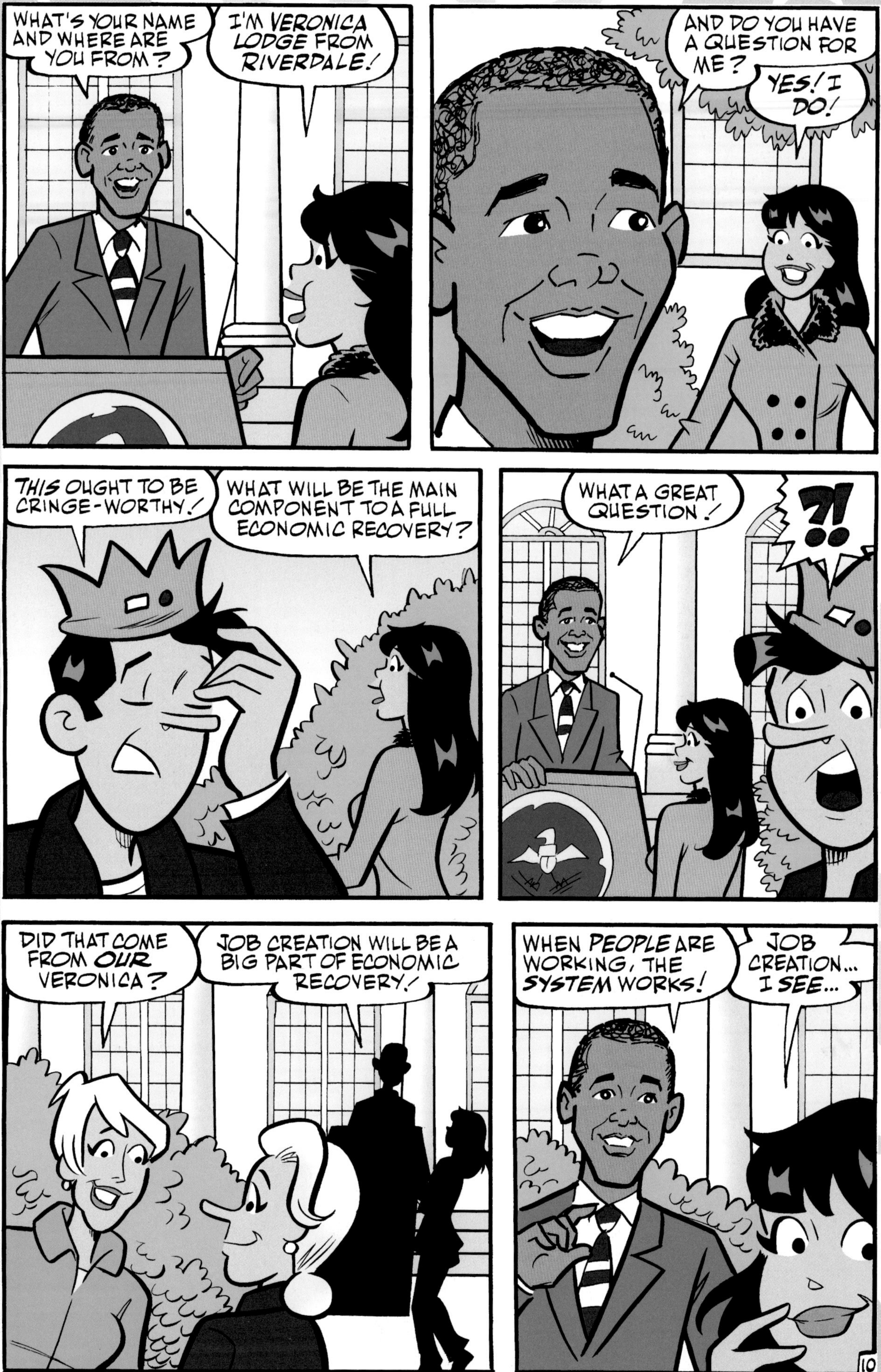
WHAT'S YOUR NAME AND WHERE ARE YOU FROM?
I'M VERONICA LODGE FROM RIVERDALE!
AND DO YOU HAVE A QUESTION FOR ME?
YES! I DO!
THIS OUGHT TO BE CRINGE-WORTHY!
WHAT WILL BE THE MAIN COMPONENT TO A FULL ECONOMIC RECOVERY?
WHAT A GREAT QUESTION!
?!
DID THAT COME FROM OUR VERONICA?
JOB CREATION WILL BE A BIG PART OF ECONOMIC RECOVERY!
WHEN PEOPLE ARE WORKING, THE SYSTEM WORKS!
JOB CREATION... I SEE...
10

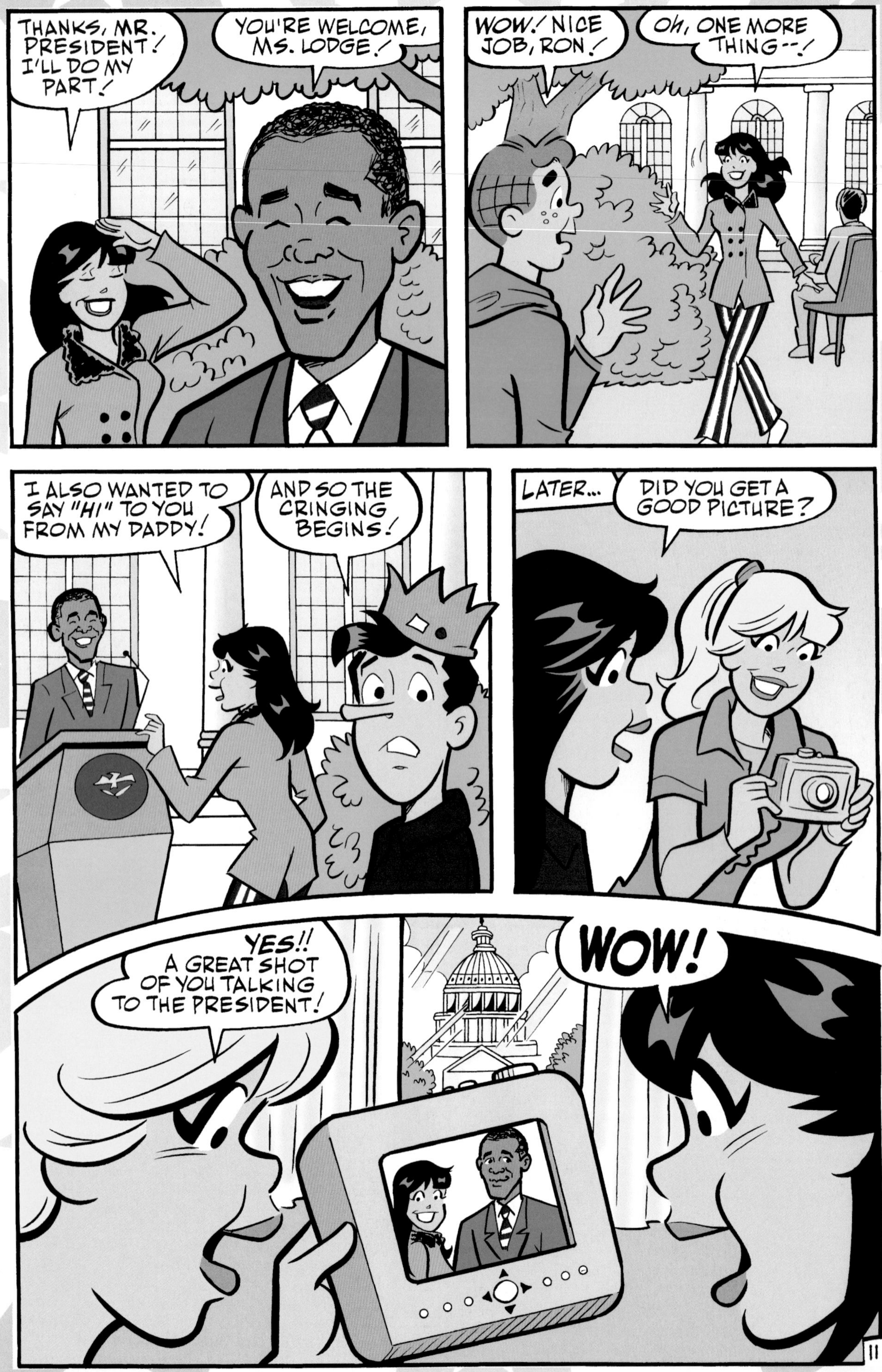
THANKS, MR. PRESIDENT! I'LL DO MY PART!
YOU'RE WELCOME, MS. LODGE!
WOW! NICE JOB, RON!
OH, ONE MORE THING--!
I ALSO WANTED TO SAY "HI" TO YOU FROM MY DADDY!
AND SO THE CRINGING BEGINS!
LATER...
DID YOU GET A GOOD PICTURE?
YES!! A GREAT SHOT OF YOU TALKING TO THE PRESIDENT!
WOW!

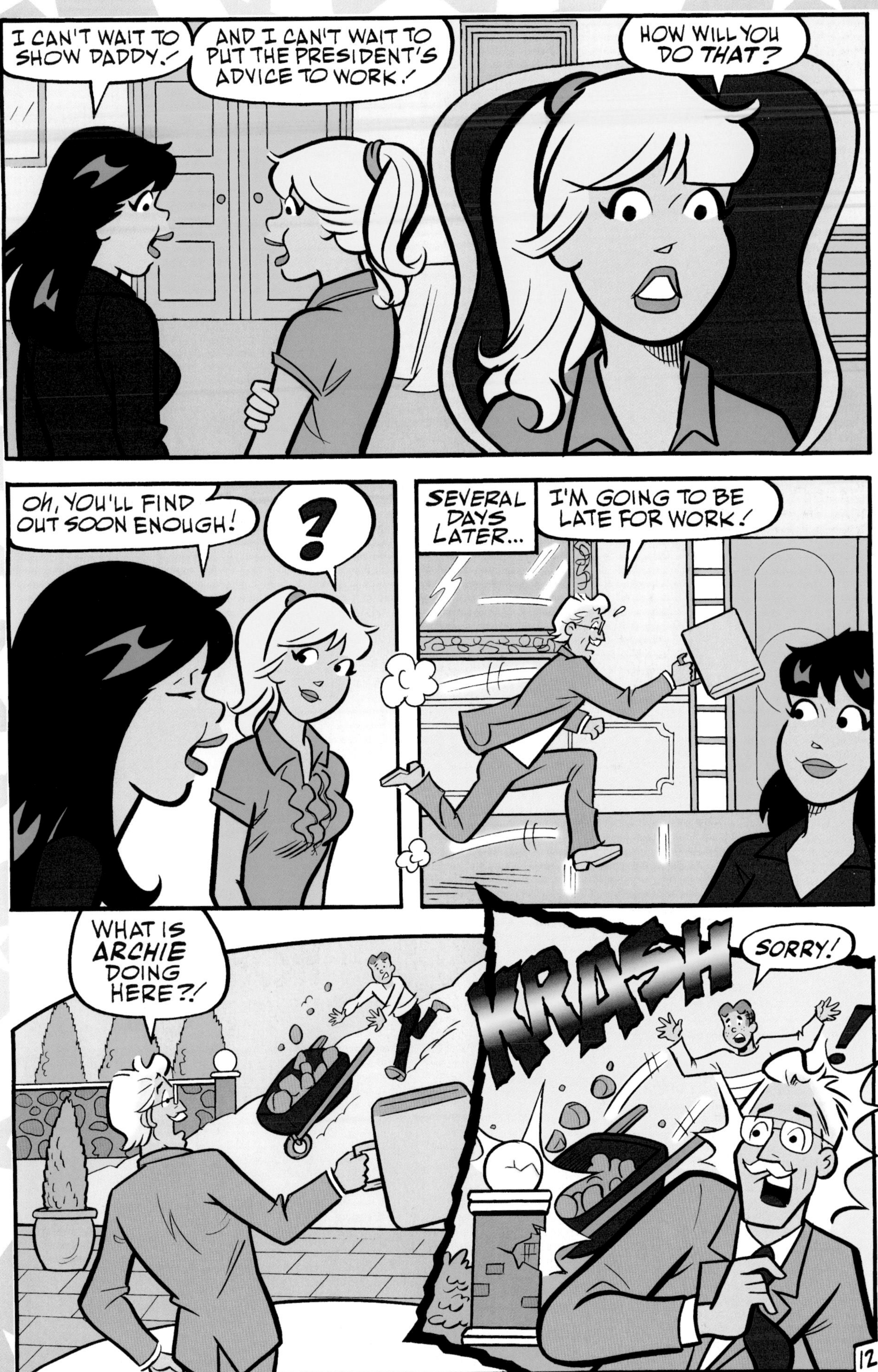
I CAN'T WAIT TO SHOW DADDY.!
AND I CAN'T WAIT TO PUT THE PRESIDENT'S ADVICE TO WORK.!
HOW WILL YOU DO *THAT*?
Oh, YOU'LL FIND OUT SOON ENOUGH!
?
SEVERAL DAYS LATER...
I'M GOING TO BE LATE FOR WORK!
WHAT IS *ARCHIE* DOING HERE?!
KRASH
SORRY!
!

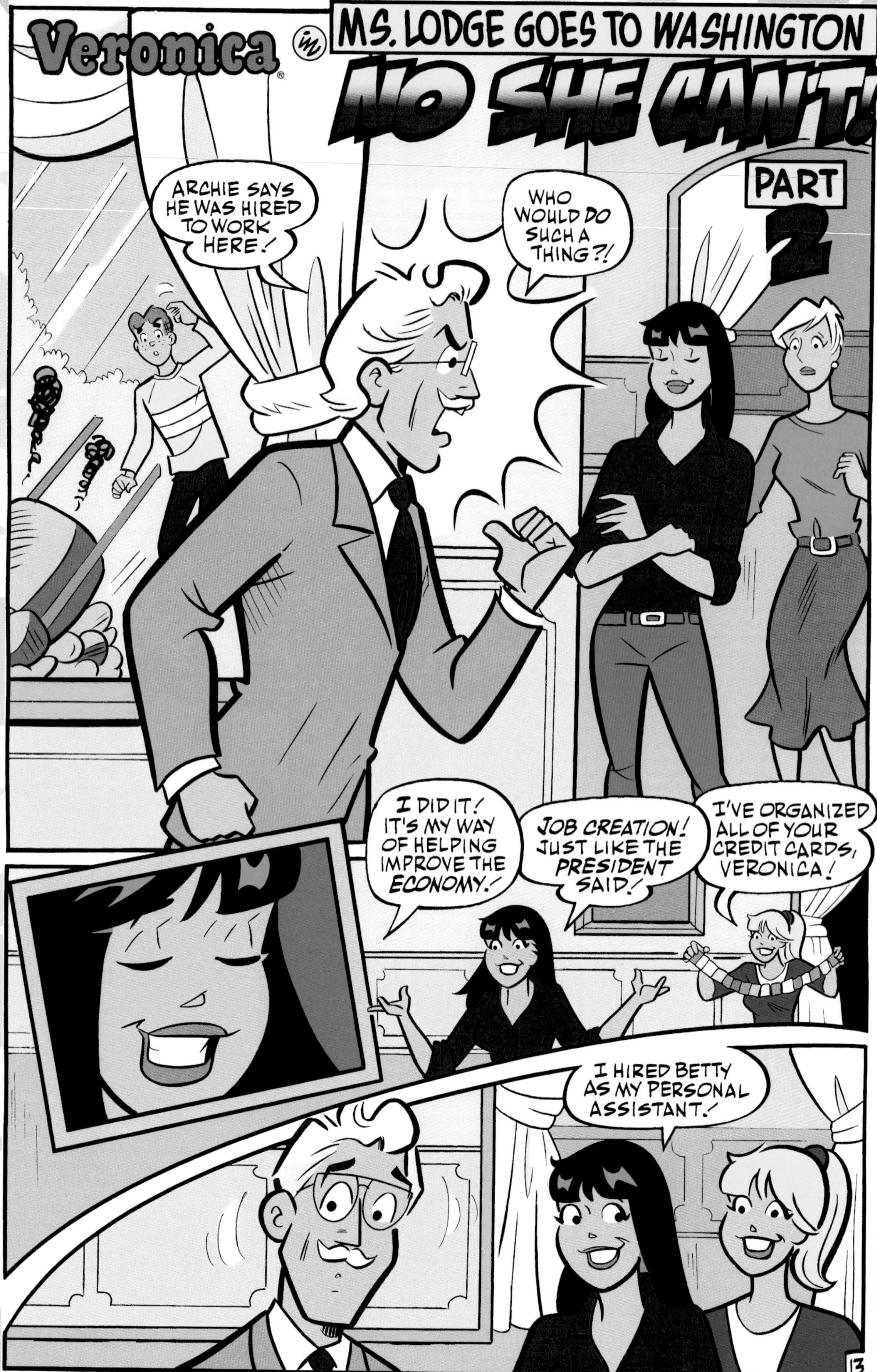
Veronica in
MS. LODGE GOES TO WASHINGTON
NO SHE CAN'T!
PART 2
ARCHIE SAYS HE WAS HIRED TO WORK HERE!
WHO WOULD DO SUCH A THING?!
I DID IT! IT'S MY WAY OF HELPING IMPROVE THE ECONOMY!
JOB CREATION! JUST LIKE THE PRESIDENT SAID!
I'VE ORGANIZED ALL OF YOUR CREDIT CARDS, VERONICA!
I HIRED BETTY AS MY PERSONAL ASSISTANT!

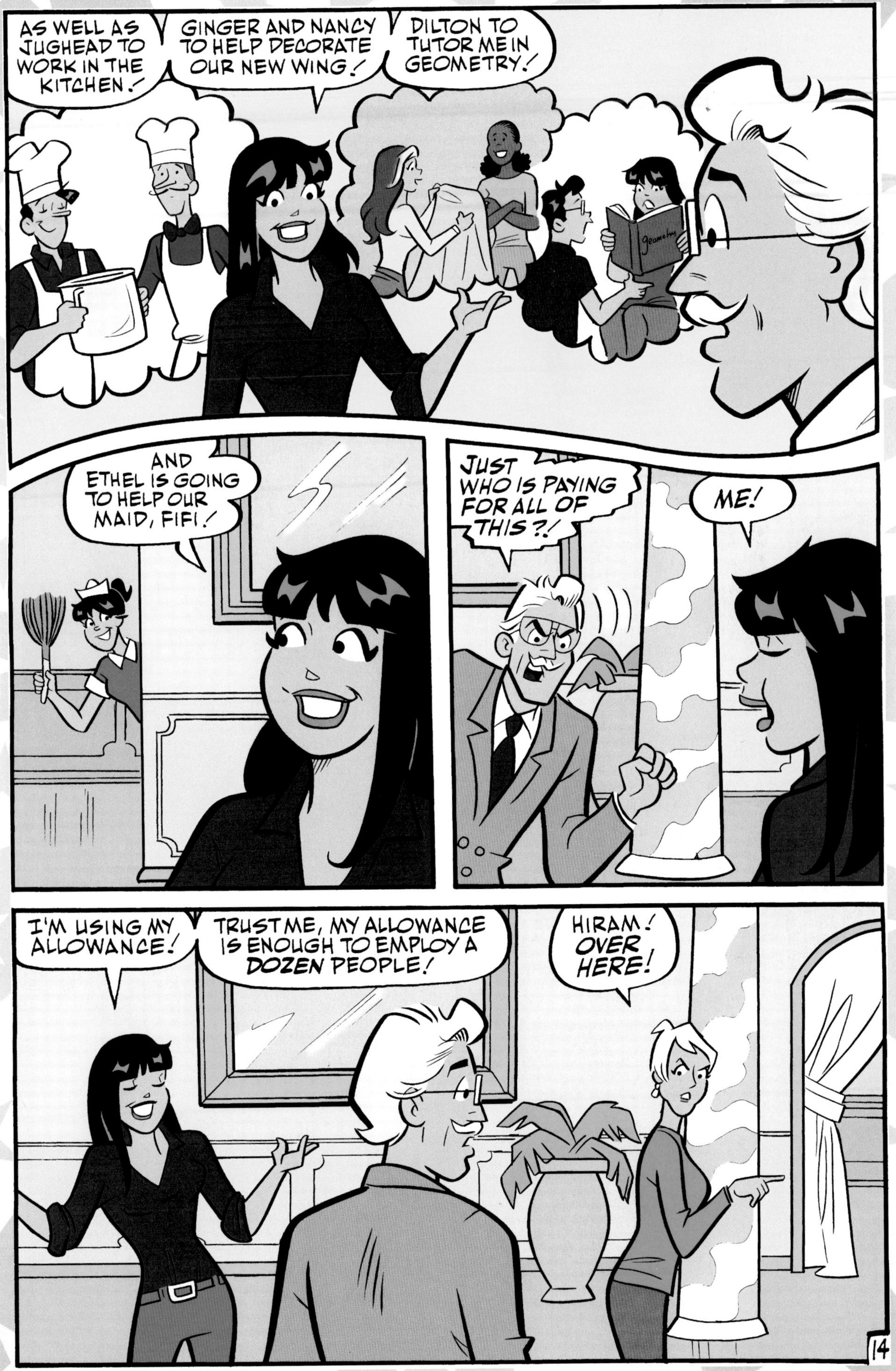
AS WELL AS JUGHEAD TO WORK IN THE KITCHEN!
GINGER AND NANCY TO HELP DECORATE OUR NEW WING!
DILTON TO TUTOR ME IN GEOMETRY!
geometry
AND ETHEL IS GOING TO HELP OUR MAID, FIFI!
JUST WHO IS PAYING FOR ALL OF THIS?!
ME!
I'M USING MY ALLOWANCE!
TRUST ME, MY ALLOWANCE IS ENOUGH TO EMPLOY A DOZEN PEOPLE!
HIRAM! OVER HERE!

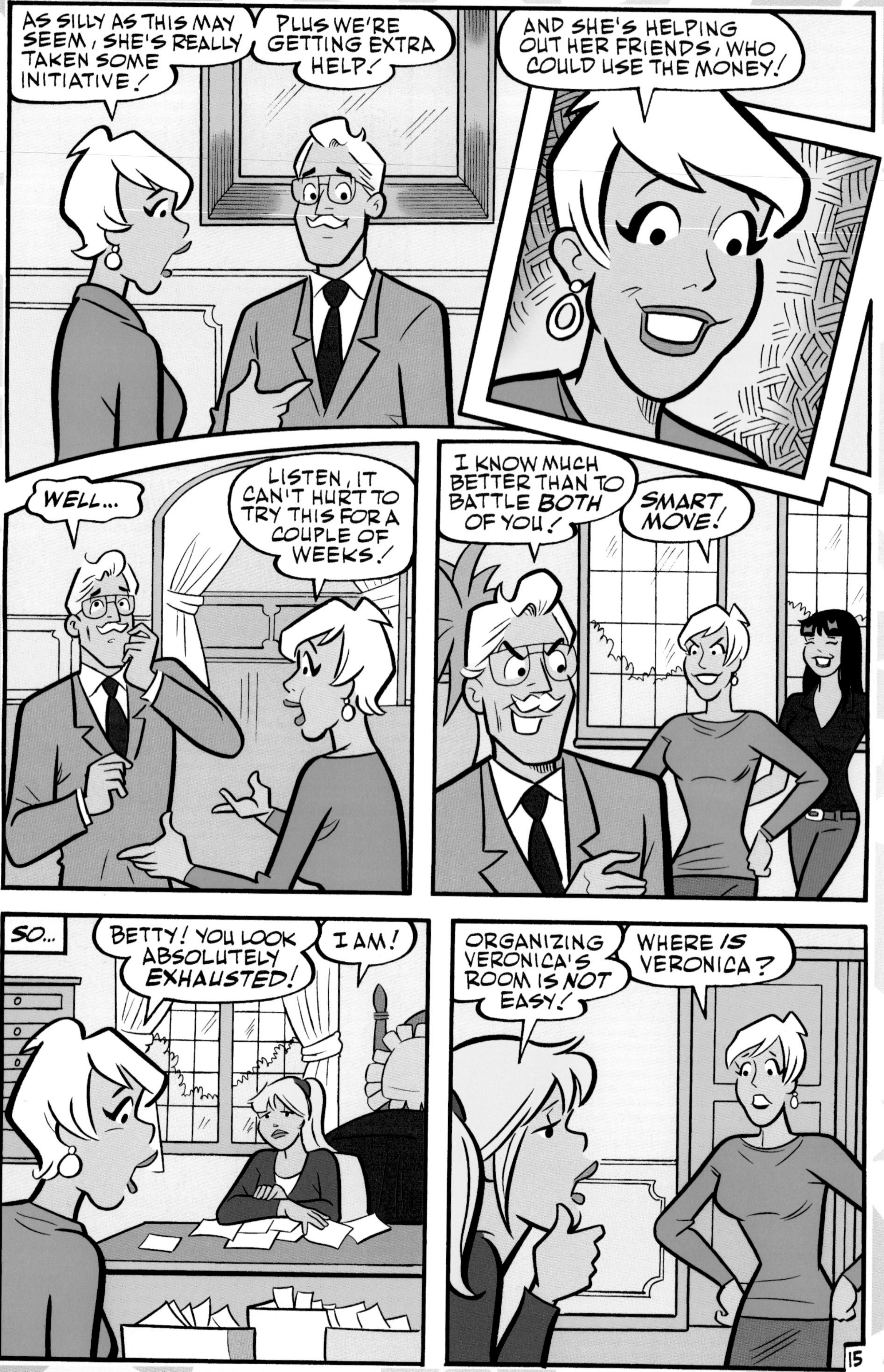
AS SILLY AS THIS MAY SEEM, SHE'S REALLY TAKEN SOME INITIATIVE!
PLUS WE'RE GETTING EXTRA HELP!
AND SHE'S HELPING OUT HER FRIENDS, WHO COULD USE THE MONEY!
WELL...
LISTEN, IT CAN'T HURT TO TRY THIS FOR A COUPLE OF WEEKS!
I KNOW MUCH BETTER THAN TO BATTLE BOTH OF YOU!
SMART MOVE!
SO...
BETTY! YOU LOOK ABSOLUTELY EXHAUSTED!
I AM!
ORGANIZING VERONICA'S ROOM IS NOT EASY!
WHERE IS VERONICA?

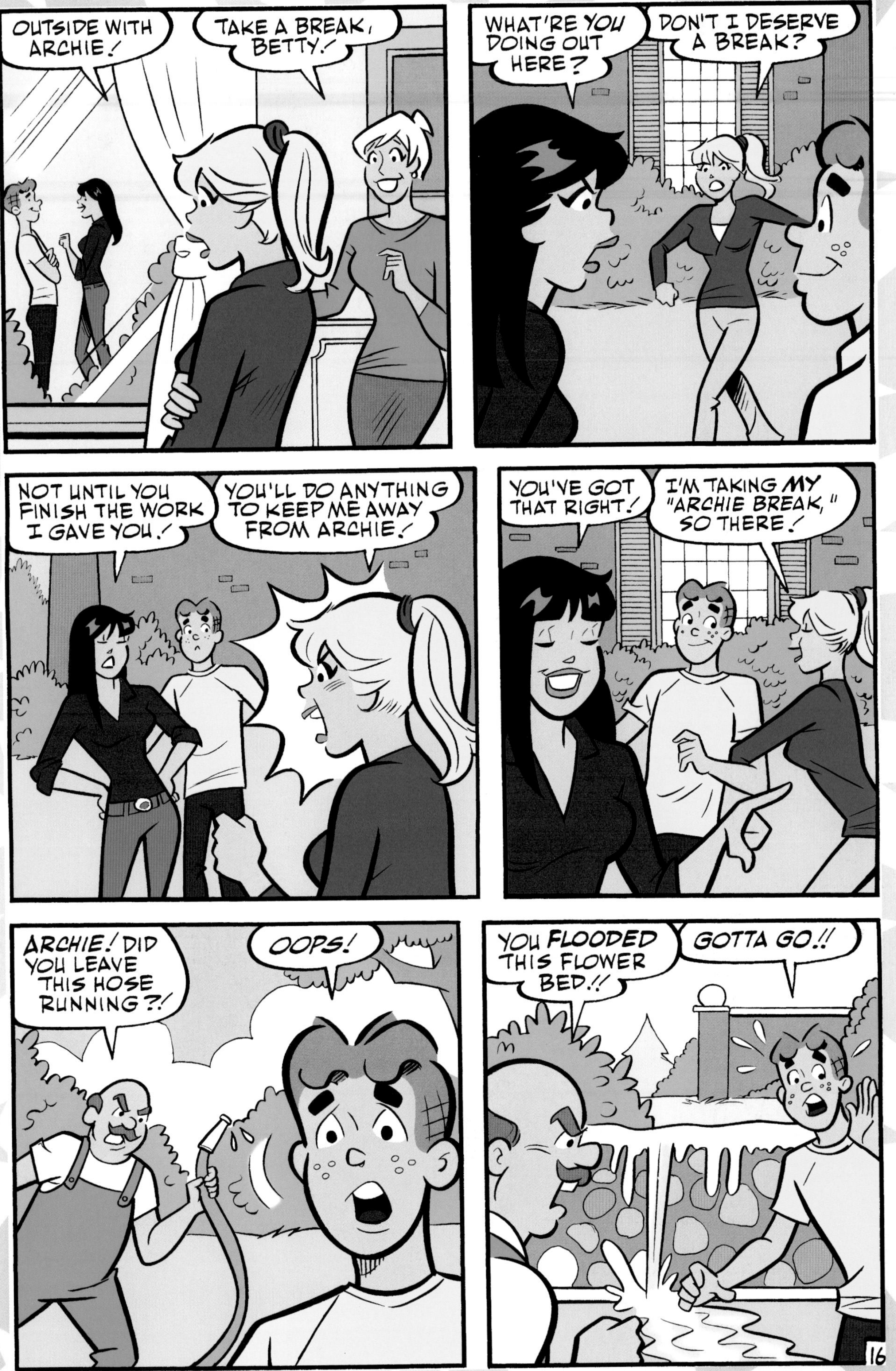
OUTSIDE WITH ARCHIE!
TAKE A BREAK, BETTY!
WHAT'RE YOU DOING OUT HERE?
DON'T I DESERVE A BREAK?
NOT UNTIL YOU FINISH THE WORK I GAVE YOU!
YOU'LL DO ANYTHING TO KEEP ME AWAY FROM ARCHIE!
YOU'VE GOT THAT RIGHT!
I'M TAKING MY "ARCHIE BREAK," SO THERE!
ARCHIE! DID YOU LEAVE THIS HOSE RUNNING?!
OOPS!
YOU FLOODED THIS FLOWER BED!!
GOTTA GO!!

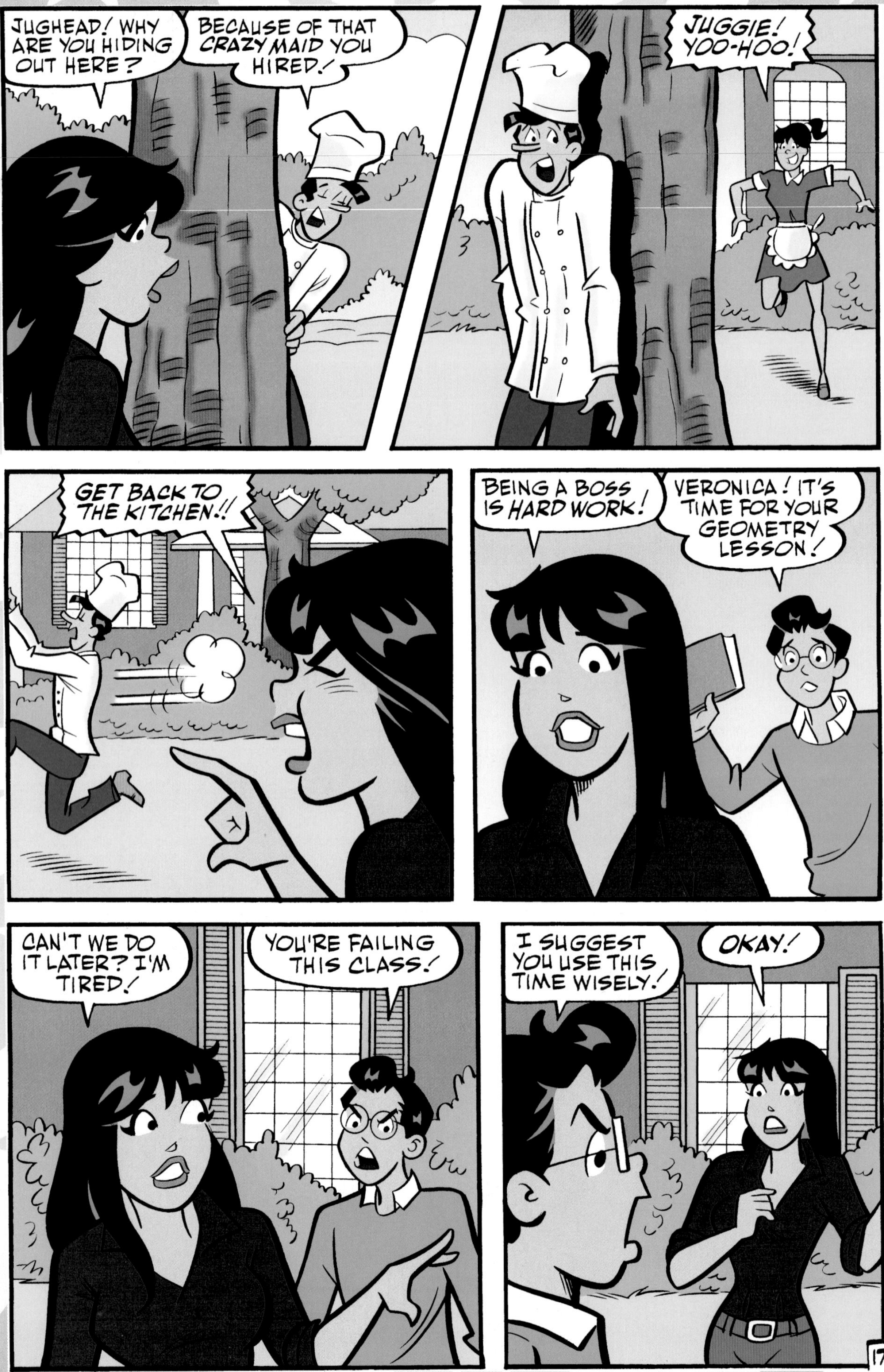
JUGHEAD! WHY ARE YOU HIDING OUT HERE?
BECAUSE OF THAT CRAZY MAID YOU HIRED!
JUGGIE! YOO-HOO!
GET BACK TO THE KITCHEN!!
BEING A BOSS IS HARD WORK!
VERONICA! IT'S TIME FOR YOUR GEOMETRY LESSON!
CAN'T WE DO IT LATER? I'M TIRED!
YOU'RE FAILING THIS CLASS!
I SUGGEST YOU USE THIS TIME WISELY!
OKAY!

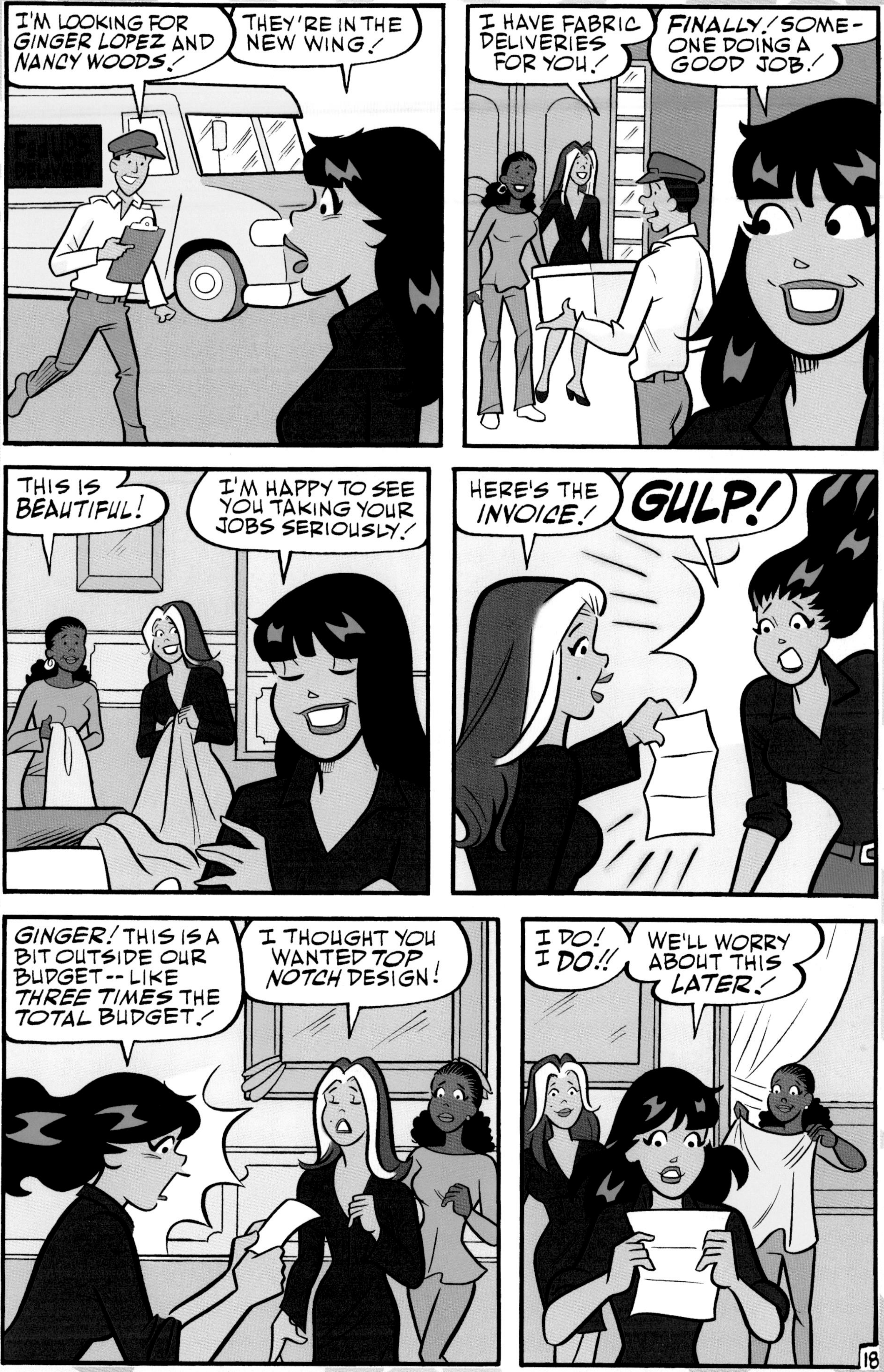

I'M LOOKING FOR GINGER LOPEZ AND NANCY WOODS!
THEY'RE IN THE NEW WING!
I HAVE FABRIC DELIVERIES FOR YOU!
FINALLY! SOME-ONE DOING A GOOD JOB!
THIS IS BEAUTIFUL!
I'M HAPPY TO SEE YOU TAKING YOUR JOBS SERIOUSLY!
HERE'S THE INVOICE!
GULP!
GINGER! THIS IS A BIT OUTSIDE OUR BUDGET--LIKE THREE TIMES THE TOTAL BUDGET!
I THOUGHT YOU WANTED TOP NOTCH DESIGN!
I DO! I DO!!
WE'LL WORRY ABOUT THIS LATER!

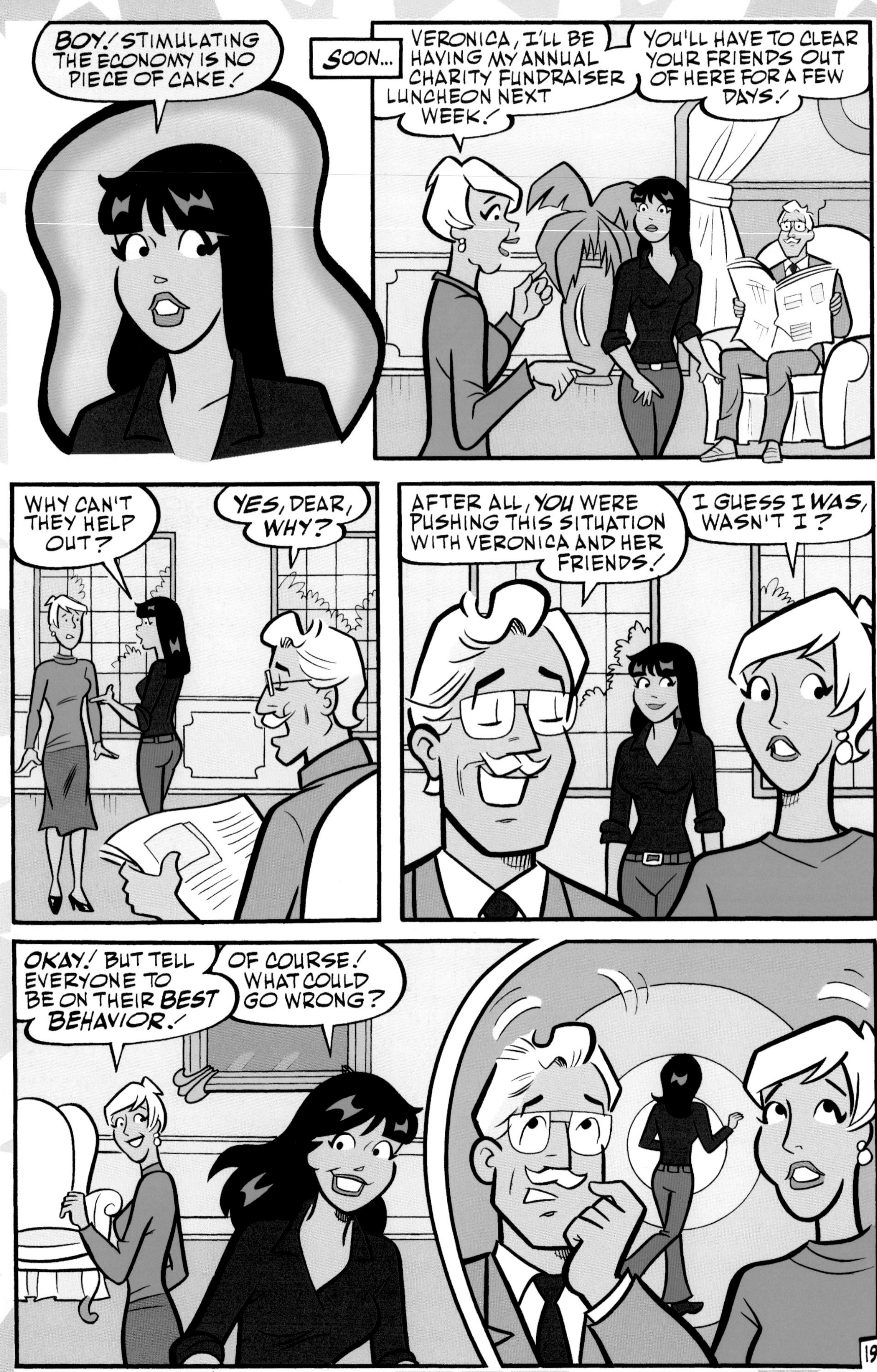
BOY! STIMULATING THE ECONOMY IS NO PIECE OF CAKE!
SOON...
VERONICA, I'LL BE HAVING MY ANNUAL CHARITY FUNDRAISER LUNCHEON NEXT WEEK!
YOU'LL HAVE TO CLEAR YOUR FRIENDS OUT OF HERE FOR A FEW DAYS!
WHY CAN'T THEY HELP OUT?
YES, DEAR, WHY?
AFTER ALL, YOU WERE PUSHING THIS SITUATION WITH VERONICA AND HER FRIENDS!
I GUESS I WAS, WASN'T I?
OKAY! BUT TELL EVERYONE TO BE ON THEIR BEST BEHAVIOR!
OF COURSE! WHAT COULD GO WRONG?

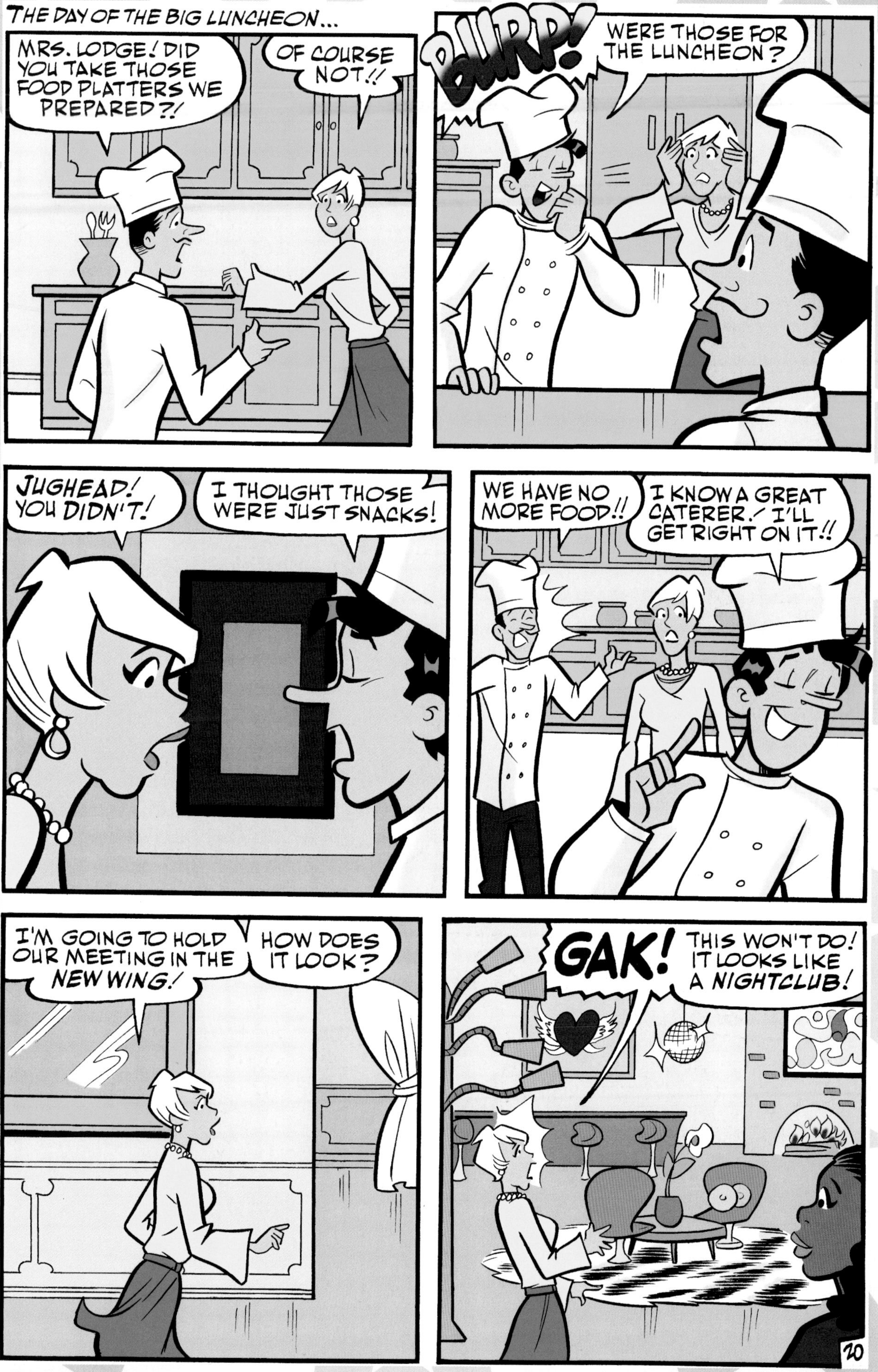
THE DAY OF THE BIG LUNCHEON...
MRS. LODGE! DID YOU TAKE THOSE FOOD PLATTERS WE PREPARED?!
OF COURSE NOT!!
BURP!
WERE THOSE FOR THE LUNCHEON?
JUGHEAD! YOU DIDN'T!
I THOUGHT THOSE WERE JUST SNACKS!
WE HAVE NO MORE FOOD!!
I KNOW A GREAT CATERER! I'LL GET RIGHT ON IT!!
I'M GOING TO HOLD OUR MEETING IN THE NEW WING!
HOW DOES IT LOOK?
GAK!
THIS WON'T DO! IT LOOKS LIKE A NIGHTCLUB!
20

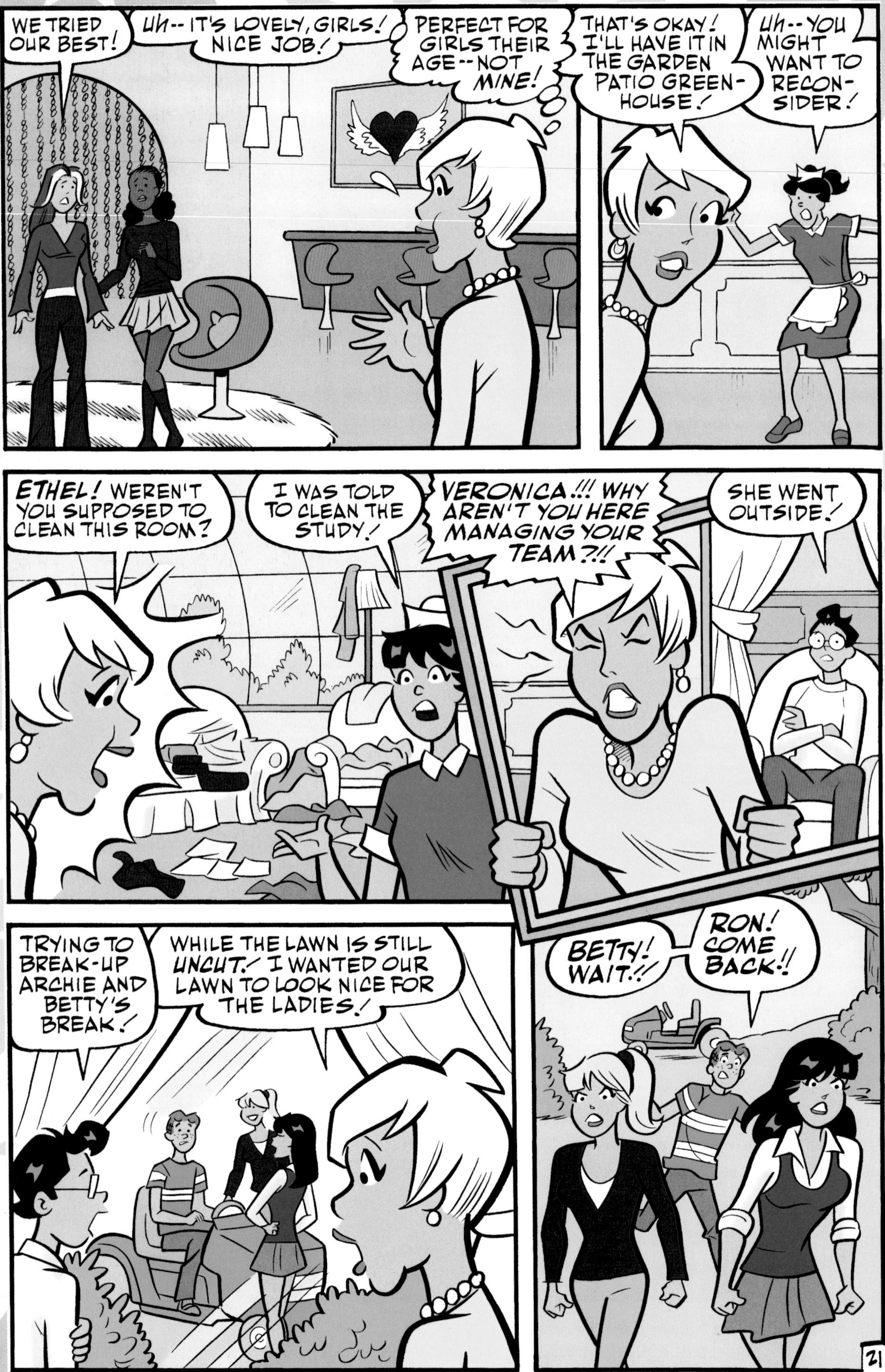
WE TRIED OUR BEST!
UH-- IT'S LOVELY, GIRLS! NICE JOB!
PERFECT FOR GIRLS THEIR AGE--NOT MINE!
THAT'S OKAY! I'LL HAVE IT IN THE GARDEN PATIO GREEN-HOUSE!
UH-- YOU MIGHT WANT TO RECON-SIDER!
ETHEL! WEREN'T YOU SUPPOSED TO CLEAN THIS ROOM?
I WAS TOLD TO CLEAN THE STUDY!
VERONICA!!! WHY AREN'T YOU HERE MANAGING YOUR TEAM?!!
SHE WENT OUTSIDE!
TRYING TO BREAK-UP ARCHIE AND BETTY'S BREAK!
WHILE THE LAWN IS STILL UNCUT! I WANTED OUR LAWN TO LOOK NICE FOR THE LADIES!
BETTY! WAIT!!
RON! COME BACK!!
21

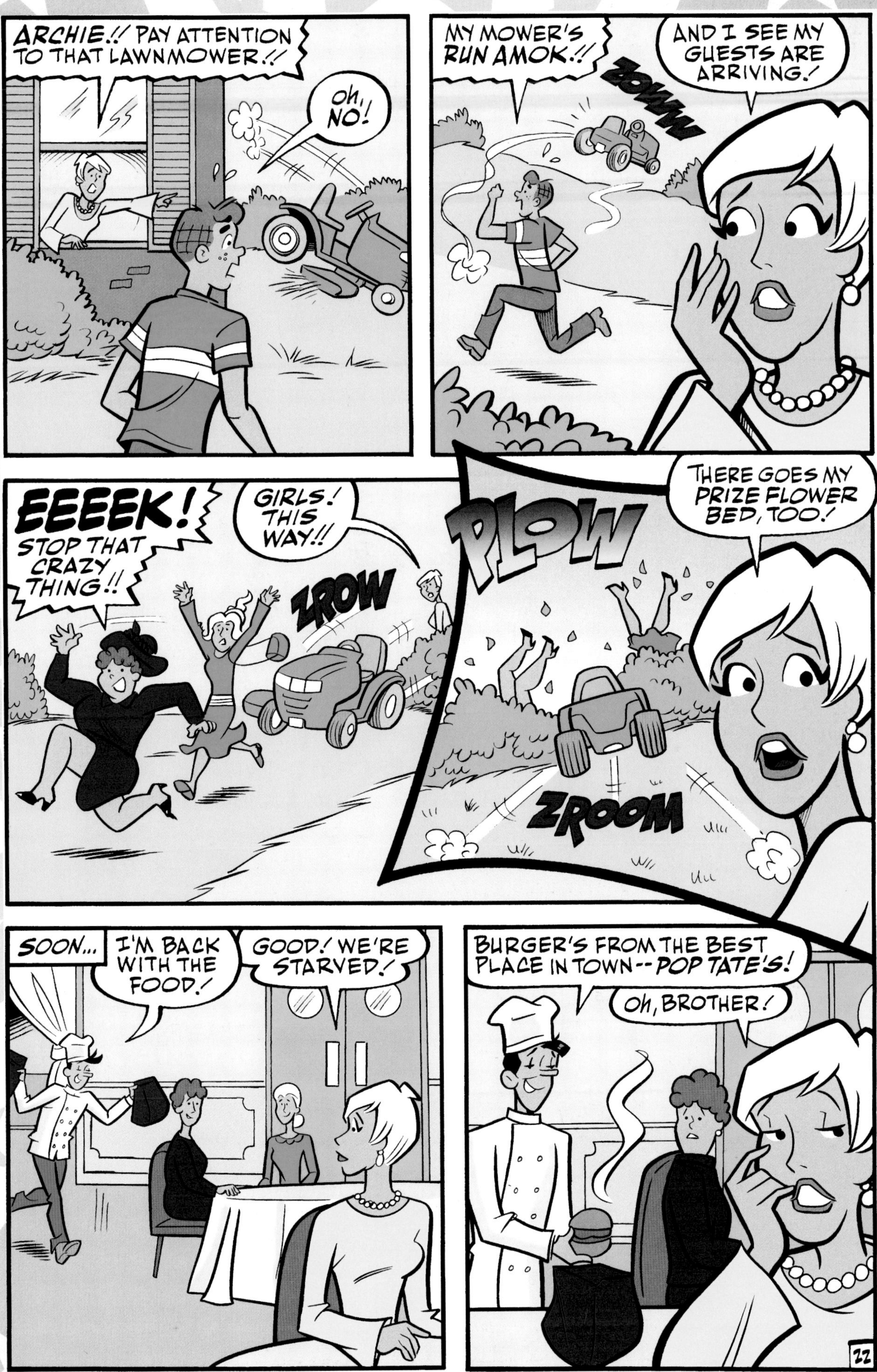
ARCHIE.!! PAY ATTENTION TO THAT LAWNMOWER.!!
Oh, NO!
MY MOWER'S RUN AMOK.!!
ZOWW
AND I SEE MY GUESTS ARE ARRIVING.!
EEEEK! STOP THAT CRAZY THING!!
GIRLS! THIS WAY!!
ZROW
PLOW
THERE GOES MY PRIZE FLOWER BED, TOO.!
ZROOM
SOON...
I'M BACK WITH THE FOOD.!
GOOD! WE'RE STARVED.!
BURGER'S FROM THE BEST PLACE IN TOWN -- POP TATE'S!
Oh, BROTHER!
22

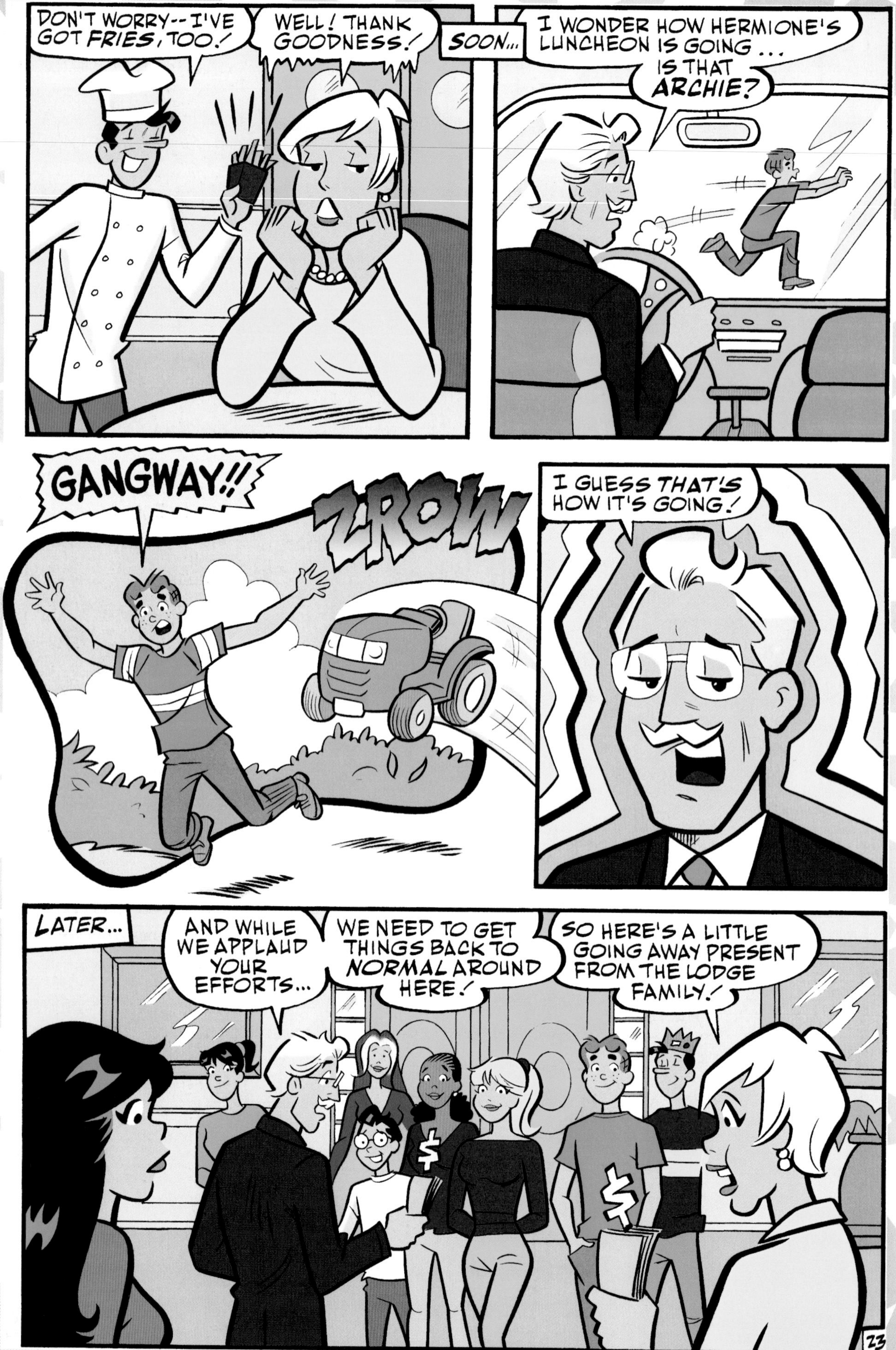
DON'T WORRY--I'VE GOT FRIES, TOO!
WELL! THANK GOODNESS!
SOON...
I WONDER HOW HERMIONE'S LUNCHEON IS GOING ...
IS THAT ARCHIE?
GANGWAY!!
ZROW
I GUESS THAT'S HOW IT'S GOING!
LATER...
AND WHILE WE APPLAUD YOUR EFFORTS...
WE NEED TO GET THINGS BACK TO NORMAL AROUND HERE!
SO HERE'S A LITTLE GOING AWAY PRESENT FROM THE LODGE FAMILY!
23

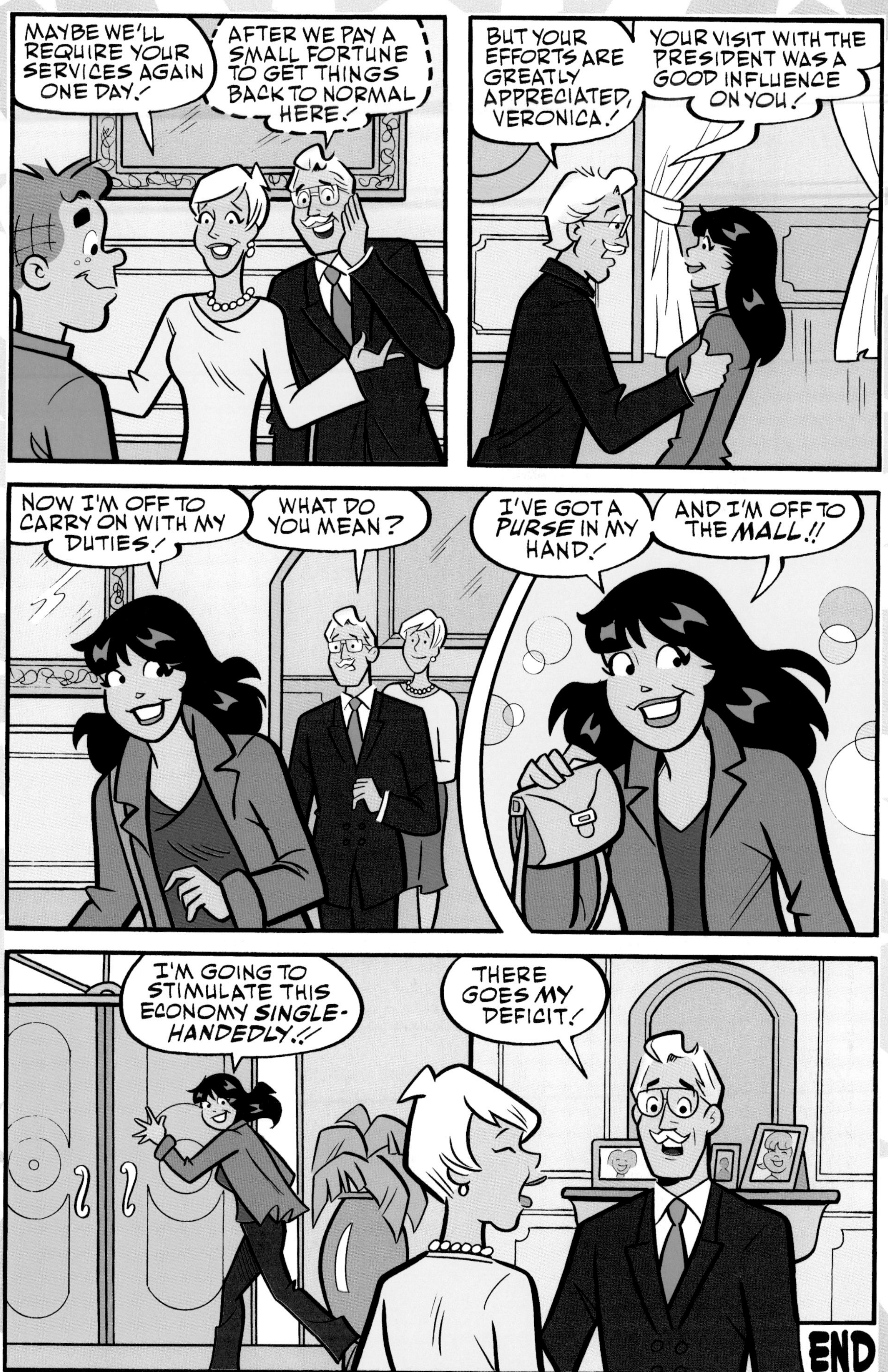
MAYBE WE'LL REQUIRE YOUR SERVICES AGAIN ONE DAY!
AFTER WE PAY A SMALL FORTUNE TO GET THINGS BACK TO NORMAL HERE!
BUT YOUR EFFORTS ARE GREATLY APPRECIATED, VERONICA!
YOUR VISIT WITH THE PRESIDENT WAS A GOOD INFLUENCE ON YOU!
NOW I'M OFF TO CARRY ON WITH MY DUTIES!
WHAT DO YOU MEAN?
I'VE GOT A PURSE IN MY HAND!
AND I'M OFF TO THE MALL!!
I'M GOING TO STIMULATE THIS ECONOMY SINGLE-HANDEDLY!!
THERE GOES MY DEFICIT!
END

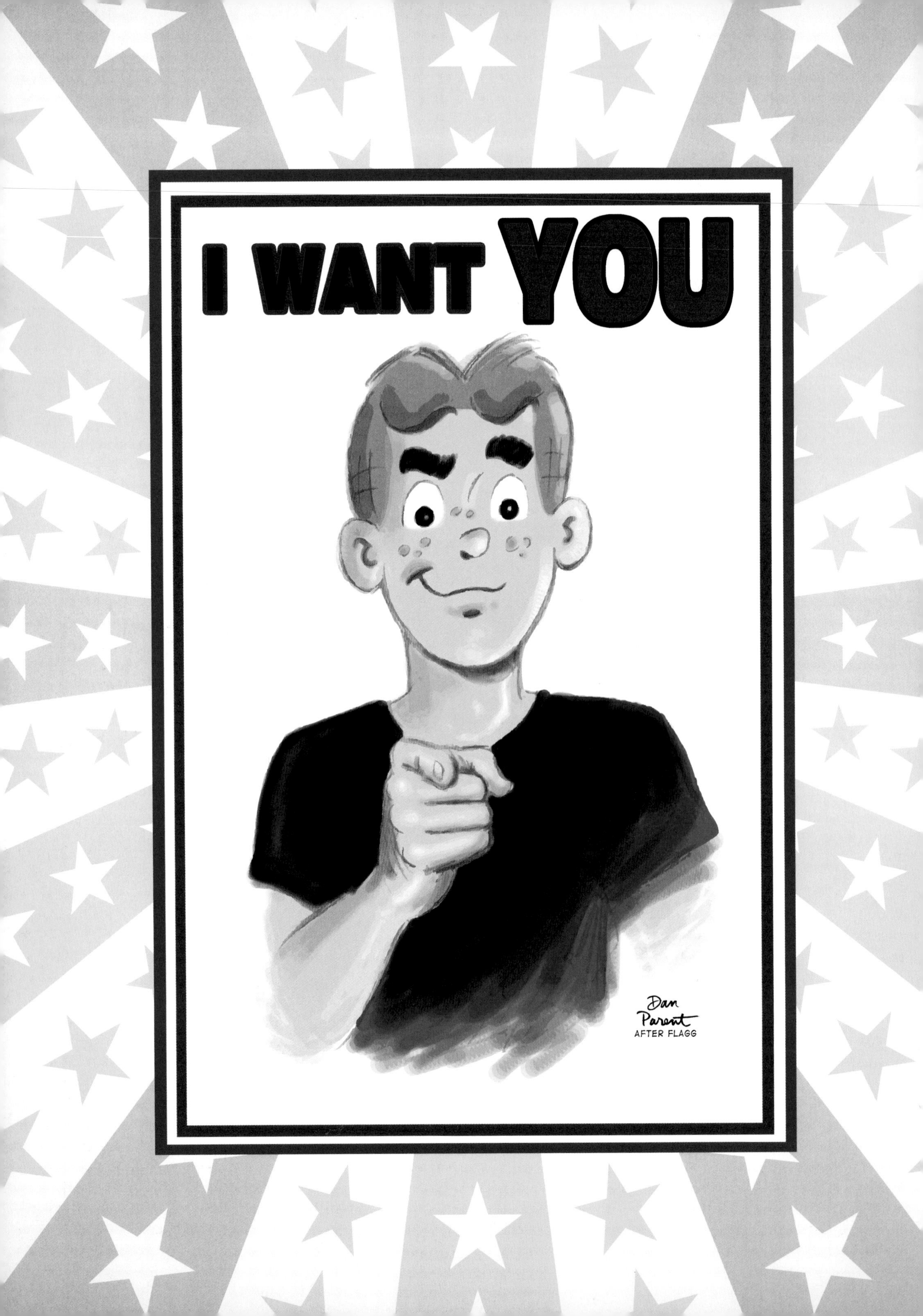
I WANT YOU
Dan Parent
AFTER FLAGG

Did You Know...

Before any artist turns in a cover image to a story as huge as **Obama & Palin in Riverdale**, they have to draw several sketched ideas for the editor to choose from. Here are some of those early sketches.

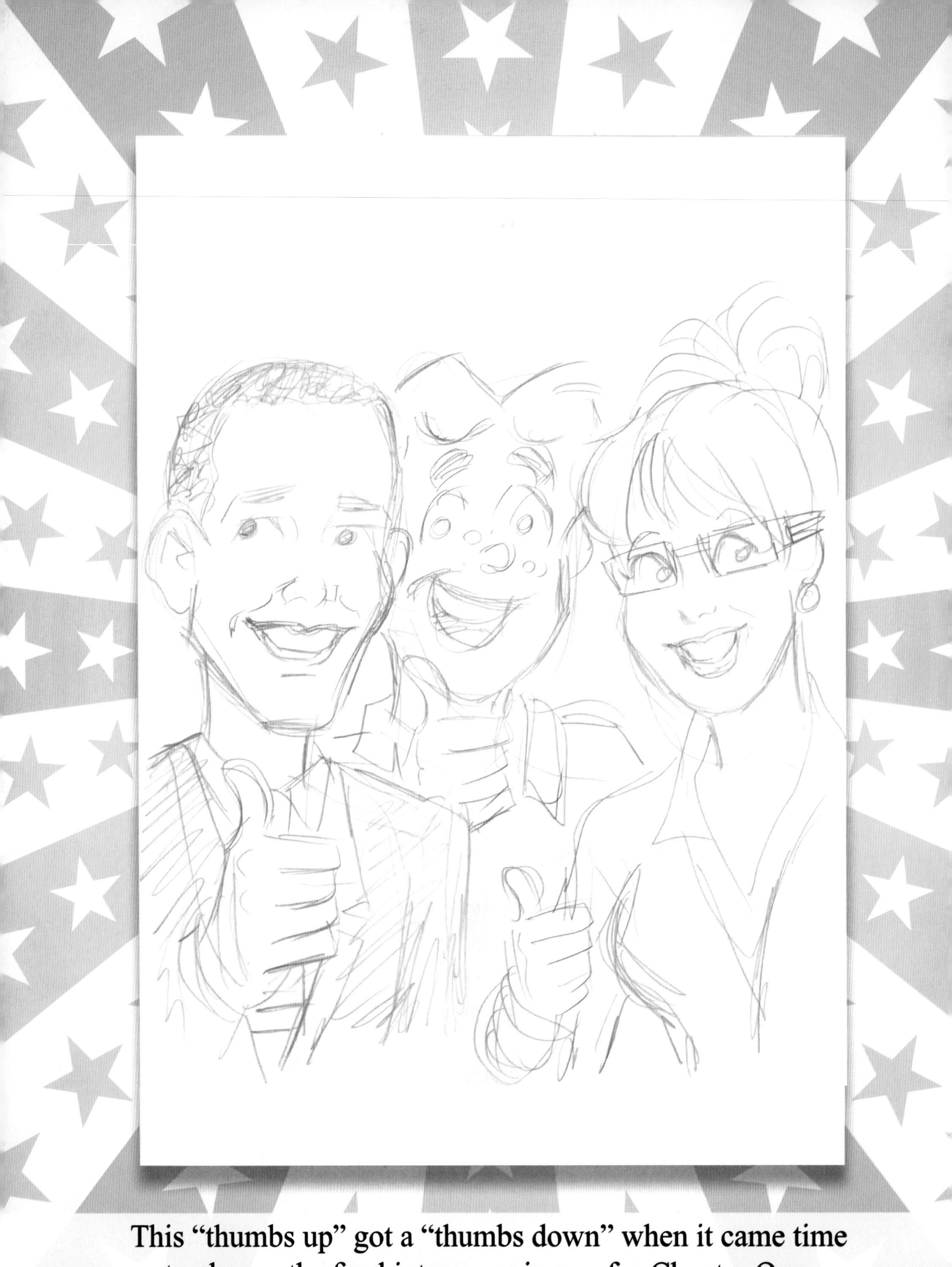

This "thumbs up" got a "thumbs down" when it came time to choose the final intro page image for Chapter One.

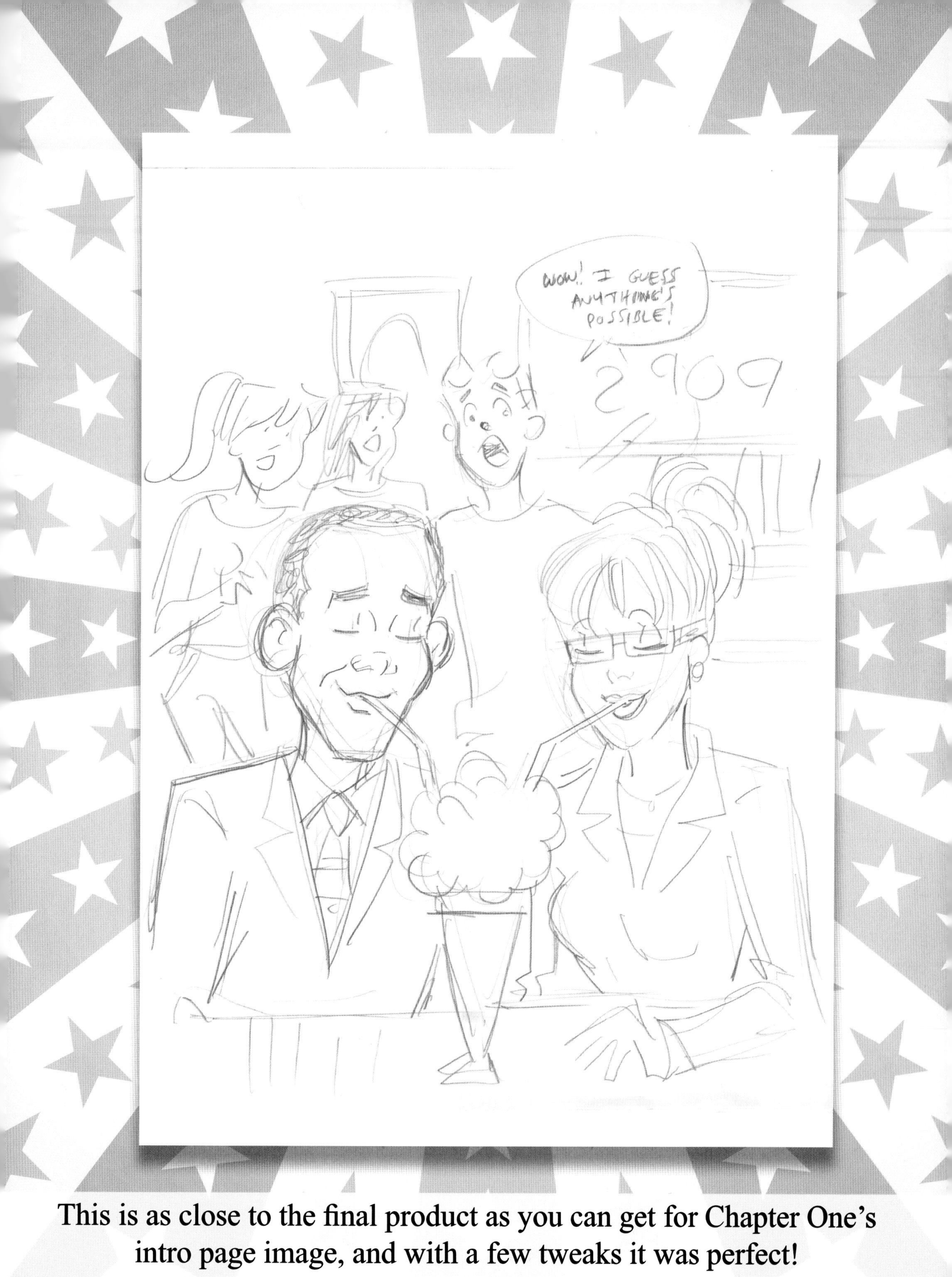
WOW! I GUESS ANYTHING'S POSSIBLE!

This is as close to the final product as you can get for Chapter One's intro page image, and with a few tweaks it was perfect!

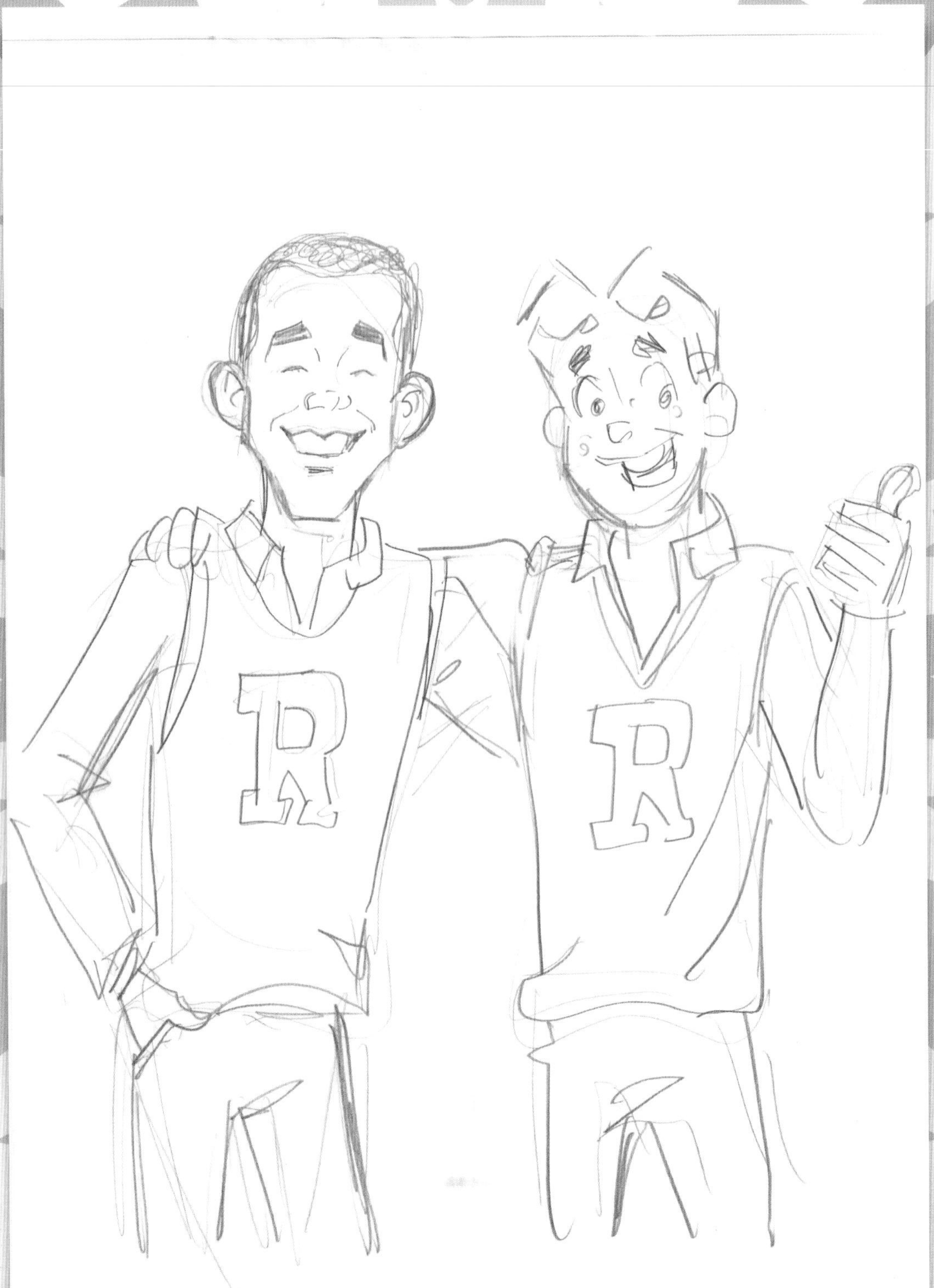

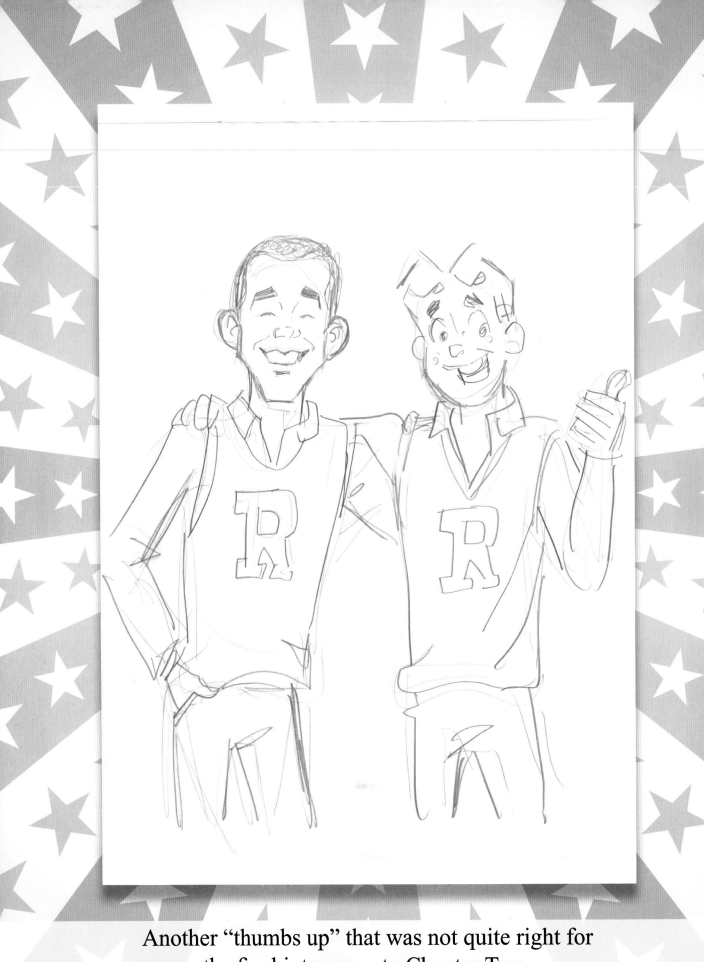

Another “thumbs up” that was not quite right for
the final intro page to Chapter Two.

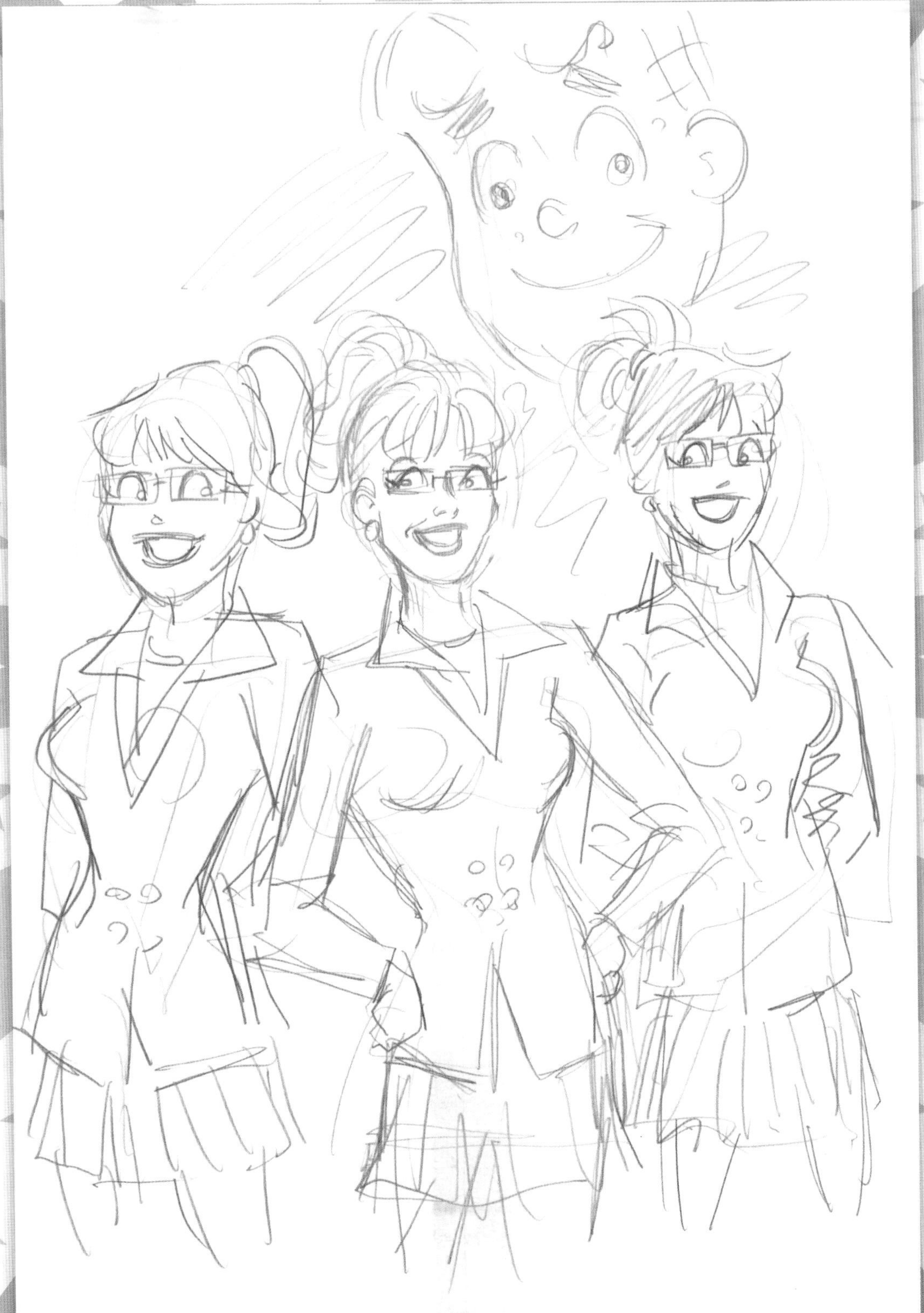

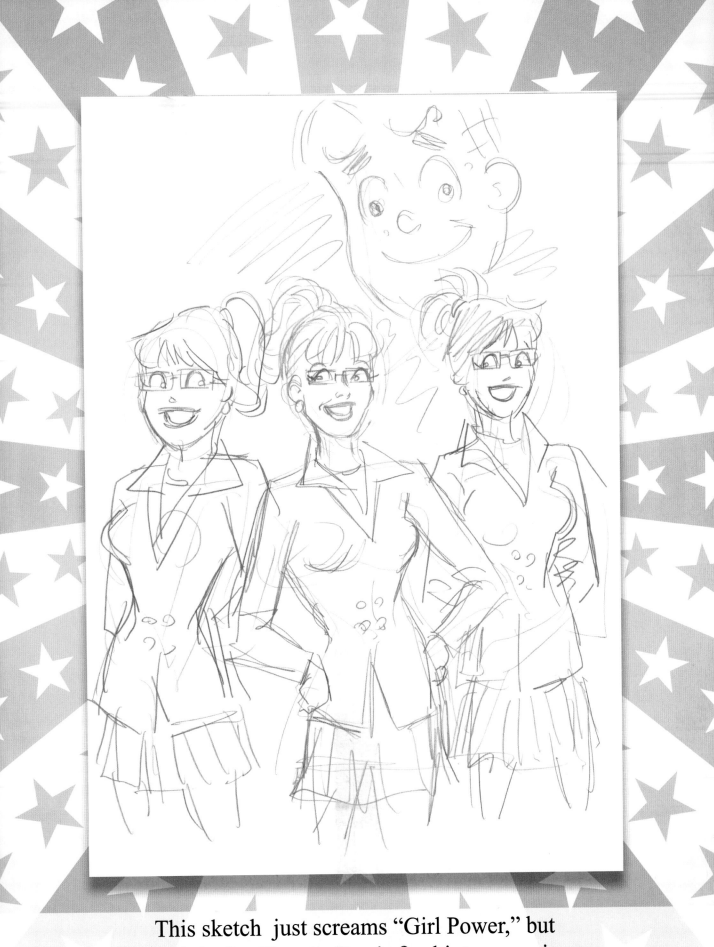

This sketch just screams "Girl Power," but wasn't right for Chapter Two's final intro page image.

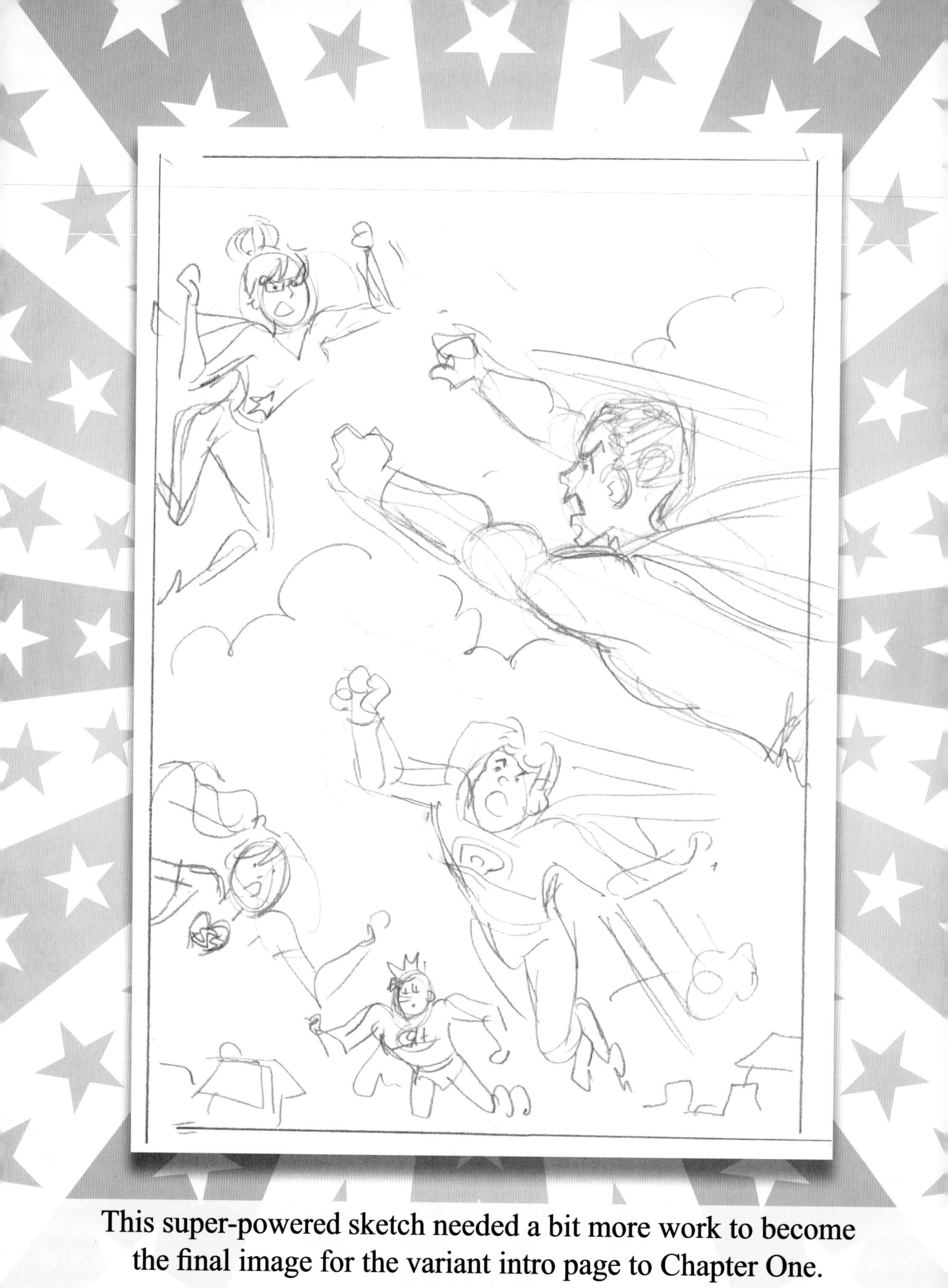

This super-powered sketch needed a bit more work to become the final image for the variant intro page to Chapter One.

Did You Know...

Before drawing what would become the variant intro pages for Chapter One and Chapter Two, artist **Dan Parent** sketched out a few parodies of some famous superhero comic book covers.

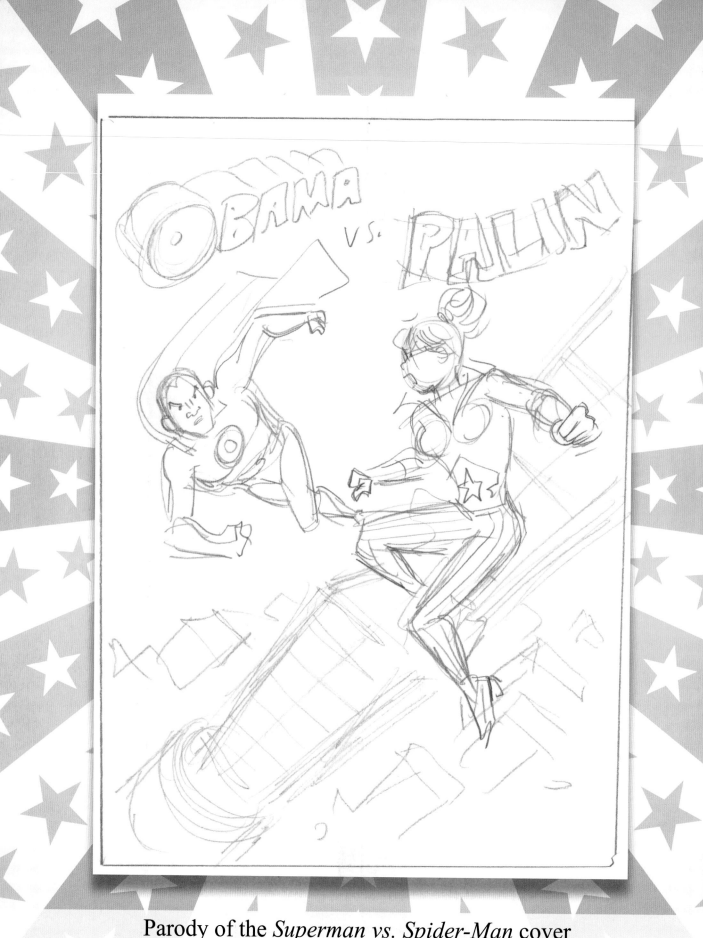

Parody of the *Superman vs. Spider-Man* cover
originally drawn by Ross Andru and Dick Giordano.

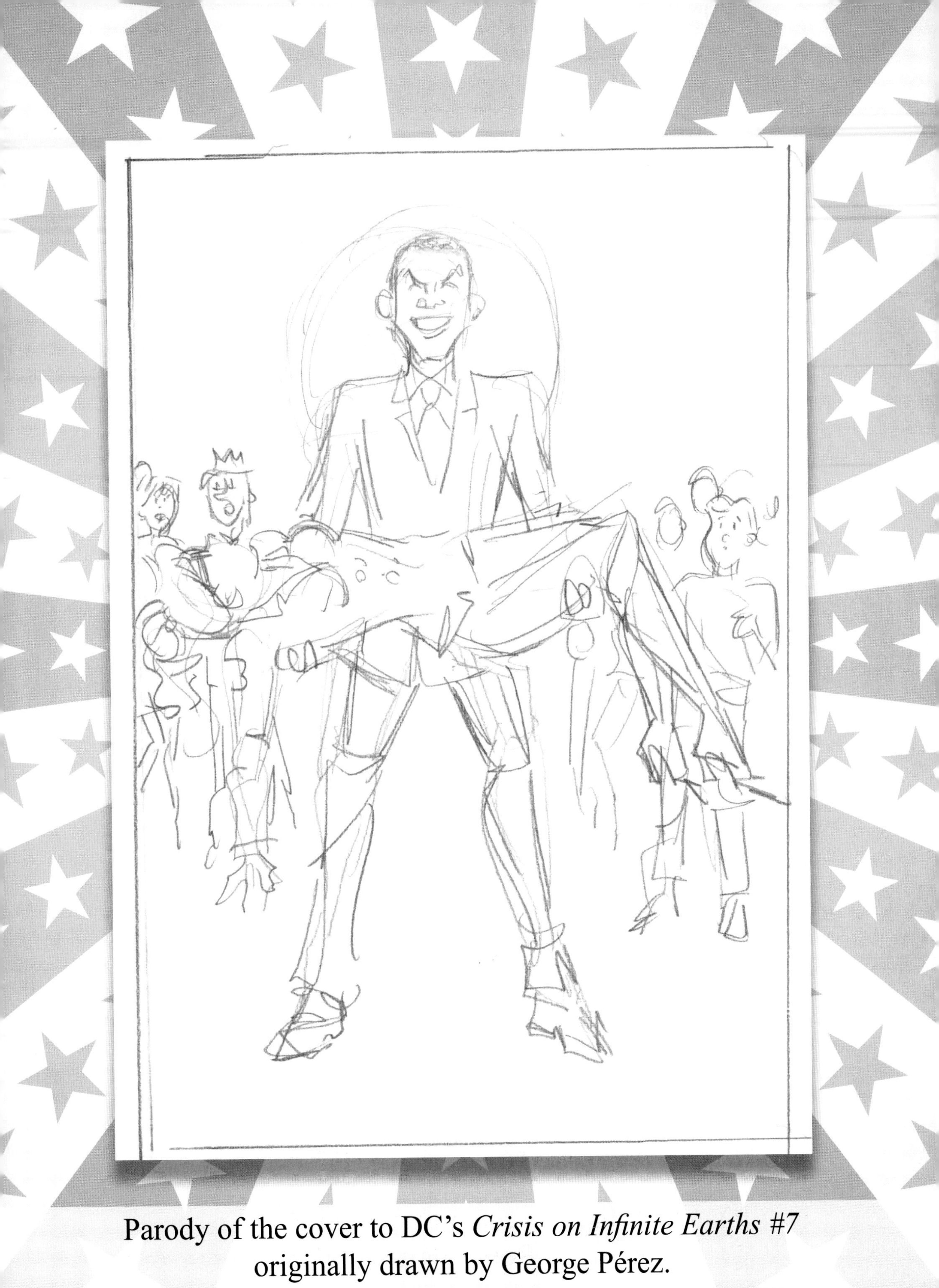

Parody of the cover to DC's *Crisis on Infinite Earths* #7 originally drawn by George Pérez.

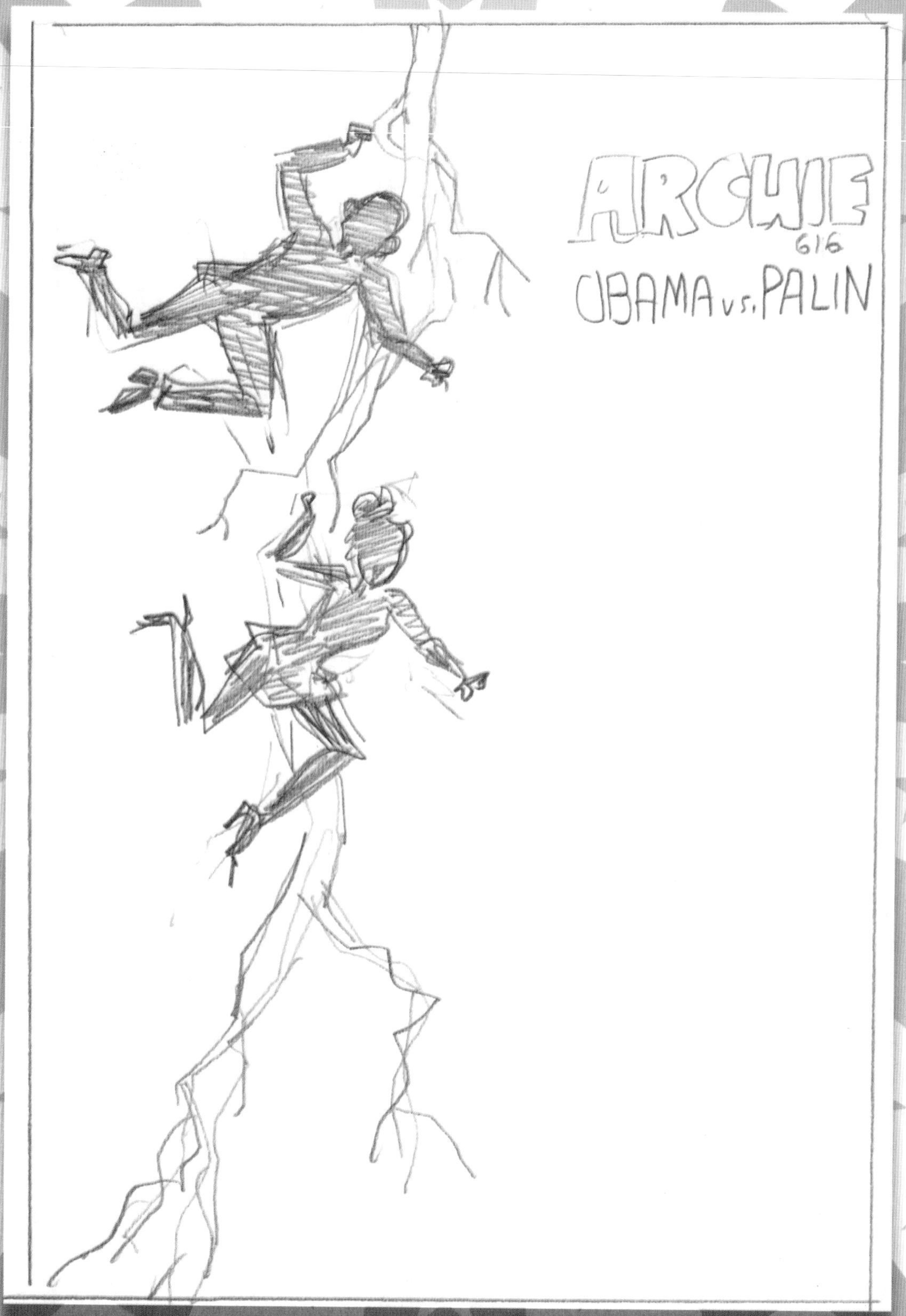
ARCHIE
616
OBAMA vs. PALIN

Parody of the cover to DC's *Batman: The Dark Knight Returns #1* originally drawn by Frank Miller.

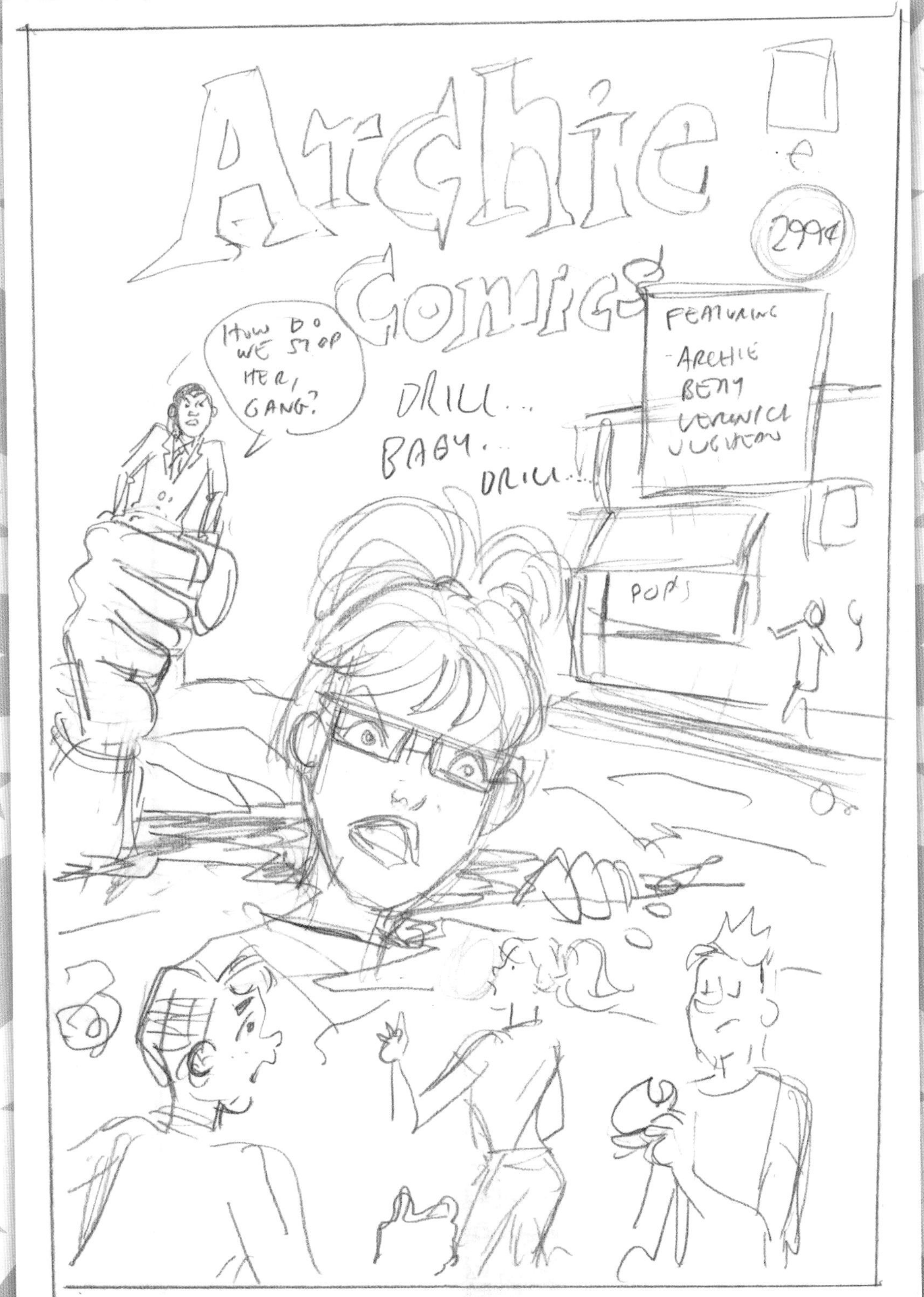

Archie
Comics
HOW DO WE STOP HER, GANG?
DRILL... BABY... DRILL...
FEATURING
ARCHIE
BETTY
POPS

Parody of the cover to Marvel's *Fantastic Four #1* originally drawn by Jack Kirby.

The Archie Babies

The Archie Babies

Before they ruled the halls of Riverdale High, Archie and his pals were kings and queens of the playground!

ISBN:
978-1-879794-72-6

Archie & Friends: Night at the Comic Shop

Classic comic characters leave their four-color worlds to wreak havoc on Riverdale!

ISBN:
978-1-879794-69-6

Archie & Friends
Night at the Comic Shop

Archie
Freshman Year
Book Two
The High School Chronicles — Book Two

Archie: Freshman Year Book 2

The coolest freshmen at Riverdale High are back for an all-new semester of hilarity!

ISBN:
978-1-879794-71-9

The Archies & Josie and the Pussycats

Two of the hottest bands get together to make some sweet music!

ISBN:
978-1-879794-61-0

The Archies & Josie
and the Pussycats

Best of Jughead
Crowning Achievements
American Idle

Best of Jughead: Crowning Achievements

Get ready for a buffet of comedy with everyone's favorite foodie, Jughead! "Bon appetit"!

ISBN:
978-1-879794-67-2

Sabrina: Animated

Sabrina's not your average girl... she's secretly a witch!
Based on the hit animated series!

ISBN:
978-1-879794-80-1

Sabrina

Betty and Veronica
Storybook
The Wizard of Oz
Cinderella, Sleeping Beauty
Alice in Wonderland

Betty & Veronica: Storybook

The ladies of Riverdale live happily ever after when they take center stage in four classic fairy tales!

ISBN:
978-1-879794-60-3

Archie: World Tour

Archie and friends go on a globe-trotting expedition full of excitment and adventure!

ISBN:
978-1-879794-73-3

Archie
World Tour

Archie Comics

LOOK FOR THESE AND OTHER GRAPHIC NOVELS AT COMIC SHOPS AND BOOKSTORES EVERYWHERE!

ALSO AVAILABLE ONLINE AT ARCHIECOMICS.COM